Gargaphia:

Where History Means Murder

Robert T. Jones

Southern Yellow Pine
Publishing

Published by:
Southern Yellow Pine (SYP) Publishing
4351 Natural Bridge Rd.
Tallahassee, FL 32305

www.syppublishing.com

This is a work of fiction. Names, characters, places, and events that occur either are the products of the author's imagination or are used fictitiously. Any resemblance to actual persons, places, or events is purely coincidental.

The contents and opinions expressed in this book do not necessarily reflect the views and opinions of Southern Yellow Pine Publishing, nor does the mention of brands or trade names constitute endorsement.

ISBN-10: 1-59616-041-1
ISBN-13: 978-1-59616-041-5
ISBN-13: ePub 978-1-59616-042-2
Library of Congress Control Number: 2017955150

Printed in the United States of America
First Edition
September 2017

For Brooke

Prologue

Some people know. They research and stumble upon something important, something groundbreaking, or something threatening to someone powerful. That wasn't me. My research couldn't have been more innocuous. Ancient history…, literally ancient history. You know, the kind about old guys dressed in togas living on a flat deity. My thesis altered the perception of a handful of gray haired and pompous men, but none of them are dangerous. You throw a ball in their direction, and they wouldn't know whether to duck, let it hit them in their face, or analyze its rotation as they remain naïve to its trajectory. They are all cowards physically, but more importantly, they are all completely self-obsessed. You can't feel threatened when your narcissism overshadows your thoughts of jealousy. Their lives are entwined in research, and my findings gave them an outlet for countless publications at my expense. Narcissism begets the thought of tearing me apart on paper, but never real life.

The station was cold. The kind of drastic change that produces goosebumps when the summer sweat seemingly freezes to your arms. The kind of change when a hundred-degrees becomes sixty-five at the drop of a hat. My head swirled, and a tension headache split my brain in two. Minutes, or even seconds, and my entire life changed. I finally brought myself down off the adrenaline soaked high. I brought myself down enough to think about what had just transpired and the questions I had already been asked. I couldn't think about what happened before that moment, at least not meaningfully. One distinct interaction filled my memory bank as if the rest of my being never existed before that fateful time. The intense focus was an obvious defense mechanism for a body and mind shocked to its core. Slowly, items began to filter in which allowed me to discern the events as they happened.

***

She sat directly in front of me, smiling when her face split open. Blood expelled from her forehead, pummeling what was my joyous face. I saw her because she was in my eyes, the purest of reds. I tasted her because she dripped from my lips, warm and bitter iron. I heard and felt her fill my ears. I smelled the sweetest of lavender perfumes mixed with the horror of her metallic insides. She was on the floor, her skinny features being overcome by blood, when I heard the sound of the shot. I didn't have time to panic before the next shot clipped the right side of my jaw. I twisted rapidly and fell over the desk chair stationed directly behind me. I felt myself. It was an odd reaction as the adrenaline decided whether or not to freeze me or let me free. Everything was intact. There was blood, but all bones were formed and fit where they should. Relief spread over me until my eyes fixated on Professor Hogue's lifeless body sitting in a cartoonish amount of blood and brain matter. In shock, I rose. It was a pathetically inept reaction to the carnage. Fight? Flight? More like a deer in the headlights reflex. The next shot was impeded by the building prior to entry. Red dust poured in from the brick that saved my head from the same Hogue explosion lying in front of me. Flight? Yes, flight. I bolted out the door as the final shot penetrated the back of her office. The cute stickers and inspirational quotes were marred by four rounds of a 308. Such devastation. Such effective destruction. Sheer panic took over, but I couldn't help but find my brain wandering to the efficiency in which my life had just been destroyed. Four rounds. Four simple rounds.

The McMullin building for Humanities was a few decades past the need for reconstruction. This wasn't Oxford, Harvard, or even Melbourne. The University of Newcastle upgraded departments based on their ability to bring in funds, and to date, the humanities department wasn't quite a cash cow. Why else would they let a thirty-one-year-old business man, which is what I was four years ago, into the PhD program?

2

Sure, I had an MA. Many do, but my theories were strange and completely unorthodox. I didn't just aim to enhance the field of ancient history. I aimed to destroy it. I aimed to target everything they held dear to the world and crush it under my new multi-disciplinary interpretation of Herodotus. I talk tough, but such an ambition caused less arousal amongst my peers than a Buddhist Temple at prayer. There was no reason to think I was a target. Here, less than one week from commencement as a PhD, Hogue had been the only Professor to take my research seriously. Luckily, as one of the more distinguished faculty members, she had enough clout to pass me through. Now she lay face first in a suffocating deep pool of her own making.

I caught my breath at the end of the hall near the top of the stairwell. Screams echoed throughout the building. It was summer, but there were still ample signs of life around campus. No one else ran outside their rooms. I found that odd. Frozen in space and time, it was as if I moved whilst the world was stuck on pause. I thought I had survived a run of the mill school shooting. Sure, Australia didn't have many, but it's not as if the world down under had run out of tormented souls that must hear their name before they die. It's hard living, and it's hard not fitting in. No one is immune to the world making them feel small. I remember a tear rolling down my cheek and my heart racing. I continued to have a similar reaction simply thinking back. Hogue was dead no more than fifty feet from me at that point. I loved her like a mother. She gave me hope, but even better, she gave me an opportunity when the world seemed to run dry for me. Anger filled my soul. It was quick, like falling through a frozen lake and feeling the shock freeze every warm morsel in my core. It was also short-lived.

When he appeared, I thought he had to be the largest man I had ever seen in person. Awe-inspiring size proportionate to a giant, but that wasn't the first thing I noticed when looking at him. He had the coldest and largest eyes I had ever seen. They drew me in. They pierced through me and stunned me in place like they had some sort of cosmic power. He was rock hard and smooth with one major exception. He had the oddest scars on each cheek, mirrors of one another. He wore a black shirt, nothing written on the front. This wasn't the type of person who needed

3

brand recognition. He wore dark pants, but I couldn't tell if the colors matched, and that bothered me. It's amazing what you think about in the fractious moments of pure terror. I enjoy symmetry and matching, but my colorblindness makes my effectiveness at the latter terribly frustrating. At first I marveled. Like I said before, I wasn't worried about anyone being *after* me despite the shooting a few minutes earlier. Not only was my research tame for real world application, I was likely the most non-confrontational person on the planet. I had made an art of it. I avoided the chance of conflict, not the conflict itself. I made sure my interactions didn't have the opportunity to escalate into something confrontational. I accomplished this while still holding a competitive edge. Game and sport were the one avenue where I could express myself completely. It was controlled. It was confrontation in an environment suited for me. Soon, my agility would be my own saving grace.

At first, I found it strange the monstrous figure didn't take his eyes off of me. It was extreme focus as if he and I were the only two animated figures in a building full of stagnancy. I could tell that the screams around him were of no bother. This man was used to screaming. Violence must have bred him. I finally started to surmise that I was the only target he had in his mind. The cold stare was meant for me alone. By the time I registered this threat, the silenced 1911 was pointed down at me. He wasn't next to me like you might imagine. The man was so large that he was still far away and the gun was pointed down like he was on the floor above me. He didn't say freeze or any other nonsense. He simply fired once, twice, three, and four times. I juked like a jumping spider approaching the triple jump. Somehow I was clean. By the time the third and fourth shots were fired I was speedily, and not so gracefully, shuddering down the stairwell. The monster above finished his seven-round magazine as I completed my decent from the second floor and bolted out of the side entrance to McMullin. I stumbled as concrete met grass, but continued through the discomfort of trauma induced exhaustion. I wasn't in the best shape of my life. Illness crept in on me when I was twenty-seven and had left its mark. Remission was good to me, and I was fast, but my bones were weaker and my muscles wobbly in comparison. I tired quickly as I made my escape, but for the time being I had been freed from a monster.

Pavers lined the ground and tidy gardens accentuated the walkways in between buildings. Clamors of people were now speedily running nowhere. Time not only sped up when looking at these people, but it was like they were on fast-forward running in circles. Pepper in a bowl of water after a drop of soap has been applied. Or insects being smoked out from a hive. By the time I realized the monster wasn't alone, the neck of a poor student running in front of me was, from what I could gather from the day, mistakenly sniped down. The shot was undeniably meant for me. He went down in a heap and wailed in pain grasping his neck. I didn't have time to play doctor. Survival was the foremost concern even as the guilt of the young man entered intimate levels of my mind. I had been fortunate of dumb luck so far. I calculated that I had made nearly a half-dozen dimwitted mistakes and got away predominantly unscathed. I had to think. The grounds were open next to McMullin, but a full assortment of summer-lit trees was on its periphery. I had to take cover.

The pounding of my heart was at unsustainable levels, but my survival instinct was determined. I wore a T-shirt, gym shorts, and Crocs. Luckily for me, I wore Crocs with the heal strap fastened. I could run with little worries, and I could zig and zag with my head lowered toward the cover. At least, this is what I convinced myself of as I attempted the escape. For the first time, I had been completely proud of my choice of outfit. I enjoyed comfort, and while I knew there was a time and place for finer dress, I usually based this solely on what my peers would find acceptable. Professor Hogue was never one to care. She enjoyed my arguments and never looked down on my choice of comfort over fashion. In fact, she often admired it. Unlike the Monster's head, mine was simply shaven down with clippers, not with a razor to the skin. That takes too much time and is way too shiny. I wore a five-o'clock shadow that was customary to my appearance. My pockets contained my cell phone and a wallet, but nothing to slow me significantly. One more shot was fired as I ducked into the trees and out of the sight of my assailant. It too was a miss, and this time nothing was harmed in its wake. The sirens poured

5

in after the last shot was fired. My assumption of safety was backed up by the police vehicles that flanked my position soon thereafter.

***

It wasn't until the Police station that I realized I had escaped a near death experience. It was an assassination attempt on my life, and I had survived. I was alive. Hogue wasn't. What was going on? When the questions came in, the surreal nature of my experience came to light. When asked to give my account of the happenings, I was caught in obvious confusion:

"Professor Hogue was the only reason I was even in Australia today. I literally got off the plane from Brisbane two hours ago. Hogue picked me up and took me to the University. I was going to stay at her vacation home in the Blue Mountains for a week of relaxation. Next week…" I struggled to hold it together, but I did: "she was going to hood me at commencement. That's why I'm here…, I graduate next week."

I thought to myself how important this was to her. The culmination of four years' worth of research for both of us, but these cops had cleaning up to do. They didn't need some American getting soggy eyed in their precinct while they had two dead bodies over at the University. Detective Chief Inspector Clive Ricketts had the body language that shared these sentiments. He was noticeably leery of me and glared at me without cracking a smile throughout our short time together. He was a middle-aged man. He sported a rough looking comb-over, crooked but white teeth, a stocky build, and pointy features. He was not an attractive man. A taller Penguin from Batman kept popping into my mind. He leaned in closer as to discern something important. He spoke harshly in a high-pitched accent:

"Dr., I mean Mr. Appling." The Dr. in front was an obvious dig as I had just mentioned the graduation. Or was it a would-be graduation? I hadn't thought of that until now. He kept going: "I understand you have been attacked and someone close to you has died, but I have two dead bodies. I need to establish a motive. You have arrived and people are dead…." He gestured to get me to open up to him as he raised his eye

6

brows and threw up his arms dramatically. The room was starting to feel hostile towards me. Unlike the University, the precinct was ultra-modern and almost too clean. The small room sported an aluminum table and chairs, a Styrofoam coffee cup, white walls, and black coffee. The walls were too white and the coffee was too black. To its credit, this was coming from someone that doesn't actually drink coffee. The contrast was simply too much to handle. Being mildly obsessive meant that my reaction was physical as much as mental. My skin began to crawl simply being in the room. The wobbling from the air vent felt like enough to make me confess to whatever they wanted. I was an innocent man, or at least that's what I thought before I came to the police station. Everything about the precinct was designed so the most innocent of people could feel like criminals. That, and an impatient DCI staring me down as though I had stolen his daughter's virginity.

I calmly collected my thoughts. I spoke with a touch more purpose now. "DCI Ricketts, I'm unsure what you are trying to get from me here." Ricketts tapped his fingers on the table and the echo was loud in the tightening room:

"Just the facts Mr. Appling. And try to sum it up quickly." It seemed that Ricketts was the very first Australian ever to want to do anything quickly. At least, that had been my experience ever since applying to my first Australian University so many years ago. I leaned forward and pressed my open hands on the table. I began speaking with an obvious hint of nervousness. A tinge in my throat made my words shaky at best:

"I've known Professor Hogue for around five years. For four of those years I have conducted research with her as my supervisor." I took a deep breath. "My reading committee used to have two, but the other had to take sick leave two years into my research. We hadn't heard from him since." Ricketts motioned for me to move with more haste. Perhaps he thought some of the details were irrelevant. I wasn't sure how he did that so effectively. A combination of eyebrows, eye rolls, and hand gestures made it happen though. "Ok..., to the relevant parts. I am a student. I study for UoN but live in the United States. We worked this deal out at the beginning of the program. I have visited Australia several times, but we—"

7

"Professor Hogue?" Ricketts interrupted.

"Yes, Professor Hogue" I confirmed. "We spoke mostly over Skype."

"And this is on the web somehow?" Another interruption.

"Yes. It was a more efficient way to communicate for me as a non-traditional student with a family and roots." Ricketts nodded with an apprehensive understanding and I moved forward: "I conduct research on Herodotus." Ricketts expression made me realize he didn't care, but I moved on: "I work in conspiracy theories in ancient history and have been successful in identifying some remarkable trends that suggest an ulterior motive to Herodotus' *Histories*. I have even been able to prove, in theory anyway, where many modern historians... you know, within the last few hundred years, have been inaccurate as to pertinent locations of events."

"Why that is remarkable stuff Mr. Appling," Ricketts said with heavy sarcasm. "So how does this make you a target for an assassination attempt? How does this lead to what happened today? Who have you wanked off? Who wants you dead? Because I seriously question that it's because of a one hundred-year-old book." Ricketts seemed to be playing dumb, but I wasn't going to bite. The research I study is nearly two thousand five hundred years old and one of the first histories ever recorded in detail. Somehow, I thought Ricketts wanted me to correct him so he could act upon me being pretentious. This was not something I would give him the satisfaction of. Luckily, before I had a chance to continue, the door burst open. A much younger, probably mid-twenties or something girl walked in. Obviously pissed, Ricketts snapped again with sarcasm so thick it could act as its own atmosphere: "What can I do for you, Constable Shen?" Yaravela Shen was beautiful. She tried her best to appear pedestrian, but even without makeup, her hair pulled back, and an unflattering uniform, she was beyond simply attractive. Her complexion was olive, her eyes a mysterious gray, and her shiny black hair was breathtaking. Definitely the product of Caucasian and Asian breeding, but I couldn't be certain as to her ancestry. Honestly, it didn't matter. Her curves were near perfection, and I couldn't help but notice when she bent over. This was despite her whispers into Ricketts' hair-filled earlobe. It was like she knew men had to watch her, and despite her prideful attempt at dressing down, she couldn't help but use her looks to her advantage. I couldn't tell what she was saying. It didn't matter. I was half delirious from panic, terror, and a minor side of jet-lag, and the new Constable was a pleasant sight disruption from Ricketts.

Ricketts slammed his hand on the table in disgust. He waddled up from his chair and made his way to the door. He didn't bother speaking to me, but did offer a scowl of condolence for his premature absence from his interrogation. This was punctuated by an inaudible promise to return. I nodded to Ricketts, but had become increasingly more focused on the other figure in the room. Constable Shen passed me a seductive but rather sinister smile before winking at me. I was taken aback for a moment until I saw the flat-headed screwdriver wielded in her left hand. With cat-like precision, she angled the tool up and shoved it deep into Ricketts' carotid artery before he opened the door. He instinctually flung his hands up to grasp his neck. Blood, a sight I had seen too much of since arriving in Newcastle a few hours earlier, was everywhere.

I was rendered speechless, slightly desensitized from the blood and panic earlier in the day. My shock turned to fear as I saw Shen pull the screwdriver ferociously from Ricketts' throat. Ricketts went down in a heap and convulsed on the floor for around a one Mississippi count before dying a few feet in front of me. Shen averted her attention to me. She made a gun out of her right hand and mockingly pulled the middle finger back as if she were shooting me. Although dazed in hysteria, I couldn't help but notice the right hand wasn't gloved like the left. Her beautifully manicured nails, highlighted by some sort of elaborate pattern, caught my eye. She winked once more before her sinister stare turned quickly into tears of horror.

She screamed in terror. "AHHHHHHHHH Help!" She tossed me the tool and I… well yes, I caught it. It was instinctual. With all of the commotion, the last thing on my mind was being framed for murdering the pandering DCI Ricketts. That is, it was the last thing until it was the only thing. I was holding a bloody screwdriver by the handle. The beautiful Miss Shen was clutching Ricketts' neck "trying" to stop the bleeding. I was up shit creek, in shock, and very tired of being Down Under.

Chapter 1

It had now been more than two years since Miss Shen was kind enough to frame me for murdering a Detective Chief Inspector. Somehow, when I shouted, "It was her! It was her!" it didn't have the effect I was looking for at the time. The wheels in the Australian justice system turn slowly sometimes. In my circumstance, sloth would be the appropriate animal for description.

My case had been a slam-dunk for the prosecution. Shen was young, but respected among her colleagues. She was also a cop. Coupled with the preconception of some sort of guilt left behind by DCI Ricketts, I was dead in the water. My primary lawyer, Edward Gillway, had wanted me to plead guilty from the start. He said my cooperation would give me the best chance for leniency in holding. This was almost tempting to me. I had been permitted to see my family one time in the first year of my incarceration. My wife, once a beautiful and calm veterinarian, had turned into a skeleton. She was still so beautiful, just like the first time we laid eyes on each other in middle school, but the prospect of my never returning home from Australia had taken its toll. I stayed strong where she seemed broken. I remained calm on the surface:

"How are our babies?"

She sat up straight and put on her toughest face to tell me that Atlas, my sweet brindle boy, had fallen ill while I was away. Bren and I never had kids. It was a bone of contention early in our relationship, but as time passed, sickness and depression clouded our thoughts on a pregnancy. Where we didn't have human children, we did have our other babies. Our immediate family consisted of two dogs and two cats inside our home. We always seemed to take on a group of fosters in addition. Mostly kittens, but there were the occasional puppies as well. Then there were the animals that roamed the farm. An assortment of rescued cows, horses, mules, goats, and reindeer. They were collectively our babies, and I missed all of them terribly, but none more than Atlas. He was connected to me and we bonded from four days old when Bren and I bottle fed him and a few of his brothers. Atlas meant everything to me, and it terrified me that I was missing precious time with him. Time where we could play. Time where we could snuggle. Time where we could drive late at night in search of a snack or a quiet walk downtown.

"Well how bad are we talking?"

"I'm not sure how much longer he can hold on." She could no longer hold back her tears, for she knew the news shook me to my core. I saw that she regretted telling me almost immediately. I reached for her hand to let her know it was ok but stopped myself short. I could feel the cold eyes of the guard piercing into my back. She continued to cry. All I wanted was to hold her hands, to roll her wedding ring through my fingers. I stared at the intricate custom scroll work that I designed for her as the light sparkled off a central row of diamonds.

"I needed to know." I forced a smile trying to comfort her, and she placed a sympathetic kiss on my lips. It wasn't cold, but I could tell that the anxiety had built up and she no longer cared about the rules. I hoped and prayed that it didn't turn into resentment. Our minds can do funny things and emotions can manifest into so many interesting solutions to deal with our problems. I placed my hand on her cheek and brought her close. I didn't have to say it, but I did anyway:

"I didn't do it." Our eyes met and tears fell from all four. Without thought, she pulled me in for an embrace. A whistle blew almost immediately. A young and cocky guard slammed his nightstick on the door and shook his head. We knew the rules, but both of us knew it was worth it. I kissed Bren's hand once more before she exited the room.

This was the only close contact I had with anyone in my family. I would see glimpses of my mother, sister, and Bren in the courtroom, but I wasn't permitted to see them in person. It took a near act from the gods to let me see Bren one time after I was locked away. Too much was riding on this case. It was as high profile as it could possibly be. I could feel

12

their eyes almost penetrating the back of my skull as I looked forward in the court room, unceremoniously cuffed to the desk in front of me. I would finally get a few seconds of eye contact when we would recess for the day. I split the seconds between the three of them, and was forced to watch their eyes grow dimmer each day I wasn't free.

My case was a media circus. They called me, and although innocent I really enjoyed it, "The Bloody American." To the public, there was no doubt that I was guilty, and even my defense seemed to question my involvement in the crimes. The photo some media scumbags tracked down was taken from my Facebook page. It showed a bearded, and rather thuggish looking twenty-two-year-old. The photo was taken in the dead of winter. I had a fluffed up full beard and glared in the camera for fun as if I was trying out for an episode of *Cops*. The photo couldn't have cast a worse light on the well-kempt man they pegged for cold-blooded murder. I couldn't help but laugh as I looked at the photo. It was cropped, and I remember holding a tiny foster kitten that had just peed a step prior to the litter box. It was Halloween, and we dressed the kitten in an adorable set of bunny ears. If I was guilty of anything in the picture, it was pissing the kitten off for the sake of its brighter future in getting adopted. Hindsight, it worked. Funny how misconstrued things can become when taken out of context.

Regardless, all they would see is the bearded murderer plastered on every media outlet in Australia. I was never particularly fond of shaving, but I would grow out a beard and clipper it off when it became a hassle. I tried to keep it fully in check, but sometimes it would take me a few weeks before I got around to grooming. When I was young, the few weeks would be months. That's where the photo spawned from. Full on Unabomber beard, which was hardly the ideal perception for an innocent man. Nothing was going in my favor. They wanted to pin me down on all three murders. Murder One for Ricketts and an accessory to Hogue and Kyle Bengham, the student who was killed in front of me as I escaped from the clutches of the monster.

For an entire year, things seemed dreadfully bleak. While they couldn't establish a clear motive, the prosecution had me with the murder weapon in hand while a fellow officer acted and would testify as a

13

witness. Then three items finally happened in my favor. First, a forensic investigator named Dr. Molly Templeton, decided to take on my case. She was hired by the team of lawyers I used as consultants from the States. They spared no expense, and added pressure from the U.S. Embassy offered her the chance to check out the finer details of my case. The first thing she found concerned the murder weapon. Templeton had studied thousands of homicides. She deduced that the screwdriver I supposedly used to kill Ricketts had a very awkward arrangement of fingerprints relative to the angle in which Ricketts was stabbed. She deduced that I couldn't have actually stabbed Ricketts in that manner. It was physically impossible for an intact human wrist to bend that way. Of course, I knew this. I had been claiming that Shen wore a glove. She simply hid it from sight as she attempted to "save" Ricketts. Unfortunately, this detail didn't give me the means to turn the tables completely in my favor, but it was a start for reasonable doubt.

The second item was the awkward disappearance of the footage from the suspected murder. Everything was filmed prior to one minute ahead of Shen's arrival into the room. Mysteriously and not completely out of the ordinary, so claimed the prosecution, the footage vanished. The prosecution simply deduced that my network, the one that assisted me in the murders of Hogue and Bengham, must have hacked into the system. They claimed the lack of CCTV footage around Newcastle disappeared in the same way. The footage, therefore, worked against me in the twisted courtroom. It was actually a rather sad plea, but the proverbial witch hunt for the "Bloody American" seemed to turn most items in their favor.

The third item, and controversially the one that would free me, happened when Yaravela Shen went missing the day prior to taking the stand against me. At first, there was outrage in and around the courtroom. Speculation persisted that I was the one who was responsible for her vanishing. I was the easiest scapegoat. After all, I was the rich American murderer. The wheels, previously moving at sloth's pace, then grinded to a near halt for an entire year as a hunt for Shen turned up nothing at all. There were no signs of anything. It was like she never existed. Then, and finally, a cavalier media member named Rick Matthews decided to search just a bit further. He didn't search for a body, he searched for an identity. To everyone's astonishment, he found that Yaravela Shen never existed at all. Yaravela Shen was a false identity used to infiltrate the police academe; and just as quickly as she was able to surface, Yaravela Shen disappeared without a trace. Shen had been at the station for two years prior to her disappearance. One of the years was completely shrouded by her involvement as a witness to one of the highest profile murders in Australian history. At least that's how everything looked before Rick Matthews, Molly Templeton, and seemingly Shen herself came to my rescue as the clock struck 11:59 p.m. in my trial.

Today I'm to be released from this rotten hell-hole of a prison. It's been two years, two months, five days, one hour, and fifteen long minutes since Shen framed me for murdering Ricketts. Life in prison was a mixed bag for me. In one respect, despite my fervent defense, most of the congregation thought I had killed a high-ranking cop. That, as frustrating and morbid as it sounds, was an appealing attribute to the vast majority of the prisoners. However, to the guards, I was a perfectly grilled steak ready to be chewed and spit out. I had been beaten more by the guards than the prisoners. This also gave me sympathy to the congregation. I was never raped or anything like that, either. I was a rich boy from America. This is true. Prior to studying history, I had an MBA and I had made a very nice living growing several businesses. I still owned them despite being jailed in another country. My warehouses thrived, my multiple apps were rising in usage, and my rental properties were full. I had my best friend, Ethan Davies, to thank for this while I was away. Ethan had been the loyal rock I needed. Not only while I was imprisoned, but before that while I studied, and before that while I battled cancer. Ethan saw the mental anguish the cancer left me with. I wasn't the same after treatment, and he knew it. I was a shell of my former self and completely unfulfilled despite living how most people would only dream. He took over operation of the businesses and nodded when I told him I needed to make the life changes that resulted in my studies at Newcastle.

Being rich, or at least what the prisoners would call rich, added a certain amount of resentment to the population. People didn't know what

15

to do about me, and so they chose distance above all else. I made one friend, and that was in my second year when I actually had a cellmate. You see, for the first year, fears that the congregation might have some sort of inner link to my assailants on that fateful day, made me request solitary. This was granted without question for as long as I wanted. While the prisoners didn't know what to think of me, neither did the leadership at the prison or even the judges. I was a mystery. Most of the prosecution and the judges probably started to believe I didn't kill Ricketts once my defense started to harden midway through the first year. Constable Shen's disappearance just before her official testimony one year into my stay, cast a very large shadow of doubt on my guilt. That said, I had entered the country, and within a few hours there were three dead bodies around me. That wasn't a resume builder for innocence, and as long as there was a single shroud of suspicion, the wheels of the justice system moved entirely too slowly.

I looked at my prison sentence like the romantic adaptions of my favorite movies. Above all, there was the *Count of Monte Cristo*. It was beyond fitting for my situation and my person in general. I could hardly restrain myself from screaming "What's my crime!" at the top of my lungs. There were other links as well. I plotted, and I thought. Something you never want to give someone like me is the time to think about, well, anything. I am not Einstein or Hawking, but I am a proficient mind when I ignore my quirks, or simply let my quirks take over. Most of these quirks have to do with being obsessive, but not quiet to the point of compulsion. I have what I'd call the opposite of ADD. I have ultra-concentration, but I must be narrowed in or I lose it all. What I mean by this, is that I can do or think about any topic in the world under the correct set of circumstances. Being locked in solitary to me was the right set of circumstances. When I have the desire, any idea, puzzle, problem, or creative solution would usually fall right into bed with me. I'm very lucky in this gift, but like most that find these portions of life easier than others, I was cursed with spiraling downward. I was plagued with the thought of being just another statistic for the world to spit out. I battled depression, but never took the edge off with substance or alcohol. Not that it was an option in prison. Regardless, it wasn't my style, and I

16

feared being out of control even more than the pains of depression themselves.

Sleep also eluded me prior to prison. However, in that hole, it became almost impossible for me to get more than a light few hours. I would think, theorize, and envision my next moves as if they would come any day. Until that day, I would stay at the height of anxiety. I would stay in shape by using my confines as a gym, a positive part of the prison experience that kept me from madness. See, I always knew I would get out eventually. It was only a matter of time until my defense team from home, which I paid handsomely for, unlocked my door. I was, after all, an innocent man. I also knew there were major holes in the prosecution. There was no motive for me to kill any of the three people. Hogue was about to hood me at a graduation ceremony and had already accepted my thesis defense, or dissertation defense in American terms. The student that was killed, a twenty-two-year-old English major from Sydney, I had never seen in my life until he died merely a few inches from me. Ricketts was the easiest to explain away. Simply put, if there was no evidence to link me to A and B, then why would I kill the link toward expediting my freedom from the madness that had just ensued? In a police station, no less? Come on! Cooperation was my only, and a very wise, bargaining chip. Even if I had been linked to killing the first two, why would I cement my grave by killing an Inspector in cold blood? Again, in a police station? Hardly the wisest of moves for someone still claiming to be sane, a person less than a week away from his doctorate. On top of everything, there was also the missing video footage from the time Shen came in until Ricketts was dead. They had the footage from before when Ricketts was interrogating me. Well, they had a lot of it any way. It couldn't be a mere coincidence, and something finally proven in my favor when Shen was nowhere to be found. After two years of, pardon my language, trying to bend me over and fuck me in the ass, the Australian justice system had come up dry. There were no more proverbial wells to wish in for my conviction.

So, I thought. I basked over the research I had conducted over four long years of my life. Where was the link? No one had killed me in prison. Not a guard that was paid off or an inmate in my second year.

17

Where was the link? I used my cellmate Jules Englewood, an American from Atlanta, GA, to help ponder my questions. He obliged because I could help him with his own plights. He obliged because in prison, he was my only true friend. You see, *Count of Monte Cristo* alive and well. I wasn't sure who was Edmond and who was the Priest, but I still loved it. It brought me a smile any time I thought of the links. Jules was a beefy ex-football player that missed his chance at a full ride playing for Auburn. He was a five-star prospect ranked twenty-fourth in his class by Rivals. He didn't rob a bank or shoot someone, he simply got the wrong girl pregnant at the wrong time. This girl was a congressman's daughter from the state of Alabama named Missy Powers. She was a month shy of fifteen when she told her parents. The act was consensual, but Congressman William H. Powers III sure made poor Jules' life difficult from there. Jules was an extremely talented kid who played linebacker for Booker T. Washington in Atlanta. By the time Congressman Powers was done with him, he was a scared black seventeen-year-old who had forced himself on his daughter. Missy was nowhere to be found. Mysteriously, she had vanished without a trace. Out of fear, Jules ran away before the spring semester of his senior year, and before the inevitable trial. He was a smart kid that knew what life was to be if he stayed and faced the music that was coming on way too loud. He abandoned all hope for Missy and his unborn child, as well as his single mother. He hated himself for what he did when he ran, but what choice did he have?

Jules made his way west. He was a huge kid at seventeen, some six foot four and two hundred and sixty pounds of muscle. With that kind of size, he had a skill-set. He took cash and changed his identity. His fists were bloody by the time he was twenty. By the time twenty-two rolled around he had committed unspeakable atrocities for some of the most powerful crime bosses on the west coast. At twenty-four, he used his cash, of which he had a remarkable sum, and ran once again. He watched Steve Irwin as a kid, and dreamed of sleeping under a tree where he might spot a koala in the wild. It was a simple flight to Australia, so he booked it. He arrived down under and blew through his money at a staggering pace. Before his twenty-fifth birthday, he was sentenced to three years on multiple assault charges. His demons had finally caught up to him. He was serving his second year when Thomas Appling, a biscuit white intellectual from Tennessee entered his cell.

I promised Jules to help him meet his daughter. This was something I was more than happy to help with. See, when I looked at Jules, a huge man riddled with scars, tattoos, and way too many bad breaks, all I thought about was giving to him. We connected almost immediately. It was something that neither of us could really understand. We didn't come from like circumstances or have hardships in common, but both of us had witnessed the harsh side of luck. Both of us loved passionately and would give ourselves completely to those we loved without question or fear. That passion was the greatest explanation we could ever find for the reason we got along so well.

Jules listened intently to my tales. He wanted to learn more about Herodotus, Thucydides, Plutarch, and all the historians I had mastered. He wanted to learn about the battles of Thermopylæ, Salamis, and Platæa. He called me "Doc" to credit me with something I worked so hard for but was taken from me right at the finish line. Something he was all too familiar with as well. You see, the University of Newcastle refused to grant my PhD under the circumstances. I could hardly blame them, as it would be nothing short of scandalous to award a suspected murderer with a degree. I often wondered if they would ever reconsider. I suspected they would, but I wasn't sure.

"I'll see you in a month, Doc." Jules' voice was raspy today. The big man had been crying, but tried to hold it back. He was to be released in thirty-four days, almost a full year early for good behavior. However, I knew the time by himself would hurt. Unlike me, Jules was intently social. Solitude was an exceptionally dark place for Jules. He needed people. He needed friends, associates, or the comfort of wildlife. I could almost see him turning into a crazy cat man if he never found love.

"Fluffy," I replied as I always did when he would get so sentimental or emotional. He smiled and his bright white teeth reflected off his brown skin. His features were soft. Jules was handsome with light blue eyes that contrasted his enormous body and sleeves of tattoos. His look was the exact opposite of fluffy, but that's the nickname I gave him. He was

19

fluffy because his true interior was koalas, pandas, cotton tails, and marshmallow fluff. Sure, he had committed some pretty rough crimes. You could even say Jules Englewood was a thug, but to me, he would always be fluffy. There were few in the world I would trust more than him.

"Stay cool, Dr. DrApp." He winked at me and we embraced in a hug for the first time. I was Dr. DrApp to him ever since the second day we knew each other. Two true southern boys, our first stab at comradery happened when I reeled off an early Three Six Mafia verse after we spoke about music for a bit. We spoke of music and how we missed it. He told me he liked Dave Matthews, something he never told a soul. I told him I'd been listening to Triple Six since fifth grade. He didn't believe me, so I had to prove myself. When I started rapping, his jaw hit the floor. My nickname of App from childhood mixed with Dr. Dre. Dr. DrApp I was, and I sensed I would forever be, to at least one person. You never know someone like you know a cellmate. There's little to be gained by posturing, so in the right circumstances, some of the truest bonds can be built. A level of trust has to be earned, or disaster could ensue. Few bonds worked out as clean as Jules and me, but I knew of some others that took place. Hell, I knew of a few marriages that were arranged from prison cells. Life is funny, and while I wasn't going to marry Jules, I certainly knew we had built a life-long bond in our one year as cellmates.

The guards unlocked my cell as the prison erupted. The chorus was loud when I left. The only one that was quiet was Jules. The only one who knew who I was, what I had gone through, and where I had to go.

Chapter 2

July fourth in Birmingham, Alabama felt as if the fireworks were constantly blowing up inside Mr. Powers' yellow Polo shirt. The poor shirt wasn't helped by a significant beer belly doing its best to snap every strand. Mixed with the almost comical amount of sweat terrorizing the shirt like the spin cycle on the washing machine, it's safe to say that, if anthropomorphized, the shirt would seek suicide as an alternative to the closet. The heat plaguing his early round of golf with the area's more illustrious businessmen was nothing short of daunting. Sweat beads squeezed their way to the brim of his hat, dropping off to the scorched earth just short of his Odyssey Putter. Alabama summers, the land where humidity and heat produce an air so sticky and hot that, well, just don't go there. Through seventeen holes, Powers was down a skin and another ten grand. Without dropping a birdy on eighteen, this would make five straight rounds and more money than most Alabamians make in years.

His ProV1 lipped out, and he received a callous slap on the back from Grady Hedges.

"Tough break, Will." The snide remark left Powers speechless as he hadn't lost five straight rounds since, well, a time all too terrifyingly familiar. A time he tried to forget about through Tennessee Whiskey in the clubhouse. A time some ten years ago. He nodded and forced a smile:

"At least it was closer this time, Grade. I'll be back next time." He shook Grady Hedges' hand and piled into his EZGO in route to the clubhouse, a filet, and his whiskey.

The southern clubhouse. Old and crispy rich men, cigars mixed with aged cologne, and more pretention than Lord Cornwallis in Charleston, South Carolina. Waiters dressed in tuxedos each and every day.

Members wore expensive shirts pocketed with stains from their rounds. No matter, they rarely wore the same shirt twice. Powers sat with three others while he scarfed down his fifty-dollar "lunch special." The burgundy sauce paired well with the filet and the fingerling potatoes. Butter oozed off the potatoes and mated with the dark sauce. The spices were perfect, the whiskey was woody, and the meat sublimely medium rare. Powers ignored most of the ranting of the other men. Hedges talked about some kind of investment in the background. Powers noticed that Samuel Emory Talbot and Roger Samford Fletcher, the other two in the group's foursome, were intently listening to what must have been a provocative proposal pitched by Grade. There seemed to be little out of the ordinary from Powers' perspective. Par for the course, if you excuse the pun. Grade was a charming business man that must've been worth tens of millions by now. In this company, Grade might as well have been poor, but he brought a charisma to the table. He was good looking, even in his early fifties, and sported a trim physique unique to the table. He wasn't overly ripped, but carried himself nicely. He was also the only one at the table that could be called "new money." Powers pondered and admired Grady for a few moments as he slopped up the last of his steak. Sauce dripped from his lips onto the brim of his belly. Perhaps the yellow polo would receive the mercy of a trash can. He didn't listen but for snippets as his loud chewing clogged his ears and closed his mind. A normal man would feel remorse, but Powers was no normal man.

"I'm sorry, Grade. My head is not here today. Can you come by the house tomorrow if this is something serious?" The three men around the table smirked at Powers, but understood all too well his plights.

Grady Hedges stood up. "I'll come by at one, Will. You alright today, buddy?" Grady flashed genuine concern, and Powers nodded slowly:

"I'm fine, man. Just not here right now." He stood up and threw back the remainder of his whiskey. He shook three hands in the order he felt socially obliged to follow. He then gasped and exclaimed: "I'll be back at it tomorrow, boys!" He smiled superficially, which was something the others understood and let pass. He turned away and walked out of the club. He nodded and spoke pleasantries to a dozen or so people on his

22

way out, which was customary. The valet already had his beautiful 1967 Aston Martin DB pulled up with the door open. "Thanks Jack," he smiled. He gave John Willow a fresh one-hundred-dollar bill. John didn't care what he was called as long as the hundreds kept coming. Powers plopped in his car and cruised with the wind hitting his thinning dome.

When he returned home, the whiskey mixed harshly with reminders of the ten years his only daughter and her unborn child went missing. She was fourteen-years-old at the time, almost fifteen. At the time of her disappearance, he was a U.S. Congressman for the State of Alabama. He was far less crispy back then and married, although unhappily. He wasn't a candidate for anything major at the time. At least not by the standards of one of the wealthier men in the country. He probably had a shot at Senate and perhaps Governor, but no realistic expectations or drive for a higher office. Now, he was a widower of one year and ten years removed from his daughter's disappearance. After his daughter went missing, he played the sympathy card toward an easy position as a U.S. Senator but lasted just one term before retiring from politics. He received ample pressure to run for President on the Republican ticket but folded when the questions of his daughter began burning his insides. A few years later, his wife committed suicide. The note spoke of nothing. It was pure gibberish and an obvious sign toward a drug induced stupor. Will Powers hated his wife, but resented even more the thought of being worse without her. Now, he was lonely. He couldn't order take out without picking up the phone. He couldn't arrange a tee-time without scheduling it for himself. Everything that used to lay down for him suddenly became increasingly more tedious.

He sold out of his raw materials company that had been in the family for four generations. Entitled beyond compare, Will Powers never had to lift a finger for the finer things in life. He didn't have all his assets in one place, but if he did, he'd be just shy of the billionaire moniker. Will Powers wasn't short of friends, and even had three living sisters with large families of their own. But he was alone. He was completely alone with the exception of hired help. He couldn't trust a soul and spending all the money in the world couldn't bring back his daughter. In fact, he had been trying continuously for ten years. He had spent millions trying

23

to find Missy, but the girl was gone and probably buried somewhere. He slipped off his golf spikes and took off his socks. His toes soaked in the cool marble slab foyer, which gave him the sensation to stare above toward the tacky but monstrous crystal chandelier above him. He tossed his key on a ring and stumbled toward his theatre. He left the spikes, socks, and copious amounts of grass for some nameless housekeeper to pick up later. He unpaused the episode of *Dexter* he had been watching and scooped a giant cone of ice cream out of his custom designed theatre ice-cream booth. His dominant left hand-held remnants of the scoop on its knuckles. In lieu of wiping it down with a wet paper towel, he simply licked it off. The chocolate mixed with cherry chunks, and he felt as if he were eleven years old at the old soda shop. He plopped into his massive suede chair and sucked the ice-cream away from the cone ferociously. A tear rolled from his eye and he thought about Missy. Will Powers would sit in the same position for the next twelve hours.

Chapter 3

One thing would never change with me. Despite Rick Matthews, I still hated the media as a whole. Prior to my pseudo-celebrity as a murderer, I always hated watching the news and how they would manipulate stories for their own personal gain. It sickened me to see people vilified or glorified based solely on the perception of a newsfeed. It sickened me that media members would ask questions solely to get a human-like response from someone they interviewed, all in an attempt to destroy them if they would fall prey to their ruse. This drove me insane when coaches would be interviewed during games back home, purposefully at the height of their emotions. It didn't make it more real for the fans. It simply made them look like assholes or superficial dorks. For me, it started when I was interviewed during my processions to court. For someone like me, there were only a handful of times I could be asked why I killed someone I didn't before I yearned to become sarcastic in my response. Luckily, I held my tongue despite wanting to go on an insensitive rant about the details in which I stabbed Ricketts, and my villainous plots to overthrow the entire government of Australia one DCI at a time. Thankfully I was tactful all the way through. I simply stated that I was innocent and moved on.

The flash bulbs were piercing as I made my way out of the facility and down the few steps leading toward the flock of media members blocking traffic below. Screams ensued the second my head popped out from the door, the first time as a free man in over two years.

One person yelled, "Justice!" All to a split chorus of cheers and jeers.

"You'll always be our Bloody American!" This even got a short chuckle out of me when I saw Rick Matthews peeking behind a stout long-haired woman.

"Murderer!" Another person screamed from the far background. To my astonishment, that yell received more boos. It was the first time I felt the split crowd begin to turn just slightly in my favor.

"What will you do now?" A woman hopped up trying to gain a view of me. More questions came pouring in as I smiled brightly, put my head down, and completely ignored the massive crowd. That, in my estimation and after two years of scrutiny from the same crowd, is true justice.

Bren, Diane my mother, and Lori my sister, waited eagerly in the car for me. Tears and a group hug consumed the four of us. It was, without doubt, one of the sweetest moments of my life. For just a few seconds, I began to forget about plans and precautions. I was a husband, a son, and a brother for the first time in so very long.

"Well, now what?" My tone and demeanor were indecisive. Before the embrace, I thought I knew a semblance of a path toward my future, but now everything was unclear. What does a person do when they are freed from a wrongful prison sentence? What would I do with myself? My newly acquired support staff, especially when together, was never short of advice.

"It's been a long few weeks, Tom. It'd be nice to get back to the hotel. We love you so much!" My mother spoke first and flashed a genuine, but seemingly forced smile. Her words were very simple, and I could tell how tired she was when she spoke them. All in the car felt tremendous relief, but the anxiety from the past few years rendered us nearly comatose for energy. Understandably, no thoughts of action filled our hearts at first. When the car began to ease away from the mob of media members, a sinking feeling hit me like a punch to my gut. I hadn't thought about her in months. It took me a long time in solitary, but a few months in, I finally stopped seeing Hogue's blond hair soaking up her own blood. For so long after my imprisonment, it was one of the most vivid images I held. Then, after months of reconditioning my mind, I rarely thought about it. Then, I rarely thought about her. Now, and finally free in the physical form, she's back in my mind. It's funny how our minds and emotions build parameters and invisible fences. Feeling caged, I felt the words project from my mouth as if I were trying to break down a mental wall:

"Where's Dr. Hogue buried?" The three relieved smiles in the car reverted into uneasiness. Confusion shrouded their faces. Bren smirked a bit before beginning a shuddered response:

"We...," She looked for confirmation from my mother and sister. "We haven't been there. We weren't even in country when they held the funeral." I nodded. I wasn't in shock or even confused by their absence of knowledge about Hogue. None of them were close to her. Only Bren had met her, and that was for less than a few hours on a visit.

"Sorry, that's a dumb question. If it's alright..." A stupid thing to state when I knew my request was more than reasonable. "I would like to visit her grave before we go home." Lori nodded but didn't speak. She was constantly supportive of anything emotional. She had always been this way. She was in tune with other people's feelings to an almost damaging level. She wanted so much to help, and many times hurt herself in the process of giving so much of her vulnerability to those closest to her. The pain led to drugs. I didn't know if she was still using, but the new tattoos on her face suggested that perhaps she was still battling. She shrugged and smiled as if to say of course. I knew Lori, and knew her reaction to something like this. It was very consistent, so was the reaction from my mother.

"Our plane leaves really early in the morning." The statement was as a matter of fact. It wasn't that she was trying to prevent us from seeing Hogue's grave. She just couldn't resist bringing up something that might get in the way. Something that had to be planned around. My mother is a very scheduled person. She has anxiety and throws herself into social situations despite feeling uncomfortable on the inside. Many of her burdens stemmed from a childhood where a set of leg braces subjected her to serious ridicule by insensitive kids. Kids can be some of the cruelest instigators. In my mother's case, the torment was harsh and the lasting effects, damaging. She didn't like talking about it, but she created defense mechanisms to cope. One major mechanism was her toughness. She would never bow away from an intimidating situation. She was up

27

for anything when it came to public situations. She flocked around with friends and she desired attention to build her self-esteem. Her decisions, in many situations, were hasty due to this reflex. She was impulsive and fun, but needed control. Hence the statement of the plane's departure.

Lori shot my mother a scowl. The two argued as most mothers and daughters will, but they loved each other and would do anything to protect one another from outsiders. They were equally protective of me. To all three in the car, I was the super hero that could do no wrong.

"We will find out where it is now." Lori tried to be the ultimate calm in stressful situations. She had a near superpower to be optimistic when the times were at their roughest. She hadn't always been like this, but experiences of her own humbled her and shaped her into one of the more giving people I had ever encountered.

Lori and I were not particularly sensitive to our mother's insecurities. In fact, our mother pushed us very hard toward ignoring the items that she struggled with. She wanted us to be tough. She wasn't cold, but if we were injured, going to the hospital would've been the absolute last resort. She demanded toughness, self-reliance, and responsibility. It turned Lori and me into respectable human beings, but both of us struggled at times with the insecurities we bottled up as opposed to feeling the freedom to share something intimidating, or perhaps something peculiar like a fear. I, myself, am a master at compartmentalizing. So much so that I can be completely overtaken by the shock of an emotion if it decides to rear its head out of the blue. The guilt from not thinking about poor Hogue in so long, and almost forgetting entirely to pay some sort of respects to her, was one such feeling. Lori's insecurities flashed when she would have too much to drink. She would cry and feel tremendous guilt over ruining the time for those around her. It was if she craved the outlet but understandably hated herself for desiring it.

My persona made me feel like a sociopath, so I did everything possible to be as loving as a husband, friend, or family member as I could. The reflex is almost instinctual at this point in my life, and it makes me appear as a very selfless individual. Honestly, I try my very best to be everything my father wasn't. My father was an extremely intelligent man, a genius of a scientist. He passed on many of his intellectual gifts to me, and certainly much of his depression. Luckily, as opposed to only having the gifts of intellect with the even more damaging side of social ignorance, I was fortunate to feel empathy and compassion for my fellow humans, even if depression sometimes clouded my judgment. This, unfortunately, was something he must have really struggled with. I never asked him; and if I had, he wouldn't have shared with me. In fact, I hadn't talked to him about anything other than mundane items, such as sports, since they split up when I was young. He never tried asking about my life, what I enjoyed, or how I felt. It just wasn't him. This gave us probably the most superficial relationship a father and son could have while still staying halfway in touch with one another. I assumed he wouldn't make contact after my release. Hell, he might not even know about my imprisonment in the first place.

"We missed you so much!" Bren's eyes began tearing up once more as she hugged me separate from the others and pulled herself closer to me. I smiled once again, trying to free myself from the Hogue induced guilt that had taken me over for a short period. I pulled Bren closer to me. Her hair smelled so good. I missed holding her and felt the world melt away when she was in my arms. Things simply felt safer and better when she was with me. It had been this way since we were teenagers and first fell in love.

"Let's get to the hotel now. If there's time tomorrow, I can stop by the grave site before we take off." This statement relieved a great sense of angst that had hung over the car ever since I mentioned Hogue's grave. They weren't interested in doing anything outside of resting, getting over the awkwardness of my two-year absence, and perhaps getting us something yummy to munch on. This was the time I had missed during my absence. I had waited more than two years to get some sort of satisfaction from what had transpired on that fateful day, but desired to be with my family more than my revenge. Hell, perhaps my intense hours planning such an elaborate path toward retribution were hasty. Perhaps all I really cared about was caring for and protecting my family from harm. No matter what was to happen in the future, there certainly would be no scheming, no planning, and no action on this day.

We laughed and we cried on the hour drive from the maximum-security Cessnock Correctional Centre to the Crowne Plaza Newcastle, where the Australian government was kind enough to accommodate us. Before retiring to my soft bed and television, I would have the Fisherman's Basket of king prawns, Balmain bugs, and octopus. I washed it down with sparkling Coca-Cola and toasted my fluffy friend from Atlanta. I then had the warmest and softest brownie sundae. The vanilla ice-cream lightened the rich brownie coated with coffee beans. It was a meal fit for, well, someone that was wrongfully imprisoned and returned back to life after a few years. Perhaps it was a meal fit for a king as well, but I didn't have the experience to pass that kind of judgment. All I knew was that it was perfect in that moment. Out of prison, with family, flying home in the morning, and full of chocolate.

Chapter 4

Will Powers smiled and welcomed Grady Hedges into his personal study. The study in the Powers Estate was immaculate. Five-foot-tall, walnut-stained wainscoting wrapped around the entire room. Details had been hand rendered and fancy-painted to accentuate the wood grain. Bookshelves rose high above the wainscoting, and they too, wrapped around the entire room. Swinging iron ladders helped people reach the high books, and an iron spiral staircase brought an admirer of books to the second level of the study, where more walnut bookcases wrapped around just above a gallery peering down upon Powers' work area. It would be careless to leave out a pertinent detail of the books in the massive study. To this day, none of them had been read. That said, they did act as fine decorations and a statement to the refined nature of the perception Will Powers wanted to portray. Powers never met at his desk, but instead chose to sit in the two large leather chairs stationed in front of the limestone fireplace. The massive fireplace was impossible to miss when entering the study and also rose high into the second floor, bisecting the walnut bookshelves through both levels. Large unlit logs begged to be set ablaze, but the heat in Birmingham rarely gave Powers the desire or need to do so.

Powers offered his friend a Jack and Coke and a cigar, both of which were graciously accepted by Hedges. The two lit up and felt the smoke billow from their lips high into the air. A filtration system contained the smells, residues, and any other undesirable second-hand effects the smoke might produce if it were to escape the study. Grady was noticeably on edge about this meeting, which was a welcome sight to Powers after the beating he endured on the links yesterday. Here, in his study, Powers was king. From his chair, he had made dreams come true for those lucky enough to be granted an audience. He had also derailed the promise of "would be" inventors and businessmen. Millions of dollars had been exchanged with handshakes, drinks, and a smoke.

Powers nodded and turned his hands over in an invitation for Grady to unleash his idea. He rocked back in his chair, placed his drink on an end table, and gave his full and unbridled attention. His emotionless expression when approaching business matters caused the most seasoned sales people to prattle immaturely. There's fun, and then there's business. Nobody confused the two around Will Powers, and he knew it.

Grady placed his drink on the end table and his cigar into a silver ash tray with the appearance of stag antlers rising up to cup his cigar gently. He leaned forward and interlocked his hands. He stared into Powers' frigid eyes.

"Will," Grady started, "I've known you for what... fifteen years?" Powers nodded without allowing his expression to crack. "During that time, I've seen the inside of this room maybe a dozen times. I've taken a cigar and a drink from you, pitched an idea or two, and we've closed our meeting with a handshake each time." Grady began easing back in his chair with renewed confidence in his proposal. "I've happily taken your mostly constructive criticism, and despite leaving with more no's than yes's as is customary in business, we've managed to stay close friends." Powers again nodded and almost cracked a smile. "For the last few years, I've known you— Hell, let's call it the last ten years. I've also known that there is really only one business venture that would attract your true attention." Powers' business posture began to turn into bewilderment. Was this what Grady was chatting on about yesterday when he was half paying attention? Surely not. He almost hastened Grady to get to the point. Grady noticed this change and knew he had the focus he needed. He continued with a callous smile. "There's no easy way to propose this, Will. Let's try marketing terms. Supply and demand. I have a supply that you have a demand for." Will began to feel uncomfortable in his own skin. Grady sensed Will's impatience when he went in for the kill. In an almost too casual declaration, Grady spoke. "I have Missy, Will. I have your daughter." Grady smirked and let his revelation consume Powers.

The once frigid businessman felt ten years' worth of panic, guilt, coping, trauma, and pain all come crashing down upon him. His position of king within the hallowed halls of his study had vanished as the only Achilles Heel he had left in his world was shredded by his friend of more than fifteen years. His excitement was trumped by betrayal, or was his betrayal trumped by excitement? He didn't know, and he couldn't think. The tables were turned, and his world was jolted off its core. He had thousands of questions begging to be set free. His muscles tensed, and his face turned red. He tried to speak, but nothing came out. Grady smiled like he was Brutus stabbing Caesar in the kidney. His evil smile infuriated Powers who finally broke free from his silence:

"Wha— Where is she?" He rose to his feet and anger overtook him. The crystal glass holding his drink fell to the Persian rug. The glass landed safely but the Jack and Coke beaded before seeping into the thick rug and vanishing from sight. That's when all his power seemingly buckled beneath him.

Grady, too cunning too conniving, stayed perfectly postured in his chair. With all the calm of a seasoned assassin, Grady lifted his finger.

"No, no, no, Mr. Powers. We will not conduct business in this way. *Sit Down!*" A terrifying psychosis seemed to envelope Grady, and seemed to exorcise its will on the man who used to be Will's friend. *He must have been body snatched*, Powers thought. Why was he doing this? Why did Grady have Missy? Powers couldn't think. He simply sat back in his chair like a defeated labradoodle cowering to Grady's lion.

Grady calmly stood in front of Will Powers. He placed the cigar back in his fingers and sucked it through his lips. He blew the smoke high in the air before his stunned counterpart. From his shorts pocket, he retrieved a small envelope. The kind of envelope one would expect a "thank you" card to be in. He placed the envelope in front of Will Powers.

"Do not have any misconceptions about who is in charge here, Will. If you want to see Missy alive, there are clear instructions contained in this envelope that you must follow." From the small of his back, Grady

33

pulled out a small Kahr 9mm and pointed it at Will's chest. The shock consumed Will, and he accepted defeat as he had the day before on the golf course. "You will open that envelope and you will follow the instructions, Will. That's all you will do." Grady spoke confidently and watched the manhood escape his billionaire friend and former Senator. "I'll be in touch soon, Will."

Grady Hedges left the study and showed himself out of Powers' estate. Will sat in his chair, completely stunned, shattered, but also eager. Ten years of searching had culminated in the most bizarre circumstance. A circumstance that begged more questions than Will could possibly fathom. He tried to regain some semblance of composure as the envelope figuratively burned a hole through his very soul. After a minute of contemplation that could've been hours for all Powers knew, he opened the envelope.

Chapter 5

All four of us were tired, but none of us could actually sleep. There was obvious excitement stemming from my release, but also the uneasiness of the circumstances that led up to my trip to prison caused concern. The comfort of the fine dining and brownie earlier began metabolizing away. Were there still people who would attempt to kill me? The level of protection issued by the Australian government had cast a spotlight on potential dangers. Prior to release, time had made us soft to the dire conditions, the blood, and the terror. Time heals wounds to the best of its ability. To me, the few minutes of death might as well have been dreamt. No, it wasn't forgotten, and no, it wasn't dreamt, but over two years in prison had left me numb to the dangers of being released back into the jungles of the world. This is, well, what I initially thought, but after a few hours with Bren, Diane, and Lori, the anxiety of simply being in Australia was too much for us to handle.

The justice system was kind enough to give us armed guards and escorts for the remainder of our stay in Australia. The last thing Australia wanted was for me to be killed prior to returning to America. I was, for all intents and purposes, Australia's most protected person until my flight in the morning.

It was 5:30 a.m. when I decided to stop fooling myself with the prospects of slumber. I walked gently to the bathroom to avoid waking my family who had finally fallen asleep a few hours earlier. For the first time in over two years, I took electronic clippers and cut off my beard. The stubble left over was a welcome sight to me. I enjoyed a five-o'clock shadow, as it made me feel better than a shaven baby face. I'd felt this way in high school when my facial hair appeared sooner than my classmates. The same facial hair danced a tango with dress code violations every day of my junior and senior years of private school. I simply hated a clean shave, but St. Andrews, a tiny private school in Sewanee, TN beat my facial hair until the day I graduated. Ever since, the hair has only lost one battle, and that was on my wedding day.

I splashed water on my face and stared at myself in the bathroom mirror. The scar on my right cheek from the near deathblow of the .308 was faded now. It reminded me of three other scars with similar implications to me. I took off my shirt and placed my hand just above my heart. I used my fingers to comb away the hair that concealed the scar of my chemotherapy port. It too, had faded with time. Despite the fading scar, I could still feel the sting of the needle and smell the preservative that accompanied the saline to flush the port. I almost gagged thinking about it nearly ten years later. My fingers scrolled across to my collar bone where the lymph nodes first made their presence known. One day, it was as if they were balloons blown up with compressed air all over my neck. I smiled as I felt around and couldn't find a single one out of place. This was a ritual I conducted every single day. My hand then scrolled down my stomach, and I pressed my index finger inside my belly button. I didn't think about the gallbladder being taken out, I simply thought of the night of debilitating sickness that was a precursor to its removal, and then of course, the digestive distress that had followed me ever since. I smiled again. The man in the mirror was alive. He was alive despite life's attempts at cheap shots. He was alive despite prison. He was alive despite depression, sickness, and "hits" on his life. He was also ready to find answers. A determined stare and nod to myself came before hopping in the ornate shower of the Crowne Plaza. I let the hot water bounce off me. It was an amazing feeling to have a shower in solitude. One small luxury that I will never take for granted again.

I made arrangements with two guards to drive me to Hogue's grave. I gently kissed Bren's cheek to let her know I would be away for a few moments.

She pulled me in for a giant hug and told me, "Don't go!" This was a reaction I had missed terribly. Bren and I were almost always connected at the hip. She hated the idea of my leaving her side after so long away. Although, this was true for the absence of any time. Bren never liked me leaving a room without her, even if it was to go grab her something from the kitchen back home. The reaction now seemed the same as those times I left for the kitchen, or on a business trip. There were few varying degrees of her reaction. Two years, or one minute. To Bren, time away was time away. But, as with all the times before, she understood deep down that there wasn't practicality in 24/7 contact. The grave visit was something I needed to do alone, and she would never stop me from it. Before I designed an explanation of why I needed to go, she continued: "Ugh.... Well..., be careful!" She then threw the covers back over herself in exasperation. She would attempt to sleep, but I doubted that she'd be able to. I doubted she would be able to until the day we arrived safely back on our farm in East Tennessee.

"I love you so much." I spoke softly, pulled the covers down, and kissed Bren's lips. She smiled and nodded.

"I love you, too. Now go before I change my mind." We both smiled. We had missed each other so much. Before, we'd had difficulty being apart for days. After a two-year absence, we both felt the immense pain of intense separation anxiety. I knew it wouldn't take long for us to get back into a rhythm. That's simply what happens when you love someone. It doesn't mean there weren't scars to overcome, but it meant that we would conquer those scars in stride.

I slowly crept out of the heavy hotel door and softly shut it behind me. Two guards stood as sentinels in front of the room.

One nodded to me and squeezed the walkie-talkie attached to his vest. "He's ready." He spoke into the device before nodding to me again. "Come on. I'll take you down the hall." We left the other guard to stand fast back at the room where Bren, Diane, and Lori remained. I felt out of place with such accommodating security, but it was very welcome.

The Crowne Plaza Newcastle is stationed where the Hunter River empties into the Tasman Sea. The guard escorted me to the front entrance, where two federal officers awaited me in an unmarked Holden Commodore on Wharf Road. The guard opened the driver side rear door to the right of the Holden. I entered the car and let the cool leather

37

consume me. I didn't expect conversation from the two officers in the front, but I did receive a short amount along the thirteen-minute drive to the Sandgate Cemetery. The driver was a mid-thirties officer with the demeanor of a mid-teens female. She was way too chipper for six a.m. and had obviously soaked in the espresso at the Crowne prior to my arrival. She wore a blue button up with her badge on a lanyard. She carried a sidearm, but I didn't pay attention to the make. She had medium-length hair tied into a single tail in the back. She was a few pounds overweight but attractive with smooth skin and a pretty smile.

"Morning to ya!" She exclaimed too loudly.

I nodded and smiled, "Good morning. How are y'all this morning?" I said y'all but had very few hints of a southern accent. It's simply easier to say for me than the alternatives. I also enjoyed how it tied me to my roots. I felt the same enjoyment when an Australian would call me "mate" or someone would say "cheers" to end a correspondence. There was a time when I was embarrassed to be marginalized as an ignorant southerner, but those times were far gone. I embraced my background and loved where I was from. I had traveled the world and rarely met a friendlier place than rural East Tennessee.

"Good, thanks." The passenger side officer replied. He was genuine in his response, but obviously more taken back by the morning than his partner. He took a long sip of coffee: "I'd be better if Officer Happy knew it was six a.m." He smiled a rehearsed smile to his partner. I could tell the two had been through this routine quite a few times before. They had chemistry together and had probably been working with one another for years. The passenger was well put together and tall. He sported a well-groomed haircut and zero facial hair. I could tell he didn't have a hair out of place, probably didn't have a hair on his body lower than his head. Needless to say, he was particularly concerned with looking good on the job. Despite complaints about the time, he had obviously been awake for long enough to product up his hair. He had on a similar blue button up and badge attached to a lanyard, but he wore dark jeans in contrast to his partner's khakis.

There was an awkward silence after the passenger's remarks. I broke the silence with an ice-breaker of sorts:

"Busy day, today?" The passenger smirked and looked at the driver. He then stared back toward the road and spoke without making eye-contact with me:

"Mr. Appling. We really just want this to be over with. No offense, but this assignment wasn't voluntary." He turned back to me. He didn't scowl, but he wanted me to know we were neither friends nor enemies. This was a job for him and wasn't something envied by his peers. He and his partner were in charge of transporting the "Bloody American." Naivety jaded me over my exoneration. Just because I was released didn't change the circumstances in which I was arrested. Honestly, I was lucky that all the officers since my release had been so professional. The tension in the car, even from someone like "Officer Happy," was palpable to say the least.

The rest of the ride was in complete silence. We arrived at Sandgate Cemetery, and low and behold, another officer opened my door to escort me to Hogue's grave. The cemetery was arranged in a checkerboard fashion. There wasn't much space wasted, but some evergreen trees separated sections of the graveyard from one another. The cemetery was massive. All in all, I wouldn't be surprised if it comprised more than one hundred acres of land. The sun was just coming up, shrouding an eerily beautiful light upon the graves. Dew dripped off the headstones, making spider webs easily discernible. It was almost as if the spiders were employed by the cemetery. Their webs sparkling beacons of beauty contrasting harshly with the death below the surface. I smiled, as I did in most circumstances whether I was happy, anxious, scared, or whatever emotion consumed me at the time. My new escort pointed me through and gave me space. I read the periphery of the cemetery and saw roughly five more guards stationed around. Perhaps there were even more.

I stepped toward Hogue's dew-covered headstone. It read, *Professor Victoria Hogue: Gone Too Early*. She split her stone with her husband. It read, *Professor Bryson Hogue: Gone Too Early*. Victoria had spoken of Bryson often. She revered him, but he was taken early by Parkinson's. She spent countless hours combing through his research and publishing his unfinished documents. It was the kind of love I admired. She sacrificed so much of herself to honor Bryson and expand upon his

39

legacy. I knelt down next to the granite stone. It was obvious that attention hadn't been paid to her site in more than a year. This was understandable. She didn't have children and since Bryson's death, she had become reclusive, enveloping herself in his research. I was the last student she took on in supervision, and she had intended an early retirement to focus more upon Bryson's material.

I wiped away some of the dirt and caked on grass clippings that had attached themselves to Victoria and Bryson's headstone. The granite was cold and wet. The dirt and grass wiped away with ease. Traffic from the nearby Pacific Highway began steadily increasing as commuters made their way into Newcastle for work. Perhaps some were going to relax on the beaches as I surely would've at some point two years ago on my commencement vacation. I closed my eyes and tried to remember Victoria prior to the traumatic event. They say always try to remember loved ones at their best. Loved ones with Alzheimer's for instance, like my grandfather, you are supposed to remember them before their mind deteriorated and started the incessant ranting. They, whoever they are, don't tell you how difficult that is. How much easier it is to remember them from the last point of contact. While I remember my grandfather, it's hard not seeing him as the person who was attempting to get serum from bikini laden females while he was on a Canadian riverboat. That was him at his worst mentally. He had never even been to Canada, but convincing him of that toward the end was a fruitless endeavor. This was simply how he was at the end. How he was at his most memorable to me in time and experience. With Hogue, I remember a great woman and then I remember the blast. I remember the explosion of her face and her blood on me. I remember her blonde hair drowning in blood. How would I ever remove that memory and replace it with the better times completely? I likely wouldn't. I would likely always speak fondly of Hogue. She was, after all, an incredible person who helped me more than I can ever put into words, but I'd always remember her hair: the blonde dyed with red. That was her at her most memorable in both time and experience.

I opened my eyes and wiped my hands off on the khaki shorts I was wearing. I stayed in a kneeling position and pondered whether or not to say anything to my dead supervisor. I decided better of it. It wasn't me to say anything and simply let my feeling do the talking for me. What would I say to a headstone and cremated ashes? I figured, if the dead could actually hear me then they could probably sense what I was feeling as well. No need for corny words when they already have my corny thoughts.

I began to stand when something caught my eye. There was an elaborate array of fresh flowers to the grave just behind Hogue's. The display was grand to say the least. The flowers couldn't have been more than a day old. After the flowers caught my attention, I couldn't help but read the headstone. My heart sank before beginning to race at seemingly triple its maximum capacity. I froze before adrenaline crept into my system. I looked around to find safety in the guards. Thankfully they were all still stationed at their posts. I read and reread the stone. It couldn't say what I was reading, and I thought to myself that I couldn't handle any more of this right now. But none of that mattered. No matter how much I didn't want it. The reality was the same and this was far from over. I slowly walked toward the stone. I placed my right hand on it to make sure it was real. To make sure I wasn't having some sort of hallucination. I wasn't. The stone was real and the writing clear. The stone read, *Thomas R. Appling 1980-We are watching*.

Chapter 6

Money. Plain and simple. There were steps to follow, but the bottom line of the note Will Powers held in his hand was the demand for money. Lots and lots of money in exchange for the whereabouts of his daughter. Or more precisely, the proof that he had her.

Will scoffed. "Prick." He spoke to no one but referred to Grady Hedges, the man who held his Missy but gave no proof that he even had her. Grady had been very explicit that Will follow his directions precisely if he were to see his daughter again. Well, at least alive again. What was Grady playing at with such terrible threats? "I've been good to that prick."

Will debated the contents of the note and the steps clearly outlined. Of course, step one was, "Tell absolutely no one." He then went on to explain what no one meant.

"Prick" Will spoke aloud in his study. "Arrogant; cocky; prick" he said. "He has the gall not only to demand money from me, but he speaks down to me like some trailer trash. Prick…, arrogant prick!" He picked up and slammed Grady's whiskey glass through the glass-topped end table. The crash echoed throughout the study. The violence delighted Will. He picked up the remains of the end table and threw it to the other side of the room, connecting with the bookshelf and scattering a set of encyclopedias in the hysteria of his rage.

Step two enraged Will further. "Refer to, and reread, step one."

"Fucking Prick!" Will couldn't grasp something to throw, so he stomped like a child. He dropped to his knees in tears, wondering how everything came to this. Step three, Will read aloud to himself: "Fifty million cash in a goodwill payment shall be dropped off at the trail head at Vulcan Park. The location will be clearly identified at ten thirty p.m. CST on Tuesday. Step four: At that point, you will receive proof that I have your daughter."

Will closed his eyes and tried to contain the rage he felt for Grady. "Goodwill payment!" He slammed his fists on the desk he never used and screamed at the top of his lungs, "Grady, if one hair is harmed I will kill everyone you care for!"

Tuesday would've been short notice for a Fifty million payment to most people, but Will Powers always had ten percent of his wealth in cash. It was something his grandfather taught him, and although impractical, he continued to abide by it to this day. His grandfather did most of his business in cash so many years ago. He didn't trust banks. Will did. In fact, Will owned a majority share in a bank of his own, but he felt an obligation to his grandfather to keep his wish. If all hell broke loose, Will Powers would still have a large sum of money, even if it was worthless.

Will Powers stormed out of his study. He moved toward the staircase next to the drawing room and descended. A series of security measures stood between him and his custom-made vault. He had the customary high-end procedures, which included state of the art fingerprint and ocular scanners. Then he had something unique. He had a puzzle combination lock with a series of step sequences based on the pressure applied. A single wrong step would shut down the vault for an hour. As Will Powers got older, he tripped the sequence about two in every five times. This time, he was successful despite the anger in which he applied the steps. The door opened, and his grandfather's vault appeared. One more combination on a late nineteenth century vault stood between Will and his fortune. He entered it in, springing open the vault and presenting himself with more than ninety-five million in crisp bills, another fifty million in gold bars, and fortunes in gemstones, antique guns, and rare jewelry that his wife once wore. He lifted his right foot to step inside.

"Prick." He muttered again. He was completely outwitted and outmaneuvered. He couldn't stand the feeling, something so foreign to him.

43

   As his right foot touched down inside the vault, he felt the impact as if he were hit in the back of the head by Mike Tyson wearing brass knuckles. He didn't feel the fall to the floor that followed. A masked figure stepped carefully over Will's body, making his fortunes far too easy to confiscate. The masked assailant took everything practical. The cash, the gold, jewelry and gemstones. Left in the vault were the rare art, the antiques, and the almost billionaire lying on the floor. With little need for caution, the figure vanished, walking out of the estate the same route it entered. It was too easy.

Chapter 7

Someone went through an awful lot of trouble to mess with me. Perhaps mess isn't the right word to illustrate the circumstances. I was being completely fucked with from the moment I set foot in Australia two years ago. Now, after more than two years at Cessnock, the writing on the wall, or should I say grave, made me realize the dire nature of my survival. I spouted myself several hundred unanswerable questions. Why was I being watched? Why was I important to these people, whoever they were? I tried to compose myself the best I could. I didn't want to alert the guards just in case they were part of this conspiracy against me. I had one purpose now. Get my family and get out of Australia. I certainly didn't want to play this game while I didn't have home field advantage so to speak. I kept thinking that I hadn't been killed up to this point. I needed to take what the Australian government gave me, namely protection, and get back home.

I rose up to my feet and nodded to the closest sentinel that I was ready to go. He pressed his walkie-talkie and began walking toward me. The moment was in slow motion as my adrenaline expected something catastrophic to happen. He approached closer and closer to me. Then, he was even closer. I could hear his breath against the air and the sound of his boots touching the grass. I could almost feel the grass I stood upon move as he approached. I could almost feel his presence when—

"Let's go." He spoke calmly as if nothing in the world were wrong. I came down from my high slightly as my wobbly ankles and shaking legs produced enough momentum to propel me forward. My eyes were saucer wide at this point. I closed them tight. I breathed deeply in and then out. A guard opened the Holden's door and I entered the same way as before. Sweat fell from my forehead onto the leather as I entered the vehicle. I halfway expected a push to my back and a speedy getaway from the guards. My mind was obviously on hyper alert. I was geeking out and needed to compose myself.

The disposition of the two guards in the front seats hadn't changed. This relieved me. I needed their cold distance above all else right now. Officer Happy placed the car into gear and flicked on her turn signal to merge back onto Pacific Highway. We entered traffic smoothly and without foul play. I looked behind toward the cemetery and saw two additional police cars filter into the highway to form our caravan. We appeared to be plenty safe, allowing me to place my head on the headrest and close my eyes once more. What had just happened? I thought in my mind and even tried to convince myself I imagined it all. I didn't. Just like the shootings at Newcastle and the murder of Ricketts. Everything happened. Everything was real, too real.

Weekday morning traffic turned the thirteen-minute ride into twenty-five. We arrived at the Crowne just in time to see Bren, Diane, and Lori prepped with their luggage and ready to fly. They were flanked by an additional two guards, both armed to the teeth. I obtained a great sense of relief and comfort from that sight. Everything was ok. My family was safe, and we were about to be escorted to the airport.

I stepped out of the car. On the opposite side of the Wharf Road I could see a flock of media members being barricaded from my presence. I heard them screaming questions. After all, this was the final chance to get the Bloody American on record before he tucked tail to America. I didn't give them the satisfaction of more than my smile. I joined my family, and we all piled into the same limousine that had dropped us at the Crowne the day before. Blue lights immediately lit our path from Wharf to Merewether Street, to Workshop Way, and onto Honeysuckle Drive. We were given the protection of a president on our way to Newcastle Airport where a chartered flight in a heavy jet awaited our arrival.

I didn't alert my family of the writing on the headstone. I had composed myself and knew it could only frighten them at this point. My mother and Bren almost simultaneously asked:

"How'd it go?" I forced another smile:

"It was a grave." They all smirked at me for this one. I had been ridiculed since I was born for being one of the worst translators of information. For whatever reason, my typical all female audience desired me to open up and share the finer details of my experiences. I'm being misogynistic by saying this is a female versus male aspect of communication, but in my experience, men were short and women detailed. I had been raised by my mother and sister and had no serious male role model outside of my grandfather. This should've nurtured me into the female form of sharing. It didn't. I was predisposed toward short and sweet. Information gathering from me was like prying my teeth out. I was getting better with age, but I still wasn't up to the level of expectation the current reign of automotive estrogenical tyranny had for me. Lori looked at me:

"Aaaaaand?" I smiled in an attempt to escape opening up more. The smile didn't get me anywhere. Bren playfully backhanded my knee:

"That smile doesn't change anything!" I didn't buckle to the point where I shared the writing on the headstone, but I did begin sharing:

"It was odd seeing her there with Bryson to her side. She's really dead. It really happened just in front of me." I shook my head and my face glazed over. "It seemed so indefinite before. I guess I didn't have the closure of a funeral. Seeing the dirt and grass clippings scattered upon the grave made it very real." I was legitimately saddened, but a tear didn't escape my eyes. Lori placed her hand on the same knee Bren just playfully tormented:

"I'm so sorry, Tom. Is there anything you need?" I shook my head, knowing the three willing faces would surely give me all the emotional support I would need if I only asked for it:

"I'll be fine. I just need time for some of the realizations to kick in." Bren saw me squirm and knew I wasn't comfortable.

She changed the conversation. "It's a beautiful day to leave Australia!" We all laughed. The day outside was gorgeous. But none of us cared. Australia had left a very rotten taste in our mouths, and no matter the beauty it held, we needed the mountains of Tennessee and comforts of home.

After thirty or so minutes, our caravan bypassed normal security measures at the airport and drove directly onto the runway. We never saw the inside of the airport. We simply drove close to the removable stairs parked next to our jet. Again, two armed sentinels stood at the ready directly in front of the staircase. We stepped out of the car and walked confidently toward our ride. A massive person wearing Newcastle Airport apparel passed us by. He wore a baseball hat that concealed his face in the blinding morning sun. I did a double take as he moved toward the car to grab our luggage but caught only a glimpse of his enormous back as he grappled with our baggage. I shook my head and the illusions away as we stepped up toward the jet. We were finally going home and a smile lit up what was an inquisitive demeanor only seconds prior.

We boarded the jet and marveled at the lavish interior and full wait staff. This certainly beat the flight to Australia, where I booked late and ended up in the middle of a five-person row. I remember smelling the bodies of the men to my right and left, and praying to fall asleep to alleviate myself of the odors. Nacho cheese on one side and what reminded me of cat pee on the other. Now, despite being in prison only a few days prior, I would be traveling in peak luxury. The jet was equipped with a bedroom and chairs where we could stretch out for days. The Australians' surely didn't want us to feel like seeking reparation on our departure of their wonderful continent. The old mantra of treating them well when you've already wronged them. Like a rapist smiling and trying to pay off a victim. It kind of made me sick in a way, but I was fully ready to embody a naïve role if it brought us home quicker. The time for justice to happen would be in the future, but not now.

I plopped myself down next to the window where I saw the mammoth figure unloading the last of our luggage. I was still smiling when something terrifying caught my eye. Underneath the brim of the baseball hat I could see a scar on his cheek. I squinted, trying to rid my eyes of what had to be a horrid mental fabrication. To my dread, it wasn't fabricated at all. The Monster looked up toward me, made eye contact with me and me alone. He kept my stare as he closed the cargo door. He smiled wide and winked at me. He then pressed his index finger in front

48

of his lips and blew a ssshhhh to me. He then turned his index finger into the same fake gun as Yaravela Shen two years before him. He pulled the imaginary middle finger trigger and whispered to the air:

"We are watching you."

I debated whether or not to scream. My adrenaline was back in full force and my mind near panic. Was there a bomb in our plane? What was going on? Whom do I tell? The same Monster as two years before. The same one that emptied a seven-round magazine in the McMullin building. He had just loaded our jet with our luggage. What else did he load with it? Why didn't he kill me? How should I proceed? I was near rupturing when I escaped toward the bathroom to breath and decide what to do.

It took me less than the walk toward the bathroom to decide to embarrass the hell out of the Australian Government and their calculated preparations to keep me safe.

"I think there's a bomb on this plane." I whispered at first to the confusion of onlookers. "I think there's a *bomb* on this plane!" I yelled it out loud without thinking this time. I didn't use tact. I simply blurted out the one thing I knew would stop us from leaving that very moment. The one thing I knew would get us out and promote a search of the plane. I was right. It seemed like Australia wasn't quite done with us.

Chapter 8

By the time they were done searching the plane, I heard the words "Bloody American" uttered an almost obscene amount of times. I was questioned by a multitude of people in what was an obvious jurisdictional nightmare. The guards that escorted us were airport police, federal police, US Embassy personnel, and a slew of others I couldn't keep straight in my head. In almost robotic fashion, I explained to the detectives that a Monster, the code name I continued using for the huge man with scars on his cheeks, was one of the people responsible for trying to kill me on that fateful day.

To no one's surprise, the search of the plane came up with nothing. It took more than two hours to sweep it, and I sensed the frustration my claim had caused. By the time the questioning was over, I almost felt as if I had been the one to make this story up in my head. The Monster, of course, was nowhere to be found, but no one actually took credit for loading our plane either. The airport claimed that the shifts had been called in, and the workers who loaded our jet had already left for home. It was cheap, but I couldn't call them liars when they produced the schedule. Sure enough, the shifts were all accounted for, and whoever was supposed to load our plane did their job and left. I didn't need the added embarrassment of actually calling all of their employees to find the one that loaded our plane. I knew the results wouldn't matter if the jet didn't have a bomb on it. I just wanted to get home safe and sound.

"You've had a terribly traumatic experience Mr. Appling." The federal detective, whose name I can't even remember through his passive aggressive treatment of me started. He spoke down to me like a child who'd found out about Santa Claus too early. "I think it's best that you get some rest. It's a long flight back to America." He never said I lied. He never said that I imagined the entire ordeal from start to finish. But, and not being an expert at reading between the lines, he said just that. Everyone outside my family assumed I was a broken man who was hallucinating. And damn if that's not what the evidence in front of them suggested. Luckily for me, all I cared for was my family's opinion on such matters. Even if the three of them thought I was bonkers, at least they stood firm by my side and said to my face that they supported me.

Not helping my sanity was the headstone. I had the sure-fire way to prove that people were messing with me. It was located at the Sandgate Cemetery just behind Victoria Hogue's grave. Well, that wasn't there either. No Monster, no bomb, and no headstone with my name on it. The detectives even snapped off a picture of the unused strip of soil behind Hogue's grave where the alleged headstone was said to be. They were right. I saw the time stamp on the iPhone and it was from this morning. The headstone was gone. Had I hallucinated this entire thing? Surely not, but the evidence started to pile up against me.

"I'm sorry for wasting everyone's time." I appeared as a beaten down and pathetic morsel of the person who confidently spoke of bombs on planes and ghostly headstones. "I guess I've been under a tremendous amount of stress, and it's all gotten to me." The pretentious detective nodded and placed his hand on my shoulder.

"You've been through so much, Mr. Appling. Perhaps you just need some rest. Plenty of time to do that on your way home." He smiled through his teeth, and I so badly wanted to punch him. I wanted to punch Australia! But at least my family was safe, and there weren't bombs planted underneath us. Everyone thought I was an asshole, but at least I was a safe asshole.

We had an uneventful flight across the Pacific Ocean. The attendants were noticeably peeved at me, but still served us when we asked. They smiled, served, and cracked jokes in the background at my expense. I felt guilty about wasting their time, but I would've done it again under the same circumstances. *I truly thought I saw that Monster from before. No, I did see it! That's exactly what I saw, wasn't it? I saw the Monster and I saw the headstone. Why wasn't I smart enough to use*

51

my phone? I could've snapped the same picture at the gravesite and given myself proof. Myself I thought. Forget convincing others. I had to convince myself? *Wow, where has my mind gone?*

"Hey, take it easy." Bren clutched my shoulders and didn't let go for the majority of the flight. "We will be home this time tomorrow, and you'll get to hold your baby boy!" This brought a smile to my face. Atlas had survived his sickness, and I would get time with him. My entire family thought he held on just for me. He kept fighting for me. It was an incredible feeling when all hope was seemingly lost just a few years ago. He was such a fighter. The thought of being home with my family lifted me up through the rest of the trip. I could finally rest free from the Australian turmoil that had sent my life on a complete rollercoaster. Not short of irony, I plugged my phone into the headphones and set my play list to select at random. The first song, of course, was *Every Breath You Take* by the Police. I laughed out loud, and thought to myself in the creepiest voice I could imagine, *Every breath you take, every move you make, we are watching you.*

Chapter 9

There are cons, and then there are what Grady Hedges had just pulled off. Pure wickedness fifteen years in the making. Of course, there were variables in his ultimate plan, but a good con man makes do. He made millions off of Powers and his friends prior to Missy getting pregnant. When that happened, Grady struck gold and produced something of pure sinister magic. Grady was patient and above all, precise.

Now, Grady Hedges the Alabama business man was no more. The finer details had been planned, but the con came down to simple bait and switch and then blunt force. How simple it was to design a ruse to drop Will Powers' guard. The simple mention of Missy's name, after ten years of hope, seemingly flummoxed his billionaire friend. It didn't hurt that Grady Hedges was the primary outlet Will had been paying for years to find his daughter in the first place. Will didn't know this. Will did what he thought was his own research into private investigating firms. He selected the best one he could find and invested millions. All the while, Grady was in control. He built the domains, the reviews, the characters, the history of success, the reports, the location, and the staff. He also built the subliminal messaging guiding Will Powers. By the time Will had read everything, he had no choice other than to use Refined National Intelligence, LLC out of Atlanta, GA as the most suitable firm in the investigation to find Missy.

Grady's involvement didn't stop there. He was in the Powers' estate ten years ago when Missy announced at a party that she was pregnant. Grady remembered the scared little girl. He also remembered the opportunity. He saw the look on Will Powers' face. His friend Will was in shock. When Will asked about who the father was, Grady knew he would try to force an abortion on his daughter. Grady was right. Will demanded Missy abort the baby, and Missy hated him for it. That's when Grady, the decent con man, began infiltrating a whole new level of Will's existence. Grady the con became a legend in his own game.

It didn't take long to manipulate a scared girl of almost fifteen. With passions running high, less than a few hours with Missy had her convinced to run. That was the easy part. It's keeping a young girl in one mindset for more than a few days, and making her continuously aware of her father's brutality that would be the difficult part. It was difficult. Grady made Missy disappear directly underneath Will's nose, but the girl was needy, and her mind changed drastically. She was scared, and trust began to waiver a few months in. Grady struggled with solutions, but would come up with something.

The baby changed everything. Missy had every intention of going back to her father, her family, and approaching Jules to help raise the child. Missy did hate her father for his temper, but began looking at him with nostalgia and realizing that he might have just overreacted. He almost assuredly did. Once she actually delivered the baby, she knew everything would find a way to work out. This was simply not something Grady Hedges could have. He needed Missy out of the picture. He wasn't a murderer, but he also wasn't above blackmail, trickery, and deceit. After all, he made a very nice life out of it.

What Grady hatched was pure evil. He knew he didn't have the time to plot against Will Powers while also caring for Missy and her baby. You can say that Grady Hedges outsourced his cause. Believe it or not, there are fine lines between good, just sketchy, and the purest of evils. In Grady's case, he should've just murdered Missy and her baby. It would've been kinder. The path he chose would keep Missy away from his ultimate target, but would subject poor Missy to unspeakable evil. Grady Hedges sold Missy Powers and her newborn baby to the underground world. He didn't have to go far. Disgusting and despicable people were willing to traffic Missy Powers right in the very state of Alabama. Grady Hedges didn't ask for proof that she'd be ok. He didn't want to know what would come of her. He simply needed the guarantee

54

that she would be out of the picture. He received this. Missy was gone. Once she was, it was as if she had never existed in the first place.

Now, showering himself with the riches he just lifted from Will Powers' estate, Grady Hedges had made a very profitable deal with the devil. He intended to be one of the richest men in St. Kitts and Nevis, a tiny island in the West Indies. It was the perfect place to run. A tax haven that called itself home to a plethora of criminals from around the world. The passport was easy to buy and the identity easy to change. After fifteen years of precise planning, milking a billionaire out of pieces of his fortune and his own daughter, and likely causing the pain that resulted in Tai Powers, Will's wife, committing suicide, Grady planned to retire. He chartered a vessel and had paid the proper individuals months ago. It was easy sailing, no pun intended, for Grady to arrive in his Caribbean dream. In less than twenty-four hours, Grady completed the *coup de grace* on Will's life. It was his shining moment to be remembered through sips of fruity island drinks, rock lobster, and walks on Timothy Beach.

Chapter 10

Home. I was finally home after more than two years. My heart began to race as we pulled closer to the gravel drive. The rocks struck our tires and careened off the undercarriage. Smoky dust billowed around us. The garage door lifted slowly. It was too slow for the pace of my heart and the excitement I felt. This time, I could only feel a tinge of awkwardness. Was this really happening? Was I really here? I had plenty of lengthy departures from home before. Each time felt surreal. Each time felt as if I were misplaced in space and time. This time, nostalgia trumped all feelings of not belonging. The seldom used tools seemed to beckon me to build something. My aggressive BMW M4 begged me to feel its power from behind the wheel. I was on sensory overload when I began to hear Atlas' faint bark. Nothing had changed from what I could remember.

I was floating on a cloud. I can't remember walking to reach the door that would enter into our mudroom from the garage. I simply remember the door handle. How the brushed nickel lever felt in my hand as I turned it down toward the floor. Before I could blink, Atlas greeted me like only he could: fifty-five pounds of pent up anxiety culminating in a high-pitched hyena-like chorus. He twisted his body and wagged his curly tail rapidly. His intense excitement to see me broke every discipline I had ever instilled. He jumped on me and his nails scratched my bare arms. It felt amazing. Each scratch felt like life was granted to me. Each scratch felt like I was free to live once again. I dropped to my knees and let him lick my face. I wasn't an emotional person, but I felt the moment overtake me. Tears sprang from my eyes. The rest of the brood joined in, creating the perfect amount of chaos to let us know we were home. We were safe.

As I entered the kitchen, I softly caressed the chilled granite island. I smiled at the trials Bren and I went through to piece together our perfect kitchen out of what many thought was an early nineteenth century dump. Now, the historic and once thriving town center, eventually turned into shambles by previous owners, was alive once again. I smiled at the years it took to restore and renovate. All the work that went into raising a site from impending doom. It wasn't perfect, and it would likely take our entire lives to care for, but it was beautiful. It was ours. And now it could be enjoyed for another two hundred years because of our efforts in salvaging it.

Just like after any prolonged absence, the list of what to do was almost burdensome. Even the list of things I wanted to do and feel seemed overwhelming. I had the farm to inspect, the friends to greet, and the sites to visit. I had the local dives to engorge myself in after the prison food in Australia left my pallet ravenous for the comfort of good food. I had softball leagues, flag football, golf, and tennis to get back to. Not to mention, I had two years' worth of business neglect to make up for. The list went on, and even masked my thoughts on retribution for what had happened. Was I doing this intentionally? Was I trying to avoid researching into why I was targeted? Was I content to let the entire past slide in an attempt to regain a semblance of what I had already lost? I didn't know the answers to my own questions. Therapy, a discipline forcibly suggested by the U.S. Government along with my family, acted as a sounding board for the questions seemingly lost in the wake of my arrival home. This was something I was more than happy to participate in. I had seen a therapist, years back, to help overcome the mental and emotional healing issues left behind from sickness. One thing you hear time and time again is that cancer changes you. This statement was never truer with me. It's a shit disease, and it alters everything in your life. No matter the treatment plan, survivability, or type, you are never rid of the pain it causes. I knew my current predicament needed the same remediation and respect.

My therapist, just like so long ago, was the most joyous person I had ever encountered. Dr. Wilma Britt was short with an infectious smile that could light up the dimmest of rooms. Her blonde hair was wrapped in a ponytail and hipster glasses gripped her eager face. She could barely contain her excitement upon seeing me and immediately squeezed me tight with a hug that I would never forget. She was comforting, and she was safe. She offered me the same floral-patterned love seat that I had sat upon so many times. I eased into my seat as she seemingly bounded to hers. She plopped down in a chair opposite of me. There was a small coffee table and a medium-sized dog bed between us, where I used to play with her terrier puppy named Dawn. Dawn was such a comfort for clients, and I always enjoyed the distraction when dealing with the tougher moments of self-realization. The room was cheerful with Zen posters and a few cult-classic movie posters to make patients, such as me, feel at home. My favorite was *The Monster Squad*. It was one of my best remembered movies to this day. The sight of the poster gave me another to do on my list. Wilm crossed her legs and pulled her notebook into her lap. She grabbed her pen and popped the bottom to extend the otherwise hidden tip.

"So, it's been so long! What's up?" I hadn't mentioned the reason for my visit. She obviously was unaware of my incarceration and time spent as the "Bloody American." Wilm was never a therapist that was too concerned with checking up. She expected her clients to come to her as needed. She also wasn't much for the news of the outside world. It didn't bother me that she was so unaware of what had happened to me. It was a comfort to speak with someone where the slate was entirely blank. As was customary, I couldn't just delve into my issues. There needed to be some kind of opening up foreplay.

"Is Dawn ok?" I questioned and pointed toward the empty bed. Wilm was used to this from me. She smiled and reassured me of Dawn's safety.

"She's fine. In timeout." She pointed toward the closed door behind her. "It's never ok to pee on my shoes." She looked toward her feet, where open-toed casuals replaced her normal loafers. She smirked and let me smile at her expense for a second. "So, how have you been doing?"

Back to the point. I breathed in deeply, knowing this wouldn't be easy for either of us.

"Well, things have happened Wilm." She passed me a confused look before I detailed everything, beginning with Hogue and ending with my current conundrum. I was there because I couldn't talk to anyone else about my true feelings. The underlying feelings of action that consumed the layers of my mind not guided by the selfless outer shell. Bren would scoff at action at this point. I was home, seemingly safe, and needed to regain control in my own life. Raising issues to place my family in harm and cause pandemonium, in Bren's eyes, was foolish. This logic was hard to disagree with. I still had so much to lose. So much to keep safe. This said, I needed an outside opinion, and I needed it to be Wilm. At this point, and after listening to me for a nearly twenty-minute monologue, her face was a mix of astonishment and a failed attempt at keeping a professional posture.

"Are you fucking with me, Tom?" She wasn't actually questioning me in her tone. She was trying to gather herself and didn't know how to proceed. She dropped the, at this point, worn-out notebook to the side of her chair onto the glass-top end-table. Her stiff posture with legs crossed became loosened with both feet touching the hideous rug beneath us. I shook my head and shot her a "believe it or not" it's the truth kind of expression. She heaved the notepad from the end-table like it weighed ten-times the normal amount from the information overload. She dropped it on her lap, and I halfway expected her to crash through the floor of the two-story house. Astonishment turned to deep concern for me. She leaned forward: "How are you holding up?" It was a fair but simple question. One that I hadn't actually been asked so far. Everyone was so busy feeling the excitement of my release that it was hard to focus on the turmoil. The reality of the situation was I was facing turmoil. I had faced utter chaos. Mental and physical anguish from the beginning. I felt a bit shocked, almost assuming that I should be holding up perfectly. I was alive and I was free. Or was I free? Why didn't I feel free?

"Well, I don't know." I stuttered a bit. She didn't let me escape the question that easily. She was good like that. Too good. She stared at me through those glasses and nodded to insinuate I move forward. When I didn't, she broke the silence:

"Aaaannnnd." She lifted her brow above those thick-rimmed glasses. I breathed heavily, feeling my heart in my throat. Feeling the kind of uncomfortable I needed to feel in order to have self-realization.

"And I don't know what to do." It was a different circumstance, but the same question I had struggled with my entire life. I was lost once again. I had ultimate meaning for my family, but I was floating. It was the same thing I felt trying to gain meaning through creations, businesses, charities, and research. I had accomplished so much externally but almost nothing to satisfy my internal cravings. A man should gain ultimate satisfaction through having a family, protecting that family, and living a privileged life. I've found that this is rarely the case. It's rare to find someone satisfied with their life. I had always admired those who felt secure, calm, and content. My grandfather was such a man. He felt life. He felt honor amongst the trees as he picked up aluminum cans on his daily walks. Was this generational? Was this the content nature of someone who had lived through the Great War, Great Depression, and the many disastrous conflicts home and abroad thereafter? Would my generation, so privileged and disconnected from death and conflict, be able to feel that kind of content? Or was this just something I had to struggle with? Was I alone in this feeling? Had I alone been cursed never to feel such content? I have rarely found the same struggle in others. At least, not to the level at which I'm plagued. Why was that a question I needed to ask myself in the first place? Wilma nodded, knowing what I was feeling despite our lull in time. She smiled after regaining her composure and bringing me full circle so easily:

"Tom, I've known you for years. You've seen me sporadically. There have been lulls, but the same underlying theme appears with each visit. No one is happy all the time. What we all strive to find is the ability to be content with ourselves. This is something that chasing an adventure, no matter how appealing or exciting it may be at the beginning, will not get you. At some point in your life, you must seek the ability to be content with yourself. You're a junkie, Tom. You seek the high from exciting new things but rarely find happiness within those moments. You have found happiness only in the prospects of what life could bring you, and never in what life has already given you."

It was a response I had heard before and understood all too well. She was right, at least to an extent. I could sugar coat and emphasize the security to which a resolution would bring me, but the truth was simply that I wanted the adventure. I wanted to go after Yaravela Shen, the Monster, and all those who wanted me dead. I wanted to find the purpose behind the attempt to murder me, and when that failed, to destroy me instead. I wanted to destroy them in turn. I wanted to punish the Australian government for not believing me and taking away years of my life. I yearned for this, but I yearned for everything for the wrong reasons. All my planning in prison, all my preparation, and all my thinking had one purpose. This purpose was to harm those who had harmed me. None of the plans concerned the practical aspects of my life, which foremost should have been protecting my family and the lives that had been tampered with due to my absence. I stared back at Wilma and wanted to convince her of my nobility in wanting to chase my assailants. Before I spoke, I thought better of it. In defeat, I sighed and nodded.

"You're right. Perhaps what I really need now is stability. I can no longer seek something. Even though the subject may change, this endless pursuit of mine must end." I buckled in her presence, but knew in the back of my mind that I needed something more and that old patterns shouldn't be allowed to repeat themselves. While all of this was great in theory, my mind was already reeling for loopholes. I did not need to pursue my enemies but I needed, at the very least, to look at my research and try to determine why I was the target. I had to know once and for all if it was my research that these people were interested in. "We're watching you" kept popping in my mind and I let it slip out in front of Wilma once more in a whisper. *Scare tactics perhaps*, I thought to myself as if I didn't say anything aloud? Assuredly so. Wilma arched a confused eyebrow:

"Did you mutter something, Tom?" She enticed me to speak the words without whispering them.

"It's nothing." I spoke and smiled, obviously holding back.

61

"It sounded something like 'We're watching you.' This would trouble most people, Tom. What you've gone through…, what you've been through. A lot of people wouldn't have the resolve to withstand so much trauma."

I shook my head discreetly. "They would if they didn't have a choice. It's not like these people have given me an option not to play their game. They simply started playing. The first shot at Hogue entered me into whatever this is." I plead with Wilma. Something she didn't buy.

"Don't be modest, Tom. It doesn't suit you." She smiled and rose, disallowing any further statements from me prior to closing the session. She reached for me to give her another hug. She pulled me in close: "Just remember to breathe, Tom. Everything will be ok. Just slow down and breathe." She showed me out of the door. She walked behind as I approached the stairs: "Be safe. I'll see you next week!" I could hear a sense of urgency in her voice. It was like she didn't expect to see me next week but didn't have time to spend with more clients waiting for her. A schedule is something so difficult to keep as a therapist. Time is something so delicate and sometimes all you need is a few extra minutes. Unfortunately, life and a profession sometimes prevent those extra few minutes from happening. Therapists must be flummoxed by this relationship between time and profession constantly. All the what ifs? All the could've saids and could've dones in hindsight when you're dealing with a fragile human mind. I wanted to reassure her of my resolve to stay safe and breathe. I didn't bother.

"You too," I replied and smiled. She made me feel valuable despite the short hour and the need to keep on schedule for the others she had to give the same attention to. I always liked this about her and had since we first met in our introductory session. I knew she treated all her clients exactly the same. Gave them all the same motherly attention like they meant the most to her. Made them feel more valued than the next client clamoring for her attention the moment she was finished with you. She was great. This was her job and I knew this, but she never made me feel that way despite the strictness to schedule. The door closed behind me and I descended the stairs with renewed pep in my step.

I began to notice the season upon entering the parking lot behind Wilma's office. The tall brick building on the outskirts of town towered over a fresh spring garden flourishing in its shadow. Daffodils were making way for various species of milkweed. Butterflies fluttered above, and one in particular caught my eye as it struggled against the light breeze. It floated passed the building and out of the shadow. The sun struck and glistened against its remarkably vivid colors. It was as if stained glass was given wings.

The sporty interior of my M4 swallowed me whole, and I gripped the leather covered steering wheel prior to shifting into reverse. I loved to drive and felt alive when the movements of my car echoed off the pavement beneath me. A few moments shared between the road and me passed prior to dialing Bren on Bluetooth.

"Hey, how'd it go?" She answered the phone with cheer, and proceeded to compassionately get straight to the point.

"It went well." I could almost feel the entire Bluetooth speakers around me say "aaaaaannnnnnd," but I let Bren get that out of me.

"Just well? Nothing to report?" She had plenty of experience trying to get me to open up. She knew the best tactics were always the softest. I never responded well to being pushed. I tended to shut down or become defensive.

"Yes, just well. I'm feeling a bit better about things. I feel like I'll be able to let go and let the detectives handle things from here." It wasn't necessarily a lie. More of a half-truth. I didn't want her to worry about anything. I wanted her to know that I planned on staying with the family and concentrating my efforts toward that realm. That, in itself, wasn't a lie. I had every intention of letting the police handle the brunt of my case. The only thing I wanted was to find the missing link. I wanted to know why me. *What made me different? Why was I targeted?* I was obsessed with knowing for years, and felt I had to give myself that satisfaction. Deep down, despite all that Wilm had said, I knew I couldn't let it go without knowing. I wasn't good at waiting. When I was young, my first investigative obsession became finding my Christmas presents. I just couldn't wait for them when I knew they were somewhere in the house. I couldn't let it just be a surprise. My mother knew this and made things increasingly difficult for me each year. She became more adept at hiding, and I became more adept at finding.

I had nearly identical anticipation when it came to knowing about the events on that fateful day. Years had passed. It seemed perfectly harmless to me, but I knew knowledge of this would worry Bren. So, since avoiding conflicts is what I do best, I hid every intention of researching that link. "If it's cool, I'm gonna drive around and soak in some of home?" Also not necessarily a lie, more of a quarter-truth.

"Of course!" She said with an almost audible smile of relief: "I love you so much! I can't believe you're home!" I smiled widely as my BMW roared onto Interstate-26.

"Crazy right! I love you so much! See you in a bit." I clicked off the phone and let the music automatically kick in. Pearl Jam's *Crazy Mary* began playing, and I began singing. Like most songs, I didn't really listen to the lyrics. I knew most of them when I sang, but never paid attention to the meanings or anything. I liked the beats, and I loved the choruses. I turned the song up and took my first exit. Half a mile down the road stood a large federal style public library. Prior to my incarceration, I had slept on its books, paced its halls in search of epiphanies, and knew there were several chairs with "Tom-Shaped" indentions in them. It was like a second home to me. Over the years, I personally stocked the ancient history section. This was the small start I needed. The small start toward finding real answers to my plight.

Chapter 11

I've spent countless hours in this musty and cold building. I remember playing with my echoes off the empty halls as I pieced together my thesis. The library's once familiar chill now reminded me of an interrogation room. Air conditioning blasted as the spring day outside began to warm the external brick. It was also eerily quiet, which was something I relished. Almost no one used the library despite the many amenities offered. Comfort, Wi-Fi, reading material, and public activities such as free French language night didn't attract the crowds it might once have. My donations to the archives, roughly one thousand sources on the Greco-Persian and Peloponnesian Wars, were located on the third level. I used the stairs to stretch out my legs and avoid the weird vertigo sensation I received when moving up and down elevators. It wasn't anything too troubling to my health, just a weird and unpleasant side-effect of the chemo. I just hated that wobbly feeling.

I sat on a small stool that had seemingly been in the same position I left it almost three years ago during my last visit. Nostalgia hit me. This was the same position I sat in with laptop in tow. The same position I sat in when I pressed send on an email that would give Hogue a rough draft of my research. Did that start the series of events that would lead to her death a year later? I shuddered at the thought, and quickly purged it from my mind.

I took a seat, stared at the collection, and smiled at my accomplishment in placing it there. I never thought people would check out the books or peer through the binders full of journals, but this was something else I could leave to the world. That was a great feeling in itself. I sucked in the air and let out the entire breath. I reached up and grabbed Strassler's *The Landmark Herodotus*, an in depth edit of an Andrea Purvis translation of Herodotus' *Histories*. The book was large and felt good in my hands. I could read fiction on my Kindle or iPad, but for my research, it needed to be the real thing. I was born into the first generation with personal computers, but unlike modern technology-obsessed youth, I started with hard copies and that's what felt real to me. This was the real thing, and the same book I used as a starting point to Herodotus when I was getting my MA.

I scanned through Books VI through IX where the large majority of my research was based. I didn't know if I was waiting for a clue to pop out of the pages and hit me in the head, or if I was simply catching my bearings after so long away, but either way, nothing happened. There were no miraculous epiphanies located in the list of Xerxes' massive army, nothing Themistocles or Pausanias said, and nothing that connected to my Platæan conspiracies. I wasn't expecting there to be anything of note but couldn't help being a touch disappointed that the solution didn't just fall off the pages for me.

Despite my very short frustrations over a fifteen-minute scan, it felt good reading the ancient word. To me, ancient history just feels more vivid. It feels like, and without sounding too cliché, epic. Each word meant something. Perhaps all words that were written in free hand meant something more. The care it took to write out each word precisely and carefully. No spell check, no auto-correct, and no QWERTY keyboard making the words flow together with ease. Everything was more difficult. Not only the writing itself, but surviving in Halicarnassus as Herodotus did, or Bœotia as Plutarch did. Living in a world where everything was earned. Not just the achievements of note, but each excursion beyond your own friendly confines would be met with challenges rarely seen in the present day. The world was so much bigger to these people. Now, we can travel in a few hours what would have been impossible to our ancient brethren. It's remarkable the growth and evolution of humanity. We can kill each other with the push of a button, love each other over a screen, and worship the most ludicrous of causes. I don't romanticize the easier times prior to the crazy amount of information we are subjected to each day. I romanticize the pain, the struggle simply to exist, and the trials through which our ancestors forced themselves. Life is not a privilege, and you must earn it. They did. A psychiatrist, or my therapist, might say that my obsession with this world stems from an inability to find meaning in my own life. I couldn't care less about the underlying reasons, but I never really saw it this way. To me, the simple idea of life, something we can easily take for granted, was never given to those about whom we can read in a history such as Herodotus'. But the same life is easy to take for granted now. In a world that has simply gotten too small for its inhabitants.

I closed the book and smiled widely, letting the frustrations of years melt away in moments. I was finally back in the comfort of those that I spent so much time with over the long four years it took to complete my work. I placed the book back in its spot and searched for more to connect the dots of my plight. Pritchett, and his trials in piecing together the markers at Platæa; Grundy's topography; Wright's work on the secondary sources; How and Wells; Marincola, Lazenby, Fossey, Greene, and Burn. More and more, all with different stories to tell of the same events. All muddying the waters as a precursor to my very own research into the characters, positions, and actions that these figures took on a few fateful days some two-thousand-five-hundred years ago. So, what was it? What had I done that actually mattered in the scheme of things? For the life of me, I couldn't see a link. I pondered outside my research. Nothing. No business deals gone awry, no debt owed to the wrong people, and no lover's scorned. I had successfully navigated life without ruffling feathers. There was something in my research. Something was here, in this very mound of documents that I was missing. I just knew it. I knew it with all my being. I sat back too far on the stool and struggled to balance myself without tipping over backwards. A flood of embarrassment snuck into my mind before realizing that no one was watching me. Or were they? I didn't see anyone in front, behind, or between the stacks of books to both sides as I quickly scanned between and over shelves. The suspicions of whoever they were came flooding. The ones who placed the headstone behind Hogue's grave. The Monster that operated against me. The feeling made me uneasy and the quiet confines of the library lost much of its allure. The safety of solitude now became the anxiety of a man positioned within his own thriller.

I leapt up from the stool to seek human contact. The rows of bookshelves narrowed as I reached their end. My eyes widened as the bookshelves seemed to close upon me. There was a distinct fuzziness and the very air began to vibrate intensely. Finally, in the open, I breathed a sigh of relief as I set my eyes on an old librarian. She was hunched over, probably mid-sixties but acted mid-nineties. She pushed a cart of books as she glared at me through her cat-rimmed glasses. A chain necklace was tangled in her gray hair. Hair that could easily have acted as a bird's nest. She gave me a ssshhhhh look that would've made the ten-year-old me cringe. She seemed stuck in a time-lapse, unwilling to accept the world outside the hallowed walls of her library. This building was her sanctuary. I always felt that to her, the order of things meant complete obedience and respect to the unwritten rules of a mid-twentieth century library. I could almost feel the ruler slapping my hand with her scowl.

I was having a short panic attack that wasn't aided by the old woman. I closed my eyes and began to breathe in my nose and out of my puckered lips. My thoughts immediately jumped to my childhood. In particular, the basement my grandfather lived in when I was young. Most kids had irrational fears. My fears, what I feared the very most when reaching the stairs as a young child, brought me the most comfort in this moment. I had a Stretch Armstrong doll. Most kids did at the time. His arms, legs, and head could stretch creepily before repositioning themselves as if nothing happened. When mixed with my nightmares of *The Creature from the Black Lagoon*, I formed the most irrational Boogey Man. Each time when I reached my grandfather's stairs, I would panic and jolt up the stairs as quickly as I could to escape the possibilities of a Stretch Arm Creature that I had envisioned chasing me. The same panic took me over in the present, but now I could think back on my false Boogey Man and smile. The thought brought enough delight for me to relax from the height of my emotions. It was amazing to think, that in a world with at least one real Monster after me, a figment of my childhood imagination could bring me such tremendous comfort.

I reached the stainless-steel water fountain and took a deep sip. I moved toward the stairs and began my descent. Still a bit shaken, I held on to the handrail and took caution with each step down. I passed a young college frat kid and what I supposed was his cute girlfriend. They laughed as they moved up the stairs. They became quiet as they passed me, and I heard them chuckle when I was out of comprehensible earshot. Kids being kids, I supposed. I breathed deeply once again and turned into the second floor where the computer lab was stationed. Several more college kids sat down with the computers, checking their social media accounts. Some listened to headphones and some were more serious than others. I took a seat three chairs down from my nearest computer counterpart. She was a wild-haired teenager looking every bit of a rebellion in the making with her spiky, short, and black-dyed hair, her dark gothic clothing, and thick black-eyed make-up. She gave me a short glance before getting back to whatever injustice she was blogging about.

I moved the mouse, bringing the Dell wide-angled flat screen to life. I typed in my old user name and password, which surprisingly still worked after two years. It gave me tremendous relief, for whatever reason, knowing that some things were still the same. I loved when things just simply worked without headache. "When a plan comes together" as a member of the A-Team once said. I clicked on the Explorer link, which after less than a second, spawned in front of me. I clicked on the header and typed in jstor.org. I then typed in Thomas R. Appling and Conspiracy into the search box. After a short moment, the search results filed in. My publication from the Journal of Hellenic Studies popped up at the top. It was one of my first publications and questioned the link of conspiracy between Pausanias of Sparta and Artabazus, a Persian general who supposedly left with forty thousand troops without engaging at the Battle of Platæa. I clicked to open the article and selected the "read free online" link that followed. I was getting ready to read my article when my shorts buzzed. I assumed it was probably a text from Bren making sure I was ok. I debated whether or not to ignore the alert, but decided to read it prior to becoming enveloped in the article.

The caller id informed me that it was Bren prior to swiping the text open. With tremendous relief, I felt the need to give her all the safety and security of a quick text back. I opened her message as a smile lit up my face. The smile was short-lived. What I saw on that message shook me to my very core. The message simply stated, "We are watching."

Chapter 12

The penthouse suite at Hotel King George in Athens, Greece was an attractive destination for any wealthy tourist. The suite sported a private plunge pool, views of the Parthenon, plush accommodations, and the dining attraction expected from a sophisticated destination. The hotel rests a few steps from Greek parliament and the center of all Athens had to offer. However, the three men in the penthouse sitting area were not tourists. The meetings for the last ten years had been meticulously planned with care given to the minutest of details. Everything was controlled and anticipated. From the staff down to the guests, every movement was calculated and measured. The wine they drank, the flowers that would appear in their room, and even the pictures that hung on the walls, were all decided months in advance of their arrival. If the walls of the entire hotel could talk, only the chatter of Room 217 would be of interest. There were more than a dozen protocols upon entry, and still to this very day, none of the men knew each other's real names. They were simply the three, a tripod arrangement carved in blood. An arrangement that had moved seamlessly to give each in the trio exactly what they were seeking.

No handshakes were offered among the three. It wasn't that kind of relationship. They didn't have to like each other for this arrangement to work. They simply needed to tolerate and uphold their end of the bargain. The rest would fall into place thereafter. English was the preferred language among the three, but each used voice manipulating equipment to conceal their accents. One meeting per year was agreed upon to start their business, and this was to last fifteen minutes or less. All other forms of communication would be encrypted on a single email address that the three would share. Nothing sent or received, only saved and immediately deleted drafts.

"Notes?" The first man to speak, known only as Deliverer, was middle-aged with pale, light skin, bluish-gray eyes, a medium-length gray beard, and chin-length salt and pepper hair. He was average height, probably in the neighborhood of five foot nine and sported a light-colored, Colombia button-up shirt with short sleeves. He had started every meeting for the last ten years as was established long before in the protocols.

"One hundred seventy-five pages." The next man to speak, known only as Customer, was a fit, medium-skinned, presumably Middle Eastern man, probably a few years younger than Deliverer. He wore all white and kept his large Ray Ban sunglasses on despite being indoors. He wore the tan lines of jewelry, but wore none during these meetings. He was bald, but concealed it with a plain, blue baseball hat.

"Secured. Alpha." The last man to speak, known only as Supplier, was now an elderly man approximately in his early seventies. His skin showed signs of weathering, where too much sun had created substantial crevices in his cheeks and forehead. He was otherwise well-groomed with a mustache and a business-like haircut that wouldn't cause alarm no matter the crowd. His skin was olive, and his outfit always consisted of a black suit, white dress shirt, and the same proper blue tie.

The three men did not belong together. Anyone who saw them interact would think that within seconds. Each man nodded. None jotted down notes, held a phone, or any other device. They were all business and held each other in the strictest eye-contact plausible. The rest of their conversation could be followed in the same coded dialogue digested with little to no reaction from their counterparts.

Deliverer: "Alpha 15."
Customer: "Alpha 10."
Deliverer: "Alpha 13. Final."
Customer: "Alpha 13. Confirmed"
Supplier: "Alpha 13. Confirmed. Parachute?"
Customer: "Parachute 10."
Supplier: "Parachute 10. Confirmed."

Deliverer: "Parachute 10. Confirmed."

The three men nodded to one another prior to leaving one at a time from the penthouse suite. First Supplier. After ten minutes, Customer. After ten more minutes, Deliverer. Deliverer exited the elevator toward the main lobby of the hotel. His eight-hundred-dollar Armani shoes made a loud clacking sound that echoed off the white-marble floors and gold-embellished walls. It was the only noise in the otherwise silent lobby. While no one knew who he was or what he did, everyone that remained in the lobby knew to avert their gaze upon his exit. He stepped outside, pulled a cigarette from his shirt pocket, and lit up in relief that the meeting was over. A few moments passed before a black Mercedes S-Class pulled into the drive in between the hotel and Syntagma Square. Deliverer opened the back, right side door himself and entered the vehicle. Without speaking, the driver pulled away. Deliverer sucked his cigarette low before reaching into the console to check his cell. Through the smoke, he could discern several missed calls, but nothing of note. He dialed number two on his speed dial. When another man answered, Deliverer spoke clearly and confidently:

"Preparation for one hundred seventy-five. Thirteen days at location one. Ten passes." He ended the call after he received a couple taps from the other caller for confirmation.

Deliverer sat back in the cool, black leather seat. He opened the bottle of water that was resting in the center console cup holder. He twisted off the cap and downed half the bottle. He exhaled an almost rehearsed sigh before talking to the driver for the first time.

"Take me north to Alpha. We have work to do." The driver nodded, knowing exactly the position in which he was to travel. Deliverer placed his dark, thin-framed, Oakley sunglasses over his eyes. He reached once more into his left breast pocket to pull out another cigarette. He lit it, the embers glowed blood red as he sucked it in, and then pulled it from his lips. He blew the smoke out the cracked rear window as the S-Class maneuvered its way out of one of the busiest sections of Athens. His smoke looked as if it were casting a thin layer on the passersby. He was leaving the area close to Parliament as protestors to the Greek government flooded the area to voice their displeasure. They came in

73

waves as they did so often in their demonstrations. Deliverer couldn't blame them but didn't really care. He was simply pleased that their demonstrations wouldn't delay him. Trash covered the streets in the wake of the protestors. It was a pathetic marring of the ruins that scattered about the city, but to Deliverer, the chaos bred opportunity. He came to enjoy the devastation caused by a mob of unruly plebs. The business he tended to would thrive within the chaos of an unkempt Greece.

The driver weaved in and out of the heavy pedestrian traffic before finally hitting Hwy 8 and then E962 just north of the city. Merely a few kilometers from Athens, Deliverer was in relative seclusion. Nearly forty percent of Greece's entire population was located in Athens. The rest of a population scattered across a decently large landmass and a seemingly endless array of islands. Deliverer enjoyed this about Greece. He loved the amenities of the city, but even more so the seclusion of the countryside, mountains, and rocky outcrops. He grew weary of the constant bickering of the city. The constant protests, riots, and wilting economy helped a prospering business, but he didn't particularly like reveling in it in person.

As he moved further north and Attica transitioned into Bœotia, Deliverer returned to his phone. This time he pressed number 1. After a few rings, a deep voice answered.

"Yes, Boss." Deliverer placed his hand on his forehead.

"Give me something positive." The voice on the other line didn't waiver:

"It's still a problem, Sir." Deliverer punched the passenger headrest stationed in front of him, clearly distressed by the words coming from the other line. The driver never wavered. He was all too accustomed to such outbursts.

"Where are you?"

"Tennessee. Tri-Cities regional airport. Calling for a cab, now." The other voice spoke, knowing that his location would help ease Deliverer's frustrations over a particularly annoying set of loose ends. Deliverer was pleased, and his change could be seen in his demeanor as well as heard on the phone:

"Handle it. Whatever means. Just handle it." Deliverer ended the call, reached in his breast pocket, and pulled out another cigarette.

Chapter 13

I left the library without bothering to log out of my computer. Upon my exit, I called Bren's phone. She answered first ring:

"Hey! Having fun getting to know your city again?" The demeanor was odd given her last text. I opened my car door as I prepared my response:

"Did you just text me? Less than a minute ago?" She didn't hesitate much in her answer:

"No. I wanted to give you some space." I had made her feel insecure about not texting me now. I wasn't sure what reaction I wanted. None of them promising. Either Bren had been kidnapped and someone had her phone, I found that unlikely, or Bren had actually sent me a truly insensitive text. I found that even more unlikely. Someone must have hacked into her phone to further mess with me. Perhaps unlikely as well. Last but not least, I could be imagining things. With my palms still clammy from my panic attack a few moments ago, I was starting to feel like this was the most feasible possibility.

"Hopefully it's nothing." The phone switched to Bluetooth as I began easing out of the parking lot. "Just got a weird text. I thought it was from you, but I must've read it wrong." I looked down at my phone as I came to a halt at a stoplight. I scrolled to Bren's latest text to me. Sure enough, the text remained there. I hadn't imagined it. Or, if I did, I was still imagining it. "Can you check to see if you have a text to me?"

"That's weird. Hold on a sec." Less than a three second count and she returned. "Nope. Nothing here. What's going on?"

"I'm not sure. Probably nothing. I'm off the grid for a few years and I've forgotten how to use these things." I said it with decent conviction, hoping she would buy it. I heard a slightly mocking giggle on the other line. "I should be home in about ten minutes." I carried on in an attempt to completely mask the awkwardness. "See you soon!" She giggled once more.

"Ok silly." Again, mocking a bit but it was better than the alternative. We were about to get off the phone when Bren continued: "Oh. Ethan just pulled in the drive. Were you expecting him?"

"Oh, right. Damn I forgot. Yes, he's supposed to be there. I'll send him a text letting him know I'm running on time." We both chuckled at that one. Ethan had always been at least fifteen to thirty minutes early to every meeting we had ever scheduled. He was never upset that I wasn't ready or anything. He knew he was early, and he was happy to wait awkwardly in his car. Bren knew better than to invite him in. While he was always early, he also never wanted to be presumptuous. After invites and even begging him to come in early that first year of working together, Bren gave up on trying to be the most polite of hosts. "I love you! See you in a few." I said.

"Love you, too! Bye." She replied before hanging up the phone.

I arrived in my driveway about nine minutes later. Ethan smiled from his car in a "some things never change" type of look. I pulled into the garage and cut my engine off. I composed myself before getting out of the car and greeting my friend. Ethan and I shared a hearty handshake and a short, one-armed bro-hug.

"How ya been holdin' up?" Ethan opened after our embrace. I shook my head and raised my hands slightly with my thumbs toward the sky:

"I'm doing fine I guess. Some things keep happening that are concerning, but I'll be alright. Enough about me, what are you in to?" Ethan smirked but let it go prior to pulling out his phone. The pessimist in me halfway expected his phone to read something in the we're watching realm, but it was a picture of his baby that I never had a chance to meet. A bit shy of two years old and it looked just like him. I remember my last real conversation with Ethan. It centered on his becoming a father and joking that I better be brushing up on my soccer coaching skills. I smiled.

"Wow, almost ready to hit the field!" Ethan nodded and I could see the typical dad face spread across him. "They grow up, don't they?" Ethan nodded once more and smiled. I couldn't remember a time where I had seen him this happy. Nope. I had never seen Ethan Davies this happy. In fact, he was one of the more pessimistic people I had ever come across. He jokingly covered this persona up. He simply said he was a realist. I always called him on that BS. We worked well together because of this balance in our relationship. I created and he played the much-needed role of devil's advocate. In my mind, I couldn't even count how many times he shot down my ideas as impractical. A few of the impractical ideas made us money and a few never saw the light of day after combing through the details or beating the hopeless details to death as Ethan tended to do.

Ethan was around my height at about five foot ten. He sported a beer gut below broad shoulders, blue eyes, buzzed down red hair, and freckles exacerbated by years of sun. He was a rather fair athlete despite his constant complaints about his own performance. He was hyper competitive and had a brilliantly analytical mind. He was also a straight shooter and didn't feel the need to sugarcoat anything, especially in my presence. I had always thought he was placed on the planet to tear apart my optimism and bring me back down to earth. This worked for us. Somehow, despite the perception of friends making terrible business partners, our relationship worked. Perhaps this is because we were business partners prior to becoming friends. We became close when I hired him directly out of our MBA program. Slowly, we built a lasting friendship and several businesses together. We began integrating our lives outside of work almost immediately, offering each other the chance to play in various city league sports, golfing, bowling, or long nights of banter and video games. No matter the avenue, we worked together seamlessly.

"So. How are we doing?" The talk of business was to be expected. I had read various reports from Ethan since my release but wanted to hear and see his reaction in person. Ethan nodded without cracking a smile:

"Steady. Should be a lot better, but you left me in charge. Just fire me and get it over with." I laughed. Ethan had told me to fire him from the first day I hired him. He persisted, and every time he made the slightest error or things didn't go as he had hoped, he would toss his hands up and tell me to fire him. Honestly, sometimes I thought he was serious. He was so incredibly hard on himself.

"Soon." I laughed again and winked. "Come inside and I'll grab you a drink." He accepted the invitation, grabbed his computer bag, and we made our way through the open garage and into the kitchen. We headed straight for the dining room. I made a quick detour in the adjacent living room to kiss Bren and squeeze her tight. She was bundled up on the leather sofa as if we lived in Siberia without heat. She was catching up on some TV dramas in the background. I found the shows intolerable prior to prison. Now, I found comfort and her delight in them made me smile.

Ethan and I went across the hall, where a large dining room table filled the room. It served more as a desk, laundry folding station, or exclusive kitty observation platform, than a dining table. Bren and I were not social butterflies by any stretch. On either side of the table were a bar and chess table, the latter in front of a large fireplace Bren and I turned to gas many years ago. I raised up the bar to reveal a collection of scotch I owned solely because of Ethan. I snatched out a bottle of twenty-one-year-old Glenmorangie and poured him a glass to drink straight up. I picked up my own glass and opened a small drink refrigerator. There, I reached in and grabbed a can of cherry Pepsi Wild Cherry. I opened the can and poured it slowly against the side of the glass to avoid the fizz. I could almost feel Ethan's typical snickering, with a strong hint of pretention, in the background.

"I see prison has made you real hard. We really have to get you drinking." He spoke after taking a sip from his glass. "Then again, this scotch might be too good to share." He laughed and raised his eyebrows. I sat down so I was on one side of the dining table and Ethan the other. He placed his computer bag on the table and retrieved both his laptop and a binder. He brought up several Microsoft Excel spread sheets located within the same document. I scanned over the financial statements for a few moments before losing my focus.

79

"Sorry, man. I'm just not quite here." Ethan passed an accepting nod without even knowing what I was referring to. My head ached and I was too mentally exhausted to keep my thoughts internalized. "It's just. It's just that a theme has appeared in relation to my imprisonment."

"Huh?" Ethan said in confusion.

"Hey babe, will you come in here?" I shouted for Bren and she moved into the room and sat next to me at the table. I explained, with full detail from the beginning at Hogue's grave, the "we are watching" theme that had made its way from Australia into America. Some was obviously redundant for Bren, but both she and Ethan exhibited the right amount of nervousness over the predicament. I then showed them my phone with the text message written clear as day from Bren's number. "You both see this, right?" Both looked confused, but nodded to give me the security of not going insane. Bren removed her phone from the pouch of her hoodie. She unlocked it with her thumb scanner and opened it to her texts. Sure enough, nothing was there.

"You have any idea what these people want?" Ethan said.

"No, but the text came immediately after I accessed my journal article on conspiracy in the public library." I had connected the dots for Ethan. Bren focused on something else. She scrunched her face and slapped my arm:

"So, what happened to not diving deeper into this? What happened to driving around and soaking in some of home?" She was obviously pissed off and had a right to be. She was also worried, which overshadowed my deception.

"Sorry, I know I said I wouldn't peer into this. And I truly do want the detectives to handle the majority of it. I just need to know why I've been brought into this." Bren nodded:

"Then we will do this together, asshole." She forced a smile and grabbed my hand. She had always wanted us to be partners on everything. My idea of protecting her was never an acceptable solution.

"I just didn't want to hurt you." I spoke in defeat, staring down at the wood grain in the table. She moved closer toward me, placed a kiss on my cheek, and looked me in the eyes:

"Just don't let it happen again." She forced another smile to let me know that she understood why I did what I did. It was clear that she needed me to confide in her. I needed to be open. She needed this now more than ever as she was handling the abandonment issues that came with my absence. She obviously didn't think I did it on purpose, but the emotions still altered how she was treating me. Now, more than ever, she needed me to be close and attached to her. She didn't need omissions, despite how innocent I thought they might be.

"What are *you* going to do?" Ethan spoke and made it sarcastically clear that he meant "you" in the plural. I smiled:

"What are *we* going to do?" I looked at Bren, and she glared back at me, unamused with my attempt at using humor to extinguish the confrontation. "Seriously though, what should we do now? This is getting old." I emphasized the annoyance I felt by raising my arms and dropping them on the table. The smack of flesh to table was louder than I had planned. Nonetheless, it stressed the critical nature of the circumstance. Unfortunately, the feeling didn't last for long.

The brainstorming session placed us in the same position we were in to begin with. We simply didn't know what to do. We were far behind those who were harassing us. Even back home, the tides still hadn't turned in our favor, and there were no clues to bring us any closer. Ethan was not very helpful in coming up with a plan. He knew this was over his head. I could tell that, while he cared, being a father meant he needed to steer clear of any decisive action. He was also noticeably tired, and his brain wasn't operating at full capacity. I assumed he stayed up late writing the reports for me to look at and caring for his baby. His eyes begged me to release him from his obligation to be my friend for the evening. He was shaken. He needed to be with his family. An hour or so had passed since we sat down at the dining table. I got up after more moments of stagnation:

"E. We can work on business another time. We certainly can't do anything about this other mess tonight." He looked down:

"Ok.... Guess I'm fired again." We all laughed:

"Don't be a drama queen. Be safe getting home." I walked Ethan out and we exchanged good byes. We didn't schedule another meeting, but I assumed we'd get together, if not tomorrow, then the day after.

Early evening clouds shrouded the night with an ominous feeling. The pressure in the air seemed to guarantee a massive thunderstorm was in the making. As Ethan drove away in the distance, the first strike of lightning brought a thunderclap far too close for comfort. After another few strikes, the rains came in strong with the promise to last for hours. Upon my return, Bren stood in front of me with the two most comforting sights I had seen in far too long. She presented me with the ingredients for chocolate chip cookies, and I could already see the oven preheating in my periphery. In the other hand, she held a copy of *Monster Squad*, the very movie I most needed to see. With boxes in hand, she wrapped her arms tightly around my neck. I returned the favor, wrapping my arms over her head and latching my fingers toward the middle of her back. After a few moments, she whispered in my ear:

"I know it doesn't change what's going on, but it's a start." She smiled, turned away from my arms, and began mixing the cookie dough. I moved behind her, squeezed her tight once more, and whispered in her right ear.

"It's perfect."

Chapter 14

After a night filled with warm cookies dipped in two-percent milk, laughter of a nostalgic cult classic, and the soothing rain that followed the initial eruption of a storm, I was finally coming to grips with my situation. The next morning, my eyes were opened by a slobbery kiss from Atlas, which meant it was time for breakfast. I could swear his internal clock was set as precisely as a German train schedule. Bren groaned and rolled over with a smile as if to signify that this was definitely my turn. I had a feeling it would be my turn for quite some time. I kissed her cheek and said those magic words:

"Let's go outside!" The bed shook as Atlas and Nutty went wild with anticipation. They jumped off the bed and blasted downstairs toward the back door, where a quick bowel movement would act as a precursor for their meal. I could hear Atlas' lanky legs thunder down each step. Nutty began baying at the door well before I arrived.

I made my way downstairs way too slowly for the two very eager pups. I let them outside and watched as they ran around the yard like they were a year old again. I slowly moved toward the kitchen to pour food and prep medicines. Nutty was hoping up and down relentlessly while Atlas patiently sat as I approached the door. Upon reentry into the house, the dogs bolted for their bowls and devoured every last morsel. As was customary, Nutty finished first. Convinced that Atlas was given a larger portion, he threw his head back, let out a whimper, and stared desperately with big puppy dog eyes at the bottom of his dish in hopes that more would simply appear from thin air. He began to lick the edge of his bowl as if it were broken and this might fix the problem. Reluctantly, I dropped a few extra pieces in to give him that short, but sweet, satisfaction.

Both cats also demanded their own rituals. I turned the faucet on for Dopey, and I gave a small portion of wet cat food to Sir Didymus. Everyone inside the house was temporarily satiated. I moved toward the garage, opened the third door, and drove my Kubota RTV toward the barn. The sun was just beginning to appear. Dew gripped the blades of grass, and various insects jumped away as the RTV tires tore through the path en route toward a surprisingly missed routine. The horses were already in their stalls in preparation for my arrival. Two scoops of grain for each of them and a fleck of compressed Timothy hay kept them coming back twice a day like clockwork. The two mules approached the other side, and received similar treatment, although they accepted their rations with far more disdain for my presence. I had missed their callous entitlement. I sat down and watched them happily engulf their food before pulling an apple from my pocket, quartering it, and splitting it amongst the four. They were so happy with so little. I hopped back into the RTV and moved toward the rest of the farm to feed everyone a small treat. The sun was now peering over the tree tops that lined the hay fields. The RTV was splattered with dew as I flew through the green pasture. Grasshoppers burst to either side, narrowly escaping the charging vehicle. Some clung to my shirt before springing off of me toward the safety of the field.

It felt good to be back. The routine, established so many years ago, was seamlessly picked up once again. The air smelled good. I took my time filling water troughs and giving attention to each animal individually. It no longer felt like the burden it once did. Prison made me appreciate the lives that I could care for and protect. For a few moments, it felt as if no one was watching me. No one wanted harm done to me. Every being in my vicinity simply needed me to care for them and protect them from harm and starvation. I was good at this, and it made me shine as bright as the low-lying sun reflecting off the wet earth.

I decided to stay out for a while and think in the comfort of the land around me. It gave me so much clarity simply to be outside. I heard a gunshot echo in the background. Probably a local hunter, or perhaps someone practicing for the Ruritan's weekend turkey shoot. I walked around, touched the trees, and marveled at the elaborate nest built by a local red-tailed hawk. I could hear the nestlings calling for their mother to bring them a fresh kill. I kept my walk going and thought that this life might be everything I needed. It would be enough simply to go to the police, explain what had transpired, and see if they could offer some sort of protection for my family. There would be no adventure, no danger, and no alternate life. I could have my old life back. The one that Monsters and a shitty government tried to take away. I thought to myself that I wouldn't give them the satisfaction of succeeding in that endeavor. They wouldn't get the satisfaction of involving me in their sick game.

After nearly thirty minutes of walking and pondering, I hopped back in the RTV to return home. I was excited to tell Bren that there would be no more talk of adventures, and the detectives and PI's would pick up where we would no longer go. I was actually happy. I felt the decision give my life clarity. The anxiety began to melt away. The wind hit my joyous face and the undulations in the ground gave my ride short stints of excitement as I pressed the gas to move faster. I drove through the open garage door and closed it behind me. I entered my kitchen braced for the usual welcome. Nothing happened. No one was there to welcome me with open arms or paws. Silence gripped my household. I called out for Bren and my pups. Nothing. I shrugged it off and moved up stairs. I turned the corner toward our bedroom when my life lost any semblance of the purpose I had just given it in my walk. The Monster stood tall with his Kimber pointed down at me once again. Bren was lying in a pool of blood at his feet. She wasn't moving. He motioned for me to look in the corner, where I saw Atlas and Nutty alive, but in muzzles and tied firmly to our dresser. He spoke as though his words would have meaning:

"I'm not a monster." I hear a shot and see the Monster pull his trigger. Two shots fired, but only one impact. I reeled from the pain, but not from the bullet passing through the flesh next to my rotator cuff. I reeled from the immense pain of Bren being taken from me. I reeled from my animals being tied to an uncertain and possibly painful future. My freshly repaired heart was shattered to pieces in the span of seconds. The impact from the close-range blast sent me down to the hardwood floor. I awaited a third and fatal shot. It didn't come. As the realization of what happened hit me, I passed out. This was the easiest response with my wife dead but a few feet from me. It was finally over and I had nothing left. No one was messing with me any longer. They were truly watching, and when they found their moment, they struck me down. They struck me down in the worst way possible. They struck my family down in front of me. They had taken everything once again. The last thing I would hear on this earth were the faint whimpers of Atlas and Nutty.

Chapter 15

It took a few moments to break out of the stupor and realize the noise was coming from his pocket. The ring pierced his mind like someone driving nails into his frontal lobe. He fumbled in his pocket and finally grasped his smartphone. He pulled it in front of his bloody face and tried to distinguish the caller. It was Deliverer. He began composing himself slightly. He swiped to answer the call and pulled the phone toward his ear. He didn't need to speak. He simply listened.

"Is it done?" Deliverer got straight to the point. The Monster was dazed, but needed to give confirmation that he had completed his task. He didn't know what had happened, but he replied confidently nonetheless:

"He and his wife have been eliminated."

"Good." Deliverer said before hanging up the phone.

The Monster dropped his cell and clutched the side of his head. Blood trickled through his hands. The phone bounced off the wood floor and rested in more blood. He began focusing through the blur of confusion and blood. His head split in pain. He pressed his hands on the ground, letting all the blood consume them. Too much to be all his own, he thought to himself. He sat up and looked around Tom Appling's bedroom. Someone had gotten the drop on him. Appling was gone. So were his dogs, cats, and Bren's body. How long had he been unconscious? He remembered being struck as he pulled the trigger of his Kimber TLE Custom II. When he woke, his gun was gone and he was left for dead. No one ransacked his body. He took a quick inventory. He still carried the same IDs and cash he had prior to being shot.

He moved toward a large mirror on top of the dresser he had used to tie up Appling's dogs. He stared at the face in the mirror and marveled as blood exited the side of his skull. Some congealed to his face, illustrating that he had been out for a while at least. He pulled open the dresser drawers. First were pants. He opened another and found folded T-shirts. He grasped a white shirt that appeared to be a fundraising shirt for Relay for Life or something. He wrapped it around his head to stop the bleeding. The pressure on the wound felt harsh, but gave him the security to continue his search for some water.

He stumbled into Appling's bathroom. He turned the old-fashioned nozzles. One said hot and the other cold. He turned both to full capacity. He allowed the water to become lukewarm prior to splashing his face and eyes. He looked down toward the drain as the red started to drift away into the pipes underneath Appling's house. He looked at himself in the mirror to gauge the severity of his wound. It was deep, but a flesh wound. He opened the drawers under the sink. He placed his hand on a bottle of rubbing alcohol, knowing it wouldn't be a pleasant experience. He used a wash cloth to soak up some of the liquid and proceeded to press it against his fresh gunshot wound. He let out a massive howl upon application. He gritted his teeth and wiped the wound clean. When he was finished, he searched Appling's cabinet for some gauze. He pressed it on the wound and rewrapped his head with the blood-ridden shirt.

More determined and thinking clearly, he moved into Appling's personal study. He marveled at the collection he had amassed in ancient history. He kicked the bookshelves and turned the office inside out in a fit of rage. He pondered his next moves. He had lied to Deliverer, the only man he feared in this world. Bren Appling was dead, but his real target could still be alive somewhere and he had no idea where. The lie bought him time. Deliverer wouldn't tolerate a second failure. Not with stakes as high as Thomas Appling.

The Monster moved down the stairs and into Appling's garage. He found a five-gallon gasoline container next to Appling's RTV. He snatched the gas can and carried it upstairs. He doused Appling's study, his notes, outlines, and computers. He then doused the two hundred-year-old house and set it ablaze. He didn't stay to watch it burn to the ground.

88

He walked to the neighbors to the west of Appling's residence. The pandemonium next door, given that next door was roughly a half-mile down the road, wasn't noticed. The Monster knocked on the door and waited for Tom Appling's elderly neighbors to answer. When they did, he spoke to them kindly:

"I just ran my car off the road. I hit my head really hard." He pointed to his fresh gun wound that took off a small piece of the right side of his scalp.

"Oh dear. Call 911 Bennie." The gentle old man moved toward his kitchen to make the call, but the Monster had already cut the old phone line outside in anticipation.

"Phone is down, Edith! You got your cell?" Edith moved away from the door, freeing the Monster to enter without the frail eighty-pound barrier in his path.

"I put it somewhere around here." Edith searched for the phone under piles of magazine clippings from *Home and Garden, Good Housekeeping,* as well as other junk magazines that covered their rickety coffee table. She finally found an outdated cell covered in dust. She turned toward the Monster: "I don't use this much except on my drives over to the church. Well, that and I take it to Sissy's Market sometimes when I go out to play the Bingo." She continued on as most old Southern belles tend to do, revealing more information from a thirty second interaction than most people could in days. The enormous man nodded and smiled underneath his scar-ridden cheeks:

"It's no worry, really." He grabbed Edith's frail skull and forced it down through the coffee table. She was dead before she hit the ground. Bennie yelled from the kitchen:

"Everything ok in there? Edith?" He approached the living room, where he saw his Edith. "You Monst—" The Monster used the back of his hand in a swing to incapacitate Bennie. Like his wife, the force from the Monster on the feeble old man was just too much. Bennie died a few feet away from his wife of more than sixty years.

"I'm not a monster." He whispered before moving toward the kitchen where he obtained the keys to Bennie's 2003 Toyota Sienna. He snarled before dislodging the propane line in the back of the oven. He found one of Edith's cigarettes and a box of matches. He stepped outside the small cottage, struck the match, lit the cigarette, and tossed it into the kitchen. The explosion was deafening, quickly enveloping Bennie and Edith's freshly murdered bodies, as well as any semblances of their country cottage. The heat from the blast could be felt on the Monster's neck as he moved away from the carnage.

The Toyota Sienna's odometer read 75,000 miles, a testament to how little the old couple actually traveled. The car was maroon with tan cloth interior. The Monster looked at his face in the flip down mirror. What he saw was pain. He barely glanced at the fresh bullet wound on his scalp. He stared at the scars on his cheeks. The symmetrical divots of childhood trauma. He remembered the first time he was strung up as a young orphan living in Macedonia.

"And they all call me a monster." He reflected back on the monsters that plagued his memories. The demons that gave him the scars all over his body, but most notably his cheeks. He was nine years old. His parents, two textile workers from Bitola, were killed in a gang initiation ritual. Three cowardly thugs killed them before they could even defend themselves. It happened in front of what many now call a Monster, but then he was simply a scared child. The gang left the child to suffer on the streets, having to scrap for everything he could get his hands on. Then it happened. The monsters of his world captured him, tortured him, and broke him. What started with light beatings, turned into burns on his extremities, cuts across his chest, and lashes across his back. But the worst, and what every single passerby would notice until the end of his days, were when they would string him up. They used nails to penetrate the cheeks before threading rope through both sides of his mouth. They would loop the rope around a meat hook above him and then raise the hook. There, the young child would stay barefoot with the tips of his toes barely touching the floor for days on end. "They know nothing of true monsters." He remembered nearly gagging on his own tongue, rats picking at his bare feet, and the sudden release when the real monsters returned to feed him. To keep him alive for long enough to break him down even more.

He ignited the Sienna and placed it into drive. He would find Thomas Appling. He would find Thomas Appling or die trying. He would rather die than be punished by Deliverer, the one man he feared more than anything on the planet. The one man left that had been torturing him since he was nine years old. The one man he could call a true monster

.

Chapter 16

I didn't want to wake up. I didn't want to live in the world that had torn me to pieces so methodically. It had lifted me up for moments to heal, just before breaking me yet again. I lay there conscious for a while before I finally allowed myself to open my eyes. I lay there praying that this was some kind of heaven, purgatory, or even a hell. Even the fire and brimstone kind would be a pleasant alternative. Anything would beat the hell of being alive. As an all too familiar musty and damp smell filled my nose, I could feel my earthly body ache from my injuries, and I knew I was in the latter. I knew I was alive. I blinked several times and didn't recognize my surroundings. I felt as though I was in a basement. The exposed pipe in the ceiling contrasted to a dark carpet beneath me. The air was cave-like wet. I was on some sort of cot. I couldn't see anyone around me. I thought about calling out, but didn't.

I lifted up for a moment, but a jolt of pain from my shoulder put me back down fast. Tears of Bren flooded my eyes. My heart ached like I couldn't imagine. Why was I still alive? Couldn't I just die? My mind swirled as I thought of my mother, sister, and Atlas. Were they ok? Where the fuck was I?

"I'm so sorry." A female voice alarmed me from behind. I didn't try making the mistake of turning around before I spoke:

"Where am I? What happened?" The voice came a bit closer, but she didn't present herself in front of me.

"You are safe, but I arrived too late for your wife. I'm so sorry." More tears ensued. More pain, more doubt, and the thought of wanting to die so I didn't have to feel this agony clouding my thoughts. I almost felt myself passing out once more, but I stayed awake. I placed my hand on the freshly treated wound. "No! Don't touch it, please." She spoke with an air of distress in her voice.

"My family?" I spoke of everyone. Everyone was in harm's way with that Monster.

"They are safe, too. The big man didn't harm your animals. I dropped them off at your mother's house. I left a note. They will be safe there, no?" The "no" struck me as odd, like she didn't know the answer to her question, but assumed they would be safe.

"Who are you?" She didn't reply. "The Monster? Where is he? How do you know where my mother lives?"

"Please try to stay calm. Your wounds are extensive, and I—"

"Just answer me!" I interrupted in anger.

"He's dead at your house, Mr. Appling." Confusion. Finally, a different emotion than the pain of tremendous loss. She didn't answer about my mother. So many questions to ask.

"You killed him? Saved me?"

"You are safe here. But you must rest." I shook my head. It made the entire cot shake. I heard a ding soar through the air as if my cot bumped into a hollow metal pole. I looked and saw that I was hooked on some sort of IV on a drip. From my confused state, I assumed some sort of pain med or antibiotic.

"Who are you?" I asked once more before feeling my eyes close and passing out once again.

I regained consciousness again with the same confusion over my surroundings, but I was more lucid this time. My mind was a bit sharper and my body felt stronger. I was still alive, but why this time above all the times before in my life? Why keep me alive now? Where was I? Was I actually dead? Was this the afterlife?

"I need you alive, Mr. Appling." The female voice spooked me once more from behind.

"Please show yourself to me. I don't understand. Who are you? How could you need me?"

I heard her footsteps from behind me as she approached closer and closer. I could feel that she was just behind me when she touched my right arm just below where the bullet had entered.

93

"I'm not here to harm you." More confusion set in prior to her unveiling herself in front of me. I couldn't understand why she wouldn't answer me. When the female figure stepped into view and my eyes focused through the dimly lit room, my adrenaline soared, my body tensed, and I felt rage creep in. Before I could say a word, she motioned for me keep calm: "I'm not here to hurt you, Mr. Appling." She spoke with such compassion and care. What was I seeing in front of me? What trickery was this? I must be in hell! Was this worse than the Monster? I tried to get up. She didn't stop me, but held her hands up in an attempt to calm me once more. The adrenaline overrode the pain of my injury. I pulled out the IV, and as blood dripped from the open catheter, I moved closer to her. I moved closer to none other than Constable Yaravela Shen.

Chapter 17

My fists clenched, and my face felt as if the blood vessels in my eyes would burst at any second. I had never been so enraged. The woman who had framed me for murder was standing directly in front of me. Without thinking, I attempted to grab her. The pain shot down my right arm, foiling my attempt. I had intended on choking Yaravela Shen, or whatever she called herself at this point. It was a stupid move given Miss Shen's prowess as a cold-blooded killer and my current state, but what did I have to lose at this point? Shen could easily discern my anger. Hell, she knew I had every right to kill her with my bare hands. She also knew something to say that would pique my curiosity and halt my attempts.

"I saved your life that day." Still infused with rage, I passed a glare toward her and beckoned her to continue. "You probably always assumed that I was the one to unplug the camera feed. Well, it wasn't me. Ricketts unplugged the feed more than a minute prior to my arrival in that room. Ricketts had every intention of killing you that day." The heartache that had become anger now turned into sheer hysteria:

"What? Ricketts? Why? Why would I believe anything you say?" Despite my resolve, Shen knew she had me, or at the very least, had me calmed down.

"Ricketts, like me, was contracted by the organization that placed a hit on you, Mr. Appling." My eyes opened wide. I didn't know what to think but relegated myself to the knowledge that if Shen wanted me dead, she had ample chance to do so multiple times. Hell, I could even take joy in the fact if she wanted me dead at this point.

"What organization? And why do they want to kill me?" I shook with anticipation, only to be let down.

"Isn't that what we need to find out? It's the whole reason I saved you, twice now. Whatever you know. Whatever your research states. Something made you the highest priority for them. On that day in Newcastle, you had no less than ten people contracted by that organization to kill you, Mr. Appling." I shook my head.

"Look. I don't know what they think I have, or what they think I know. I looked yesterday at my sources, and there's nothing. I was just beginning to read my journal article when your organization," I pointed at Shen with my left hand before continuing "sent me another cryptic 'we are watching' text from Bren's..." Her name barely escaped my lips. I choked and couldn't contain my tears. I dropped to my knees with the realization that something I did, said, or researched was the cause of her death.

Shen moved to my side and tried to console me. She attempted to help me back to my feet. I didn't budge from the cold cement floor. After a few moments of uncontrollable sobbing, I began to compose myself once more.

"I didn't find anything. Whatever they think I have, I don't." When my mind finally gained a touch of composure, something else sparked my curiosity. "You said you were contracted to kill me. Why did you save me instead?" Yaravela Shen shook her head. She remained composed, but her gaze didn't lift from the floor:

"We don't need to get into that. Let's just say, we have more in common than you know, and like you, these people have harmed me in the worst ways imaginable. They must be stopped. There are no bounds to the evil they create in our world." Unexpectedly, she jerked her gaze from the floor. Her broken gray eyes connected with mine. She understood my pain. It was intimate with her and I could almost feel it matching my own. I started to empathize with her when she continued. "I've spent years trying to find answers. Trying to find a way to hurt them, but they use people to do their bidding. They have so much power. They force people to kill without conscience or question. They use leverage in sadistic ways."

She was ranting now, but she had made her point very clear to me. Whatever this organization was made a habit out of breaking people,

96

using people, and killing people. Shen composed herself. "In all these years, I've never seen them go after someone the way they went after you, Mr. Appling. Whatever you know, or whatever they think you know, can hurt them. It's big. Maybe it's big enough to bring them down. If you don't know what that is, then we have to figure it out."

She pled with me to join in her cause. I could tell that she sought a similar revenge on this organization that I did when I sat on the stool at the library when my wife was alive. When I sought revenge on the very person now trying to convince me to help her. I shook my head:

"It won't bring her back. It won't bring anyone back." What I was saying was true. The dead were dead. Revenge didn't help the dead.

"It can stop it from happening to others." Shen spoke in a sentence she thought would entice me to join her cause. Perhaps she was right. Perhaps we needed to give the dead purpose for their loss. Or was I just trying to convince myself that my cause was noble now? Now that Bren was gone? What about what Wilma said about adventure and thrill seeking. I shook off all the indecisive thoughts muddling my mind. To me, this was no longer about my own revenge. It wasn't about preserving a memory. It wasn't about saving the future from this organization's damage. Now, it was simply about crushing them. It wasn't about punishing them for what they had done. It was about finding them, and eliminating them from existence like they had done to Bren, Hogue, and anything resembling a hopeful life for me. The rage that fueled me when I first saw Shen had now boiled over toward her very cause. No more thoughts on protecting a shattered family. I would never stop grieving Bren's death or the life with her that was stolen from me, but I would do something. I would take action, and I wouldn't look back.

"Where do we start?" I didn't reach out a hand to become partners, and I didn't high five her or anything cheesy like that. I was a beaten down shell of a person. This wouldn't change with this newfound purpose that had lit a fire beneath me. My question was meant to receive a legitimate answer. I was all business in this approach and tried my very best to remain calm and collected while feeling the immense pain of Bren's death. Shen nodded. She, too, wasn't overjoyed in this

97

arrangement. This was something that she needed to take on for whatever her reasons were. At this point, her reasons didn't matter.

"I have no one I care about. You do. You have a mother, a sister, animals, etc. They needed security. They will not stop going after you as long as you keep seeking answers. If you have something to care about, they will use that against you." I wasn't shocked. I nodded because I knew now that she was right. I knew that this wasn't a safe endeavor that we were embarking on. Hell, I had nearly been executed in my own home. My wife was dead. My family shattered. I had been imprisoned, my supervisor had had her head blown off. I pondered what would happen to my family if I proceeded, but then quickly wondered what would happen if I didn't. If they found out that I was still alive, assuming they didn't know already, my family was still doomed because of me. I would make preparations and take measures into my own hands to protect them, but doing nothing wasn't an option. If I was going to take action, I simply needed to know that it wouldn't cause any more harm to those who loved me, to those whom I loved.

I began thinking of plans. I needed to hire protection for those that I loved and disappear without a trace. The first part of the plan was easy enough. I had worked private security at times through college. I still had good friends in the business who would bend over backwards for me. My family would be as safe as I could make them. Disappearing, without people assuming I killed Bren, would be a touch more difficult. Faking my own death seemed a bit drastic. Yea, I wasn't going to do something like that. There would be questions. Would I be around to answer them? I wasn't normally a person to hide away from my problems. I hated loose ends. Hated conflict. My heart started to beat rapidly.

"Where is Bren's body?" I hadn't asked this question. I wasn't sure I even wanted to know. I felt that no matter what Shen said I would be let down. How could anyone move her without being insensitive? Shen squirmed together a reply, understanding that what she had to say might be misinterpreted unless she was careful:

"For your safety, I had to leave her at your house. She's where she was when you were shot." I shook my head. Could she really be gone?

The image of her at the Monster's feet was almost too vivid in my mind. I was out of tears, probably dehydrated. I was numb. I nodded slowly:

"We need to go back." Shen shook her head:

"I don't think that's a good idea." I knew she was right. How would I explain any of this? Would there be others there to kill me? Almost assuredly so. A faint sound from outside caught my attention. Was it a seagull?

"You never answered a question of mine. Where are we?" I knew Shen was keeping something important from me. How long had I been out? What was she avoiding telling me? Shen fidgeted once more, her face crinkled up in an attempt to say something she didn't want to. I remembered the tense she used when referring to my family. "You said my family needed protection? Past tense. What's going on!" She finally relented to my pressure:

"After I shot the big man, I had to make a few quick decisions. First, I needed to get you out and to safety." She spoke of the events as if they were memories from long ago. As if this didn't happen within the last few hours like I had thought. "You were heavy, Mr. Appling. I used the rug in your room and rolled you onto it. I then pulled you toward the stairs. It wasn't pretty from there, but I was able to pull you to safety." I felt no trauma from head injuries sustained. I then realized my gunshot wound hurt, but the pain was more from stiffness. I felt the patch once again. Shen didn't stop me this time. I uncovered the wound. It had mostly healed. There were no stitches to be seen. "Don't freak out, Tom." My heart was starting to pound again and I had the look of panicking all over my face:

"How long ago was this?" Shen breathed in deeply and then out. She ignored my question at first:

"I then went back in for your dogs and cats. I just couldn't leave them there." I snapped:

"Answer the question!" She continued the story as if I weren't in the room:

"I looked for some of Bren's supplies from her truck." Bren worked for herself as a traveling veterinarian. Between the house and truck, there was a hospital's worth of medical supplies. I could almost see where the story was going. "I noticed she had isoflurane, valium, and ketamine. She had stitching and she had room in the truck." I put my head down nearly defeated:

"Please. How long?" She still didn't answer. She still continued the story. I knew now she needed me to see the whole picture.

"I was able to prop you up and roll you into the trunk. I stopped the bleeding with some emergency quick clot powder and bandages. You were out, but I gave you a shot of Buprenorphine and a broad-spectrum antibiotic. I looked in your pockets and found your phone. I spent a bit more than two minutes finding your mother's contact. I actually had to look her up on your Facebook account. She was under her first name in your contacts for whatever reason. I found her address. She was close enough. I found the keys to the truck and drove over to her house. I saw a car in the drive. I also noticed she had a backyard. I wasn't confident in my decision, but really what better options did I have? I needed to act so fast, you see. I quickly wrote a note and placed it on one of the cat carriers. The gate in the back yard wasn't locked. I unfastened the latch and let your dogs go in the yard. I then placed the cat carriers beneath the front door, rang the doorbell, and ran. By the time I was at the end of the driveway, I saw the front door open. I didn't see her, but assumed that it was her." A sense of relief passed over me that they were in good hands, and at least some pieces of my family were together. I didn't ask where we were this time. I simply asked:

"What next?" She was more at ease now when she spoke:

"I couldn't risk you. I couldn't see you go to prison, be questioned, or heavily guarded at a hospital. So, I drove. I drove west and didn't look back. I took all the supplies I could find in Bren's truck and switched vehicles. I had plenty of experience with wounds. Part of my training in Australia was as a first responder. I redressed the wound on your shoulder. The bullet wasn't in your arm, but it certainly caused some muscle damage. I could see the twitches as I cleaned the blood away. I searched online about the sedations I took. I was able to find the doses I needed to keep you out of it. Luckily, there was enough in the truck to sedate an elephant. I could've kept you out for years."

"How long?" I interrupted, hoping to finally hear an answer. "Where are we?"

"We are in Cabo San Lucas, Mexico, Mr. Appling." My mind jittered. It was flooded once again with questions. Before I could ask one, she continued: "You have been sedated for three weeks." My jittery mind almost lost control. I felt as if I was hit with a sledge hammer in the face. Bren. Bren had been dead for weeks. Another tear finally formed out of whatever liquid storage I had left in my ducts.

"How?" I didn't actually want an answer to that question. I didn't care. I felt beaten down. I felt abused. I felt robbed of mourning for Bren. I felt robbed of spreading her ashes to her favorite destinations. Robbed of even more time off my increasingly dismal life. I was kidnapped. I was taken away and stolen of any opportunity to explain to my family. Shen had turned me again into the "Bloody American."

"Do they think I killed Bren and that Monster?"

Shen breathed in again, the ultimate bearer of bad news. "I watched the news, Mr. Appling. Your home was burned to a pile of ash. No bodies were found."

Chapter 18

The Monster drove the Toyota Sienna with purpose. He thought about the body in Thomas Appling's home. He wasn't responsible for it. When he arrived, Bren Appling was dead on the floor and her dogs were muzzled and tied to the dresser. It looked like she had been shot. He never found this odd. Before, in Australia, Deliverer had sent multiple people to take care of assignments on certain occasions. They coordinated with each other sometimes, as was the case in the failed attempt at Newcastle. The Monster thought about the sniper that killed Appling's supervisor. He knew that if the sniper was to miss on either target, he would clean up the mess. It was easy. The supervisor was toast. Appling was slippery and both he and the sniper missed. The Monster assumed someone, perhaps even the same sniper, killed Bren Appling just before he arrived. He didn't even think twice about the body on the floor or the dogs in the corner. Three less things he had to deal with. He didn't think twice, until he discovered the body had vanished when he awoke.

"Probably just taken away by whoever shot me." He spoke aloud as if he were trying to convince an invisible friend in the passenger seat. He was supposed to kill anyone who was in Appling's house. This was customary in this line of work. Leave no witnesses. Tie up all loose ends. Bren Appling would've been a loose end. His phone rang, it was Deliverer. All seven feet of the Monster tightened up. How could one phone call from a man more than a foot shorter and one-hundred pounds lighter make him so uneasy? Sure, when he was nine, the Deliverer could over power him. Now, it was all mental. The Monster's body was

Deliverer's masterpiece and his mind was his playground. He was simply a ball of clay molded to Deliverer's whims.

"Yes." The Monster answered. The other line was silent. "Yes?" The Monster spoke louder. Still, nothing on the other line. The Monster nearly hung up the phone and justified Deliverer's call to a butt dial or a bad connection. He pulled the phone from his ear to press the end call button. Just before his thumb hit it, Deliverer responded:

"Business. Next flight. London." Deliverer hung up the phone, sending shivers coursing through the Monster. Deliverer didn't know yet. He would be forced to leave a loose end. He would be forced to leave a country without checking the pulse of a kill. He had, for all intents and purposes, lied to Deliverer. The thoughts of the torture he could be put through didn't bother him. He found that strange. What bothered the Monster was the very thought of Deliverer. The fact that Deliverer could be displeased with him sent panic to his core. He knew he was a dog. He had been beaten and treated like an animal by Deliverer. He had been beaten, and now he obeyed without question. Deliverer was his one and only master.

The Monster turned the car around, feeling the intense anxiety of displeasing his master. Just like a dog that ripped up toilet paper while their master was away, only to feel shame when they would arrive home, Monster knew it was only a matter of time until Deliverer found out what had happened. His only chance would be cleaning up the mess he made prior to Deliverer finding it. He couldn't do that in a different country, but right now without any leads, Thomas Appling might as well be on a different planet than him. He turned the Sienna around in route to the airport. There, he would travel to Charlotte, and eventually, London.

Chapter 19

"What do you mean, no bodies found?" I screamed hysterically. Shen seemed cold. She didn't know what was going on. After three weeks, she still couldn't figure it out.

"I shot that man, Mr. Appling. I hit him in the head and watched him crash into the floor. I thought he was going to bring the house down he hit so hard. I looked at your wife's body. She wasn't moving. There was too much blood. She looked dead." She spoke but I almost tuned her out at that point. I saw Bren's body, too. She was lying in blood just as Shen said. I couldn't give her more than a glance, but in the microseconds leading to the Monster firing, I had no doubt that she had been taken from me. Now, there was a tiny shadow of doubt? Was I trying too hard for something to bring her back to life? I couldn't help but think about the text message from Bren's phone. No. It couldn't be. It wasn't possible. How? How could she be connected? There must've been another explanation. Shen had to be lying. I was near panic once again. I tried my breathing exercises, I thought about the Gillman Stretch Armstrong abomination. I couldn't help but smile as I always did when thinking about it, but the panic couldn't be contained.

"How do I trust anyone?" I decided to speak instead of bottling my emotions. It was a new play, but I was a broken and confused man.

"Trust, Mr. Appling, is a bitch of a thing." Shen wasn't comforting. She was real, and she attempted humor as she gave me the same wink she did prior to killing Ricketts. It sent a chill down my spine. "Honestly, what choice do we have but to trust each other?" I didn't buy it this time.

"Are you going to kill me if I ever give you what you want?" Shen smiled at this one. I didn't know if she saved my pets because she wanted me to trust her, or if she did so because deep down she was a good person. At this point, I didn't know whether to trust that she actually did what she said she did at all. I only knew one thing. She hadn't killed me yet. Perhaps she was even right about the choice. Did I have another choice? Perhaps she was the only lead I had to these assholes. I needed to see this through.

"Mr. Appling."

"Just Tom, please." I interrupted. The whole Mr. Appling thing was getting on my nerves.

"Tom. Does it matter whether I say one thing or another right now? I can tell you this for sure though. I haven't killed you and I've spent three weeks keeping you alive. Trust is earned through actions, not words." Her words were chosen well. She was well educated and contained a pessimistic but real sense of the world. Her demeanor reminded me of a better-looking Ethan in a lot of ways. She was still shrouded in mystery though. She was a dark figure. Someone that seemed capable of kissing you while she plunged a knife into your heart. I had seen her kill a man in cold blood with a screwdriver and a sadistic grin perched on her face. That aspect of her was far from Ethan. It was far from anyone I had ever met.

I thought about food for the first time. I thought about the cookies I last ate and how Bren baked them to perfection. How the milk felt on my teeth and tongue. How the chocolate chips melted in my mouth. I didn't ask how she fed me for three weeks. Even more embarrassing, I didn't ask how she dealt with other less pleasing bodily functions. Some mysteries were simply better off unsolved, but I did need to gain some strength as my head was becoming dizzy.

"Is there something to eat around here?" Shen smiled and shook her head.

"Not much. Come on. I think it's time you went outside for a bit. Do you think you can walk?" I nodded. She moved to my side and gently placed a bandage on my hand to stop the slow drip of blood that had been present since my IV's removal. The blood had bothered me. I hated feeling like something foreign was on me. I washed my hands

105

incessantly after doing yardwork at home. Something about having things on my hands always triggered that obsessive emotion.

After tending my hand, she rose to her feet and walked toward a set of stairs near the far corner of the room. I hadn't noticed them before. I followed her up. When we reached the top, I couldn't help but realize how nice the main level of our shelter really was. From the basement, I assumed we were in some sort of shack. The main level felt dated, but extremely nice. It was open, spacious, and had a view that belonged on the cover of a travel magazine. I wandered from Shen's path, where I stepped out onto a wide balcony where a lavish pool overlooked both the Pacific Ocean and the Gulf of California. We were high on top of a hill. We must've had the best view on the peninsula. I didn't ask how we came about these accommodations. I didn't want to know. I assumed Miss Shen killed the poor owners and they were disposed of somewhere in the house. Perhaps the ocean. I guess at this point it really didn't matter.

"Hey, let's go. Food is this way." Shen spotted me drifting and tried to get me back on task. I nodded and scurried back in line. I felt an awkward wobble, but otherwise, remained pretty mobile. At least, mobile for someone that had been asleep for three weeks.

It was dusk as we walked outside toward another peculiar sight. Sitting in the drive was a new looking Chevrolet Camaro SS. It was aggressive and black. The interior was a rich white leather that was so clean, it looked as if it hadn't been sat on. I felt like I was in the *Twilight Zone*. This entire ordeal was so surreal and made me question once again if I was dreaming or even alive. I remembered back on the ending of the TV show *Lost*. Was I in a similar purgatory? Was I being challenged to find some sort of deep truth before being allowed to pass through to the "other side?" I was too hungry to care. Clarity never happens on an empty stomach.

I slipped into the passenger side of the Camaro and buckled my seatbelt as a reflex. Shen didn't bother. She ignited the engine, and it came alive with the roar of an aftermarket exhaust. She placed the shifter into first, eased off the clutch, and pressed the gas too aggressively. My back felt itself forced into the leather chair behind, and I heard Shen

106

chuckle as the expression on my face displayed the shock one gets when blasting off on the Hulk rollercoaster at Universal Studios.

We arrived at Chamuyo just as the sun was making its final departure from Cabo. The strip in Cabo appeared to be somewhat of a loose cannon at night, but just after dusk, the drunken crowds hadn't quite made it out in full force. For now, it was calm. I followed Shen from the car toward what I thought looked like a pretty stereotypical Mexican dive. She picked a table near the back. It was a touch sticky, but I felt that gave it some character. I was ridiculously hungry, and I wasn't going to let a sticky table interfere with my objective. We didn't speak at first. It was hard feeling each other out. Neither one of us trusted the other. Shen felt as though I knew something that I wasn't sharing. This wasn't even a question with her. It was open knowledge that she was hiding things. Even important things. I was too hungry to care in the moment. I wanted to begin my interrogation again, but the distractions of the atmosphere created by the restaurant were rather daunting. Perhaps this was Shen's plan with her choice of venue. Diverting me even more was our waitress. She was an adorable thing. Four feet nothing with hair stretching to the back of her knees. She wore hoop earrings that seemed to consume her entire head. To top off her ridiculousness, she wore a pair of hipster glasses reminiscent of Wilma's. She was peppy and had the cutest of spicy personalities. She spoke a Spanglish type blend, but both of us were able to comprehend her in this setting.

Upbeat cantina music played in the background. Televisions played replays of soccer games on one side of the restaurant, and soap operas on the other. The lighting was dim, and even the fake candles positioned on each table couldn't salvage decent vision.

Bread came out prior to a sizzling plate of charred Argentinian steak. Fresh grilled onions and tomatoes topped the steak as it rested on a bed of rice. The food was cooked well and much fancier than the atmosphere would've suggested.

I think both Shen and I felt that eating was easier than sharing feelings. I had been through so much trauma in the past few years that the only thing on my mind was the survival felt in the steak I consumed. I sensed much of the same instincts from Shen. Had we both been so unceremoniously abused in our lives? What had Shen gone through? I pondered that to myself as I watched her down bite after painstaking bite. The surreal nature of my circumstance began wearing off. Shen sipped on her second Tecate to wash down the beef. I began staring with more intent than before. The first words out of my mouth since fumbling through the Spanish to order my food were, "We can't play games." This didn't shock her. Would anything I say actually shock this woman? I couldn't read her and that really bothered me.

"There are no games now, Tom." Cryptic yet again. How could she make something so clear sound so cryptic?

"Tell me then. Why are you here with me?" I figured a direct approach would suit the situation best. She didn't hesitate to give me nothing.

"Like I said, I need you to help me destroy these people."

I showed a bit of exhaustion and annoyance. "No. Why are you here? You want to bring them down. Why? What did they do to you?" She knew exactly what I wanted from this. She knew why I wanted revenge on this organization. I had been robbed of a wife, a friend, and my life for more than two years. She knew everything about me and held all the cards. I wanted to know what she had been robbed of.

"They took something from me." She still didn't open up.

This time I demanded. "What! What did they take from you, Yaravela?" It was the first time I used her name. I felt my use of it strike a chord. I saw emotion from her. I was getting somewhere.

"Someone…. They took someone from me, Tom. Like you, they have killed someone dear to me. After saying they wouldn't if I just followed their rules." A tear. A single tear began making its way out of Shen's left eye. It didn't get to her cheek before she wiped it away as if it never existed. She postured so well. She was tough. Whatever this organization did to her was pure cruelty. It must have been to turn her into this. I nodded.

"Ok. I'm sorry. I won't pry further." She acknowledged me before picking up the check. I had no money. This was the first time I realized that I didn't have any money. No cards, no license, no passport, and no identification of any kind. "Thank you." I finally said it to her. It still

108

didn't feel right. Sure, she saved my life, but she didn't do that for me. It was secondary to her desire to find what information I could bring to her journey of revenge. I would eventually need more information from her. I would eventually need to trust this woman. That wouldn't happen tonight, and probably not for some time. As we walked out of the restaurant, I could hear the calm waves of the ocean drifting softly onto the beach. The humid air was filled with the saltiness, but a steady breeze kept it from sticking to our noses.

We arrived back in the home of ten-thousand more questions. I sat on the sofa and began pondering our circumstances once more. I no longer thought about safety for my family. I hoped, now that three weeks had passed that they were safe from my collateral damage. The thought of my family made me think about Bren even more. I never thought that she could be alive. I wasn't willing to let myself go down that dangerous road. She had to be dead. I saw her face down in blood. She wasn't moving.

The living, or entertaining room in Shen's home, or whoever's home, was open. Circular couches connected together behind a large center table with a gas fire pit in its center. It was an interesting array that I hadn't seen before. There was no television to serve as the central point of the room. The couches were red. Underneath the couches were large limestone tiles. The walls were white when they weren't windows. I couldn't help but notice that the walls were seemingly made of windows. It made sense given the magnificent views. Why hide such beauty? Shen sat in a spot across from me. Over the large fire pit, it felt like an extraordinary distance away.

"Do we have access to the internet?" For the first time, I began thinking about the steps I needed to take to start piecing this puzzle together.

Shen shook her head. "Not here." I scoffed a bit, but knew it was probably for the best. If granted access, I would be tempted to cyber stalk my family. That was another dangerous road to go down at this point.

"I am going to need access to some things."

She nodded. "I figured as much." She stood up and walked toward a different room. I think it was a guest bedroom located just off the open

109

entertaining area or living room. She returned with a clear storage container full of books and binders. "I printed off some things while searching from an encrypted server. I also gathered a few books." She had tried. I saw a few things of value within the container. Most notably, my article from the *Journal of Hellenic Studies*. There were also copies of all primary source material and a few secondary sources that played instrumental roles in my research. It was a start.

I moved the storage container in front of me and sat on the couch next to Shen. She immediately got up and moved toward the kitchen. She felt uneasy around me for whatever reason. I assumed this was due to the lack of trust. She probably still thought I was hiding some connection to my research. I didn't have concern enough to ask her. I turned to look over my shoulder. She was in the kitchen brewing the coffee. I loved the smell of coffee but couldn't stand the taste.

"This is a good start." I smiled and she came back into the room. I reached in the container and pulled out my article. I read it three times before the evening was over.

Chapter 20

Dr. Emory Chance sat in the War Studies Meeting Room at King's College London. He was surrounded by fifteen colleagues listening intently to Professor Agda Sunden. The room was quaint and full with those in attendance. Several large rectangular tables had been pieced together to make a large square with space in the middle. At the end of the room, Sunden presented a paper just published by the *Journal of Hellenic Studies* a few weeks earlier. It was a critique of an article by a PhD student, Thomas Appling. The original article was several years old, and detailed a relationship between Artabazus and Pausanias.

"After Mr. Appling's imprisonment, it was like this article never existed. Not one single peer review was ever published. It was as if Mr. Appling published this article and then vanished. Which, it turns out, he did. This topic first came to light when a grad student of my own cited this work in concerns to a project on the Battle of Platæa. I checked his sources and found this one in particular to be quite intriguing. Obviously, I'm not an adept Classicist, given that my research concerns ancient military history, I found it odd that I hadn't heard of this paper. Such a controversial topic should've been, at the very least, reviewed in depth by several renowned scholars. I guess this would include yours truly." The room rustled and sprung into a hoity half-hearted chuckle at Sunden's modest humor. She tried to read the room after her remark. She was halfway calling them out for the oversight. She would've been more upset had she not struck on something incredible through Appling's findings.

She continued. "For years, scholars have proposed conspiracy theories based on the work of Herodotus. Most are just that, theories.

Theories based on little factual evidence. Here, Mr. Appling used a multi-disciplined approach to develop something more than theory. Appling made the interaction between Artabazus and Pausanias likely. He made it likely that these two were in league with one another. He made it likely that Xerxes gave Pausanias the victory at Platæa. He made it likely that Xerxes sacrificed Mardonius. He made it likely that through the relationship, Pausanias promised Xerxes Sparta's loyalty in future endeavors. In short, if Artabazus left unceremoniously at Platæa, he would be punished to the extreme by Xerxes. In truth, he was continually honored by Xerxes as if he left that battlefield by Xerxes command, a goodwill gesture to Pausanias and the Spartans of Xerxes word to them. A word that Mardonius was their gift if they were simply to become the militaristic leaders of the Persian force."

A jeering hmmph came out of Dr. Anges Reid from Glasgow. He didn't speak, but the prevailing thought on his hmmph was that he could never agree with such poppycock. The man could be described solely as the embodiment of Santa Claus. Perhaps, homeless Santa Claus would be an even better description. Like a lot of the onlookers in the room, Reid wanted to be seen. He seldom had the opportunity to get the negative attention he sought. He craved the controversy of a decent academic bout. The same cravings made him a remarkably hated troll in cyber circles. A lot of times, he wanted to let the world know about his trolling activities. He always balked at the last moment, though. His job as a full professor was too good to give up for his true passion of making others feel small. Sunden paused for a moment to see if Reid needed to follow-up on his interruption. When he didn't, Sunden continued. She was used to Reid. The entire room had been trolled by him in one avenue or another. Sunden herself at a Classics conference in America, where he compared a woman historian to a midget trying to reach the pedals of a freight truck. To everyone's horror, he even acted out the scene. Political correctness wasn't Reid's strong suit, but he sure did revel at home to the hits he got on YouTube. He was suspended from Glasgow for the comment but reinstated when he threatened suit. To most of the room, his antics were simply part of the fabric of discussion at this point.

Sunden continued, "Appling did all but prove this through an in-depth analysis of the Platæan markers studied by so many before him. He spent days measuring out the precise distances between markers."

Again, Reid scoffed.

"Like a geographer? This is history, Dr. Sunden. I see nothing here to indicate Mr. Appling was on to anything but chasing his own shadow." The room began taking notice of Reid's outbursts.

Before others could say something, Chance interceded. "Anges! Let Professor Sunden finish her presentation without interruptions or simply leave the premises. This is her time, and we are here to listen, not comment." Sunden appreciated the backup. She appreciated even more that she didn't have to confront Reid.

"Fine! Lips are sealed. The floor is yours, Professor." Reid used his right fingers to sarcastically zip his lips closed, all to the collective eye roll of the room.

Sunden continued once again. "Appling also made it likely that Herodotus actually wrote his *Histories* as a propaganda piece to prevent the Peloponnesian Wars. In retrospect, Herodotus' attempt at glorifying Pausanias for the betterment of Greece had failed. Herodotus' attempt at unifying the Greeks under his epic portrayal of the heroic deeds of Pausanias and Themistocles had failed. Now, thanks to Thomas Appling, it appears likely that Xerxes bought the loyalty of Pausanias and Themistocles in an attempt to lure Sparta and Athens under his flag. He was willing to sacrifice the Battles of Platæa and Salamis in order to create such a relationship." The rest of the audience looked on in high speculation. They had heard such theories before, but few gave any stock to them because there simply wasn't a way to prove anything. What Sunden was presenting now did sound like pure conjecture.

They allowed her to continue unimpeached. "You all wonder why this matters. Why is this different from the speculation of the past? Well, because Thomas Appling has proposed there to be substantial proof written in the land at Platæa. In short, if Appling's theory is correct, one that we all know is plausible based on Herodotus' own words, there will be traces. Through new developments in ground penetrating radar, we can compare the lands in front of Platæa to other fields of war. Land

113

erodes and changes over time. GPR allows us to view the land twenty-five hundred years ago as if the events happened within the year. In a historically significant field, such as the battlefield at Platæa, the land has been protected by the Greek government. Due to this, it remains undeveloped. We can actually scan the entire battlefield using GPR. With this technology, we can discern how many people engaged in the actions, and even tell the difference between the Greek heavy-armed troops, the cavalry, and that of the lightly armed Persians. More importantly to Appling's theory, we could tell how many people left the battlefield to flee to Asia with Artabazus. The technology, in other words, will allow us unprecedented access into the past. We are afforded this opportunity at very few fields of war in ancient history, but Platæa is one of them. Platæa may be the most pristine location. It's flatter than Thermopylæ, yet remote enough that traffic in the area wouldn't damage our results. We can highlight the only time in history where the land was used so heavily. With a mathematical formula, also proposed by Appling, we should be able to arrive within ten percent of the actual numbers at Platæa at that time in history."

The audience became noticeably intrigued by the revelations. Sure, there were skeptics such as the pouting Reid, but was this really possible? If so, and for the first time, many items in ancient history could be proven. If so, Herodotus could have the ultimate fact checker placed upon him. They would never know the exact conversations between Pausanias, Artabazus, and Xerxes. But, what if Herodotus was correct in his assertion of the numbers under Artabazus' command? The numbers that left Platæa to flee north. If Herodotus was wrong about the numbers in Mardonius' army that actually fought, which many believed he was, then it would show a direct correlation between Herodotus' attempt to write a history for propaganda. If Artabazus was not punished and continued to be treated in high regard by Xerxes thereafter, then the likelihood of there being a conspiracy between Artabazus, Pausanias, and Xerxes seemed very high. Nonetheless, if the technology worked, an entirely new chapter could be written for Herodotus' *Histories.* One that would be exempt from the traditional slicing and dicing by the likes of Reid and other self-obsessed historians in peer review. It would change, in many ways, how history was researched. It would force historians out of the archives and into the field.

After the presentation, one which most of the onlookers found to be groundbreaking, there were a few questions spouted back and forth over the feasibility of the project. There was a round-table, or in this case a square-table, discussion over the logistics in pursuing Appling's research. Everyone involved understood the costs associated with bringing equipment into a country such as Greece. Only Emory Chance really knew the entire process inside and out. He had sat on Thomas Appling's committee prior to the paper in question's publication. He remembered a conversation Tom had with him about whether or not he should publish his findings. He suggested he not. He gave the reasons of casting even more confusion on already cloudy events. He insisted that the technology could only be trusted so far. He tried pushing Appling toward more traditional methods of explaining his theories. He had failed in this endeavor prior to leaving Newcastle, citing a family emergency to validate his departure. Now, someone else was bringing up the research, and with the funding of an establishment such as King's College, the likelihood that Appling's method would be undertaken seemed high. In a crowd of his peers, Emory Chance couldn't reason with Professor Sunden. He couldn't explain to her that there were better methods to take. Even if he had the opportunity, he had failed before with Tom. Perhaps he would fail again now.

He watched as Reid stormed out of the room like a child who had lost his Halloween candy. He shook his head and laughed. He wanted to ask if his sleigh needed its parking validated, but didn't sink to the same unprofessional level as his peer. He turned his attention toward the presenter. He stood up from his hardened plastic chair and moved through the crowd. He exchanged various pleasantries before arriving at the newly popular, Agda Sunden.

"Just one second as I have to leave." He said to Sunden. She quickly placed her prior conversation on hold, before shaking Chance's hand. Most in the room respected Chance as one of the more illustrious ancient historians. Sunden respected him even more for halting the momentum of the trolling Reid.

"Thank you for coming, Dr. Chance. And thank you for—" Chance nodded, not allowing thanks for taking Reid down a peg.

"Don't thank me for that! Anges is who he is. I've worked around him for years, and it's always the same. I keep waiting for him to step on the wrong foot, but I guess his value as the devil's most precious advocate has its allure in some circles." Sunden and Chance shared a quick laugh before he continued. "I'm sorry I have to leave so soon. I will catch up to you over email soon. Congratulations! This is most excellent work you have done!" Chance smiled brightly through his gray beard, received a genuine thank you from Sunden, and ducked out of the room.

Emory Chance exited the Department of War Studies toward Riverside Terrace, which overlooked the River Thames and Waterloo Bridge. He waited for traffic to seize up long enough before weaving across Victoria Embankment toward the Temple Pier. He walked casually toward The Yacht London, a fancy restaurant on a permanently moored yacht. Big Ben could be seen toward the southwest, which was a view Chance always loved to see upon his visits. He entered just in time to avoid a stout English drizzle. He took a seat in a white, painted wooden chair, seemingly meant for a proper tea room. White table cloths covered the tables, and fresh flowers exploded from glass vases, acting as centerpieces for each of the twenty or so tables in the main dining area. He sat across from a man who had grown from the little boy he knew so long ago. The little boy he took from Macedonia and raised as his own. He raised him to be hard. Perhaps he raised him to be too hard. He still thought of the boy, even when the seven-foot-tall man sat in front of him.

"As I expected, we have a situation that requires immediate resolution." Chance passed over a photograph of Professor Agda Sunden. It wasn't often that Chance actually got involved in the hands-on elements of his business. He had people for that. He had people for that all around the world for such pedestrian activities as handing out targets. The Monster viewed the photo and began to rise slowly. Chance reached across and grabbed his hand. Chance's hands were roughly half of the Monster's, but the Monster felt his heart sink upon the touch.

116

Chance's hand might as well have been a bowling ball. The Monster sat back in his chair, pondering whether he did something wrong and was to be punished. Chance spoke again. "Sit. I haven't seen you in so long. Have tea with me." The request, on the surface seemed kind. But underneath the layers of torture, and the years of mental and physical abuse, the request produce chills. The Monster didn't say a word. He lowered his head in respect to his Master's wish, and waited for the savories to make their way to the table. Small sandwiches and scones were split amongst the two men. They washed it down with Twining's Lemon and Ginger. A chocolate ganache torte followed. The Monster ate each individually. He felt small eating in that yacht with his master peering through his skull like he was placed on this earth only to serve him. When the two men finished, Chance looked long and hard at the Monster before releasing him from his presence.

"Ok. Now you can go." The Monster nodded, pushed back his chair, and made his way to the door. Everyone in the restaurant felt relief as the enormous and terrifying individual left and offered their assholes a chance to stop clinching in fear. That was a crude way to say that they were completely on edge at his arrival into their otherwise fine establishment. Snickers and whispers filled the air as arrogant socialites gossiped over what they had just witnessed.

Emory Chance stayed on the yacht and enjoyed his tea until the pot was empty. He pondered to himself for a while. How far did he need to take these precautionary measures? All fifteen in the room? Just Sunden? In private, he was actually quite fond of the boisterous Anges Reid. It would certainly be a shame to take care of him. He would need to monitor the others. He would require certainty that they wouldn't try picking up this research once Sunden was no longer in the picture. He thought he might have a solution. A solution to make people remember something different about Agda Sunden. A solution that would make her research feel small in comparison. He dialed one on his phone:

"Yes, Deliverer?" The Monster answered calmly and obediently.

Chance replied, "Minor change of plans. This one needs to be messy."

Chapter 21

Yaravela provided me with quite a few documents. I was pretty impressed. Clearly, she took steps to gather many of the materials listed in my bibliographies. I familiarized myself first with the journal article that was to act as a precursor to my dissertation.

I met Shen's eyes every once in a while. Earlier, during our dinner at Chamuyo, her dark eyes made me uncomfortable. I could palpate the pain as if I were some kind of soothsaying ophthalmologist. Her guard was unconvincingly fierce toward me. Her barriers so rigid that I could almost sense her fear. Then again, I was probably feeling my own fears. Shen scared me. It wasn't that I saw her murder someone in front of me. It wasn't that she had framed me for murder. It wasn't that I couldn't trust her. I think it was the exact opposite. Shen scared me because I felt that I could trust her. I felt that, despite the pain she had brought me, the years of agony, and her cold dark eyes, I could place my life in her hands. Perhaps I had no choice in the matter. Perhaps I knew that she wasn't a true threat to me. Perhaps I needed her not to be. I think at this time, I needed her protection despite the fears it brought me. Despite how much I had lost already. Despite my years of suffering. I felt the life begin creeping slowly into my veins. I was alive, and I felt vulnerability in the feeling.

Her eyes were different now. She wore glasses to conceal how dark they appeared at Chamuyo. Now the intense dark gray, black at the restaurant, became a soothing fragment of their former self. It's funny how glasses can do that to people. It's funny that they made her appear human, but that's exactly what they did. I almost felt that I could approach her for help and ask her a question or two. Perhaps I would have if her body language wasn't making me feel so uneasy. She now sat on a single stair leading toward the kitchen area in the open concept. She didn't speak. She simply stared in my direction. I think she was trying to let me work, but I felt like a rat beneath a hawk's gaze. I opened my mouth as if to speak. Nothing came out, but I could tell it piqued her curiosity.

"What?" She said in anticipation. She spoke as though everything was riding on what I had to discern from the piles she brought me. I think, in the world we were in, she was right. I was too intent and too focused to let the pressure wear on me.

"This." I turned to her. "This might take a while." I sensed her disappointment as she came off a momentary high of excitement. "I don't mean to disappoint. I just. Well, I just need a bit of time." I was trying to be subtle, but knew that I wouldn't give myself to the work underneath her stare. I think it hit her harder than that, but she took the hint well enough. She smiled and rose to her feet.

"Goodnight, Tom. I will give you the space you obviously need." I reached out in an attempt to soften the blow, but felt her wave me off a bit. Deep down, she knew I needed space to think. It had nothing to do with a lack of appreciation for her saving me. Sure, I didn't really feel a strong appreciation yet for Miss Shen. One day wasn't enough to get over the years of hate I had built against her. I had pictured myself killing her several times in prison. The fantasies helped pass time. Sometimes they manifested in elaborate stories and plots I played for myself. Sometimes, I even felt the strong correlation between extreme hate and this obvious attraction she carried. The feelings confused me. The thin lines our human emotions carry are more than we can comprehend at times; but, despite the muddling emotions, most of the time I simply hated her and wanted her to pay the price. A smile covered my face as she retired for the evening. I had hurt her feelings, but felt a touch of retribution for doing so. Perhaps it was selfish. Perhaps it was a bit immature, but I had finally made Shen hurt just a little bit. It was the kind of small moral victory I needed to get me through the hours ahead of me combing through that box of material.

It did take hours. An increasingly blurry 3:34 a.m. struck the clock on the kitchen oven by the time I finished reading my own article for the third time. I read my article, found sources of mine to compare, and then proceeded to read it again. The feelings rushed back in. I was wired with the excitement of my research mixed with the adrenaline of the diabolical adventure I now found myself on. Bren. I thought of her seemingly between each word I read. I could almost hear her voice as if she were giving me a loving, but pandering, late-night edit of a paper. Was she really dead? Could she somehow have texted me that awful message? No. I couldn't believe it. Still, I tried to rationalize everything in my head. To me, it seemed more likely that her phone was cloned by one of the people after me. I didn't know how they did it. I just knew that had to be the case. That's what I thought that day. That's what she made me think when I confronted her. Where was her body? Was Shen lying to comfort me that she might still be alive? I thought about trying to call her or message her. It had been three weeks. If she were alive, would she care that I was, too? The emotion kept hitting me as I tried to focus. Seven minutes after four in the morning. Still nothing substantial from anything I had looked at so far. Would I ever find what I was looking for? Would I find anything at all?

I tried to keep my mind free, something exceedingly more difficult to do as the witching hours wore into morning. Between the suffering over Bren and my difficulties in comprehending my own circumstance, I finally found something interesting in the research itself. In a binder full of journals, directly in front, was an article authored by Dr. Agda Sunden of King's College, London. The date was the first item of intrigue. It was published a bit less than a month ago, just prior to my incapacitation by the Monster and Shen.

"Weird." I said aloud to myself but not at a register that anyone in the house could hear. I wondered why this Dr. Sunden would just now be looking at something published more than three years ago. I assumed my incarceration completely wiped all my credibility away in the community. I guess I knew the answer to that stupid question. The work was titled *Thomas Appling's Herodotus: A Critique*. That seemed simple enough to me. At first, I assumed the journal would be spent tearing apart every last hope and dream I had when publishing my thesis. I couldn't have been more wrong. There was hope in Sunden's words. Not only hope, true life in her writing. She used words like "enlightened" and "moved" by my article. She cursed the community for "burying a fine piece of progressive thought." I almost blushed as I kept reading. It was just a few pages as most critiques are, but it was anything but critical. The professor was a gateway toward a life that I had lost when Hogue was shot. She was a gateway toward gaining a semblance of my old life. After my entire life, my beautiful Bren, my research, and my reputation had all been utterly destroyed, I could feel that stranger creeping back into my mind once again. I felt hope.

I stood for the first time in hours. I looked to the wavy textured ceiling above and breathed a short sigh of relief. This was something. This was something tangible I could bring Shen. I turned, and was shocked to see Shen standing in her doorframe, staring back at me through those dark gray eyes. I was taken aback for a moment, feeling my heart jump once again at her sight. I wondered if she would ever give me comfort. She held a perplexed look, obviously awoken from my short burst of excitement when I jumped to my feet. I didn't notice knocking the entire box of material to the floor. She wiped away some of the sleep written across her face. Before she had a chance to speak, I simply lifted Sunden's article in the air, pointed at it with my left index finger, and spoke confidently:

"London!"

Shen, increasingly more human with her dazed reaction, responded in confusion.

"London? What's London?" She squinted to see what the article was. I brought it closer to her.

"London is a place. And it's a place we need to get to." Shen rubbed her eyes with her index fingers in circles, finally realizing we had some kind of plan. She took the article from me and peered into the name. She nodded her head in agreement as she saw the link for herself. The article validating my research all this time later had to be significant. Sunden had to be the key we were searching for.

"Ok. I'll take care of it. London, it is."

I smiled. This epiphany felt similar to the one I had when history changed my future. I remembered the very moment when I thought I could unequivocally prove, not only a true battlefield recreation at Platæa, but also a major conspiracy theory linked to several high-profile characters, including the father of history himself, Herodotus. I remember shaking with excitement and the anticipation of a critique from Hogue and, at that time, my second committee member, Emory Chance.

Chapter 22

Two starkly contrasting existences. Most people would wonder how a respected professor, a PhD with hundreds of publications, could turn into something like Deliverer. How would a monster like Deliverer spring from the calm and humble, Emory Chance? Well, he hadn't. It didn't happen like that. Sometimes monsters are simply bred into this world. They are a product of nature and deny any attempt at nurture normalizing their default self. From the beginning, Deliverer was always there. He was a biological force being suffocated by the shell of Emory Chance, his birth name. He was suffocated by the pc world. A world that had lost its animalistic edge. A world where his true self would never be accepted.

Emory Chance played by all the rules. Private school in rural America sent him on a path to success. He was considered genius by most standards. He didn't necessarily have the drive to act upon it as one of those young prodigies you hear about from time to time. You know, one of those ten or twelve-year-old PhD's. Upon reaching Middlebury at sixteen, a small private liberal arts college in Vermont, Chance fell in love with his true self. As most college kids do, he explored his inner being, or what other nonsensical term philosophers or psych people might use. Funny that most people considered psychopaths probably take a psychology course rewarding and harboring their own self-expression. What most people would call his villainous side, Chance saw as a reflection on his own self-expression into the world. Like most, he started pushing the boundaries. He wasn't cruel. He never used animals in sadistic experiments. To him, animals were too pure. Their world, too much like his own. People, on the other hand, were damaged by societal growth. They were tainted by agendas and their own evolution. Human beings were his avenue of true expression. True art that could write his masterpiece. His masterpiece, a novel accompanied by pages filled with the carnage of thousands. The first ink in his story was written with the blood of Reverend Bill Plocker.

Plocker was an outspoken minister, whose rhetoric used to splash the early morning television screens. Chance enjoyed watching when others slept. Watching at three or four a.m. while letting the feelings of the shows impact his core self. Plocker preached and carried on about garbage. Well, garbage in the mind of an intellectual such as Emory Chance. Chance hated the thought of an ancient book like the Bible being misconstrued by fanatics. He felt the Bible, like most pieces of ancient history, was a purposeful tool meant for propaganda in its time. Such works were meant to be guidelines for humans to prosper with each other through the turmoil of the times. Certainly, not meant as instruments to wage war over or breed hate to fuel personal agendas. Not meant for instruments against modern scruples in homosexuality, abortion, or religious freedom. Chance believed the world had evolved beyond most of the rhetoric applicable in the ancient times, and the books used to guide humanity were in need of the same evolution. Most of the God-fearing tools meant to prevent the spread of disease thousands of years ago were pointless carry-overs for modern society. The hypocrisy of topics like sexuality fueling piety, where cutting your hair or nails could simply be overlooked, infuriated Chance. The fact that a man like Plocker would gather an audience to spew hate messages infuriated him further. Picking and choosing what to follow and calling it "God's will" or "following doctrine" made Chance cringe. Perhaps something didn't "need" to be done. It wasn't as if Chance thought the death of Plocker would stop his particular version of fustian speech. People will be people, but Chance saw Plocker as the perfect opportunity to spread some of his own message.

Omaha, Nebraska was crushed by a devastating tornado in 1975. Somehow, even a man like Plocker found his way in front of the cameras. His first message to a wide audience informed the world that the weather was simply a punishment for all the heathenry of mankind. The sermon

124

sounded more like a speech by Hitler than that of a modern minister. He cleansed the world of the non-believers, all to raucous cheers from the partisan crowd in the background.

The next night, Emory Chance impersonated a follower. He requested a meeting with Reverend Plocker at a local diner. The two carried out remarkable similarities in their disdain for fellow humanity. Plocker, because of an ancient book. Chance, because of a biological disposition in need of power. Both shared an overwhelming sense of supremacy over their fellow man. The diner housed a meal for two lions vying for a territory. By the time Plocker knew he was a target in Chance's scheme, he was cross tied in the only stall left in a barn decimated by the tornado. It was easy enough to sedate the Reverend. Tying up the "dead-weight" of a passed out two hundred pounds took more strength than Chance wanted to exert, but he made it happen nonetheless.

Plocker's eyes opened to Chance's deep stare. He wasn't gagged. Chance held a Bible in his hands and spoke with a purpose very familiar to Plocker.

"Hands that shed innocent blood, a heart that devises wicked plans, a false witness to bring out lies, and one who sows discord in brothers. Proverbs 6:16-19. Not in any particular order I confess." Chance began to the astonishment of Plocker. Plocker remained silent. Chance continued, "I think you are guilty by the paper of your own book, Reverend Plocker." Chance smiled and slammed the book shut.

"What are you doing? What do you want from me?" Plocker pleaded in fear of his predicament. Chance had stripped him naked, exposing him to the world.

"You have misconstrued this historical reference for personal gain. You receive ovation and ticket sales from something meant for people thousands of years ago. You are pathetic, a boil on the face of this planet." Chance pulled out a page from the Bible and approached Plocker.

"Wait! What?" His mouth garbled with the last as Chance shoved the page deep into Plocker's throat. The Reverence attempted to cough it out. Chance simply pushed more pages in. Chance heard Plocker's

125

nostrils pulling double-duty. He smiled at their feeble attempts at overexertion, before rolling up more pages and pushing them slowly into the nose of Plocker.

"Your audience will be so disappointed tomorrow when you don't arrive. They probably won't find you for days out here in the carnage of that storm. You will be eaten alive by the creatures that you find repulsive. Your testicles will be food, Reverend Plocker. Food for creatures you think don't belong in your heaven."

Plocker's eyes bulged wide. His face lost its color, giving him the sickly appearance of death prior to the deed. He struggled trying desperately to free himself of the confines. He struggled trying to rid himself of the pages tucked into his orifices. He heaved in and out, gasping for air not obstructed by the Bible pages. When his lungs could no longer fill with oxygen or expel carbon dioxide, his eyes burst and dilated, rolled high in their sockets. He was still. Silenced so easily. All the hate he delivered to the world, gone. Nothing was left. His head fell abruptly toward the base of his neck, slightly hindered by the thin, but present, wrinkles from his double-chin.

Thinking back from the present, euphoria filled every ounce of Emory Chance's being. He would forever remember it as the best moment of his life. The moment he finally felt alive. He found such romance in filling the mouth of Plocker with the scripture he twisted. He experienced delight as he watched him squirm and suffer till his last breath. He'd shared similar delights in many of his victims to date, but nothing would ever compare. He would go on to think about killing Bill Plocker each and every day from that point forward. Even now, with the propensity to keep his hands clean in his work, he would always revel in Plocker.

***

"Just a few more days." He whispered to himself thinking about Greece and counting down the moments to the second favorite event in his life. He sat calmly on a park bench in Oxford, England. He was happy: truly happy in the moment in a way that so many people can't find.

He slowly rose to his feet and placed his hand toward his back pocket. It was still there. More than forty long years since the Plocker incident and it was still there. The one thing that was sentimental to him. His one souvenir. One "trophy" the psych people would undoubtedly refer to it as. He grasped the edges, finding comfort in their rigidness. All four points still sharp after so long. He pulled it out in front of him. He stared at the tarnished silver cross that was being swallowed by Plocker's neck rolls when he took his last breath. He smiled and looked to the sky in remembrance.

"Coming soon." He whispered to himself and laughed once again like he had so many times before. He remembered the newspaper article in Omaha the day after Plocker's death. It still said *Coming Soon* next to Reverend Bill Plocker's photograph and a short description of his event schedule. It took the authorities more than a week to locate Plocker's body and to realize he wouldn't be "coming soon" to anything.

Chance received great pleasure from all the disappointed followers he had impacted—all the people who mourned Plocker's death like a fallen hero.

"You disappointed everyone, Bill!" He exclaimed to the sky this time, uncaring of the co-eds passing by. He thought about the many people thereafter. All those he had silenced. All the audiences he had disappointed. All the changes enacted by one man that crushed so many others in the wake. He was an artist. A true master in his craft like none other. Chance, a simple vessel. History, a simple subject. A platform he used to understand the minds of the other artists in the world. His passion was to admire those who impacted the world: The Caligulas, Vlads, Neros, and Attilas of the world's history. All artists in the craft of killing their fellow humans. Artists bringing balance and beauty back into this world. Perhaps none was as great as Deliverer. None as attentive to the details. None as elusive. None as invisible. His portfolio was immense over more than forty years, and now, he could kill at the stroke of a pen, at the type of a text.

There he stood, thinking about his time studying in Oxford's libraries where he researched for his PhD. He held his silver trophy in a hand that had written more bloody chapters than some of the worst dictators in history. The power was utterly intoxicating. His brilliance, perhaps once in a generation. His former pupil, bound for England and falling directly into a trap filled with more torture of mind and body. Torture meant for the one innocuous man who had somehow foiled his attempts multiple times.

"Your end is *coming soon*, Mr. Appling." Deliverer grinned a sardonic smile as he continued to take in the park's atmosphere. As always, he contemplated his next work of art. Perhaps this would become his greatest. The fate, or, scratch that. Yes, the tragedy of Thomas Appling.

Chapter 23

Justice L. Hutchens sat in his chair as he did months before when he first heard the news. His friend and mentor, Will Powers, was dead. Despite everything, the revelation still chilled him. The past four months had been an absolute blur; some would even call it a rush. Will Powers died, and a funeral followed. Nothing was out of the ordinary until he was forced to figure out the will. Justice had been pleading with Will Powers for years to change it. Powers never listened, and now it was left up to Justice to wade through the madness and see if he could find someone who had been missing for over ten years. The sole heir to the Powers estate, somewhere near seven hundred and fifty million despite what was stolen upon Will's death, was left to Missy and Missy alone.

Hutchens was the eldest member of Hutchens & Stern, LLC, attorneys that focused on estate law. In Will Powers' case, Justice was willing to go outside the box a bit more. Powers had used him for consultations on an array of business matters over the years. He had been in the Powers' estate just days prior to Missy's vanishing. He had also been there for drinks and a rarely seen human embrace he offered Will shortly after Tai committed suicide. He had seen Powers at his very best, and of course, at his absolute worst. He knew the only thing driving him to stay in this world was the ever-dwindling hope that Missy was still alive.

"Of course you wouldn't change your will." He spoke to himself as if Will Powers was still listening. "Well here we have it, you old bastard." He jested to himself as he held the results from the DNA test in his hands. Finally, after three months of an agonizing search that produced nothing other than a slew of false candidates rising from the shadows for their crack at the fortune, Justice Hutchens finally thought he had something. The letter showed up a month ago. It was the first in a string of evidence needed for Missy Powers to identify herself. A face-to-face meeting was set up after that. What Hutchens saw in that meeting was shocking. This stranger. This woman. It was Missy. It had to be her, even after so many years. Even after time had changed her, it was unmistakable. It took a while to feel each other out, but the two gained a subtle confidence in one another. Hutchens knew the connection was delicate. Hutchens knew that this woman wasn't someone who could be strutted in front of the public. This woman was no billionaire. She didn't come from money. At least not in the last ten years. Ten years away might as well have been an eternity for this woman: a ghost of what was Missy. Still, something about her gave Hutchens all he needed. He would've given the estate directly to her without the DNA test if it were up to him. Seeing her in the flesh was all he needed, but the lawyer in him sent out the test anyway.

The final step was in an envelope, and the envelope now rested in his hands. He would know once and for all if the mid-twenties stranger was actually Missy Powers. He would finally have his definitive proof to close out the case. To him, the letter seemed like such a formality a few days before it came. Now, within his hands, he was shaking.

"Calm down, Hutch." He spoke to himself again. He breathed in deeply and let the breath out toward his cherry desk. He placed his hands on the desk with the letter in between them. Could this really be the end? The end of all the searching? He looked toward the closed door in his well-appointed office and thought about how Will Powers paid for so much of it. He repositioned the picture of Kat Stern, his now grown daughter and partner in his law firm. It was taken at her graduation from the University of Alabama's law school. She held the degree in her hand and smiled widely. Now, fifteen years later, she would be taking over the firm. He would retire. He thought about when he would die. Would he be able to pass on his estate to her, his only child? Would he be able to give to her like Will was about to give to Missy? Obviously, he wouldn't give as much as Will, but he dreamt of the day when he'd be able to pass on everything he had accumulated over the years. Most notably, the photograph of himself standing with an elderly Bear Bryant before he passed. This prized photo was stationed on the other side of the desk from Kat's graduation photo. Both made him smile equally.

He burdened himself with the tremendous weight of the letter in between his palms. Moisture formed, and the resultant condensation began surfacing on the cherry desk from his fists. He was completely helpless in this endeavor. The results would be whatever they would be. Nonetheless, he carried responsibility for giving Will Powers this dream. He needed to see Will finally free from his demons. He felt he could give this to Will even as he lay in the ground next to Tai at the Powers' estate cemetery, freeing him from his overwhelming responsibility. Finally, after ten years of anguish, had he solved the case of the lost Missy Powers?

He scooped up the letter from both sides. He reached toward his elephant mug just in front of him. Big Al seemed to be smiling today. He gripped his sterling-silver letter opener, also emblazoned with that UA logo. He cut into the envelope and finally pulled out the letter. The moment was that of a dream or nightmare, a thriller that he was about to write the ending to. A moment in time that would define his retirement and his very legacy. He continued shaking, the anxiety building up to an almost uncontrollable level. The paper was tri-folded from LabCorp. His world was on a teetering point like he had never seen in his sixty-three years on the planet. He finally composed himself. He gave himself the strength to reveal this stranger's true identity once and for all.

His eyes immediately focused on the center of the page, where large bold font read ninety-nine percent *Match.*

"Hot Damn! It's a match." He exclaimed to himself. Missy Powers was alive. She was alive more than ten years later. There it was, officially and undeniably in black and white. He was the only one who knew and he would've screamed it from the rooftops if not for her specific instructions to keep a low profile while she regained footing in her old life. Hutchens' heart nearly leapt out of his chest and conducted a tango with his Big Al mug. He would free Will Powers. He would finally be able to give something to the man who had given him so much.

The phone rang three times before the young woman answered:

"Hello?" Missy Powers said.

"Missy." It was the first-time Hutchens actually called her that.

"Yes." She followed.

"You can probably guess what I just received in the mail." He choked back a tear. "I'm so sorry he never showed you how much he loved you, because that man—"

She interrupted. "I know." She stated. "I know he loved me. I was young and stupid. He was old, protective, and well, far too racist." She heard Hutchens laugh in the phone, and she joined him. They both knew Will Powers had major flaws. He was the product of a different time in the world. It wasn't that Will Powers was necessarily racist. Will Powers was an elitist who didn't want Missy consorting with anyone that he didn't approve of. Which, and Missy knew this when she was young, meant basically any person on the planet: black, white, blue, indigo, male, female, or both. Point being, Will Powers loved his daughter a bit too excessively, and the excessive pressures lost him his daughter as a consequence. "Thank you, Mr. Hutchens." Missy Powers stated. "I'll be by tomorrow to sign any documents that might be needed."

"Sounds great, Missy. Thank you for giving this to him. Thank you for coming forward. If there is an afterlife, which I pray there is so I can meet the Bear again, he couldn't be happier in this very moment." The two said their goodbyes and ended the call. Hutchens sat back in his large leather chair and let the moment overtake him. He began to cry, understanding how important his own relationship with Kat really was. How he was able to have everything that Will Powers lost. He picked up his cell and sent her a text. It simply read:

"I love you so much, Kat. You have made me the proudest man on this earth."

Chapter 24

There have now been two total chartered flights in my life, both in the same month, and both fresh from my release from prison. Life takes you to weird places. I didn't ask Shen about the details. She wouldn't have told me if I did. It didn't really matter who Shen killed or bribed to make such an arrangement happen, but we were able to skip the normal customs lines and enter the United Kingdom through London City Airport on forged passports. I got some sleep on the plane, something I needed desperately despite my three-week sedation. I was ready to go once again. Shen and I had one mission. We had to find answers through Professor Agda Sunden.

We didn't call in advance to alert anyone of our presence in London. Incognito was our closest friend and ally. It was clearly an old habit of Shen's, but something that I needed to adjust to on the fly. I'm not anything if not a quick study though. From the airport, we used a cab service to travel towards Kings College, London. We rarely left the side of the River Thames. Under a different set of circumstances, it would've been a sightseeing dream tour of some of London's most iconic treasures. Among the most notable items were the Tower of London, London Bridge, and St. Paul's Cathedral. As our twenty-minute drive approached its end, Big Ben appeared in our forefront to the south. It was hard not feeling an ounce of giddiness at being in such an iconic city for the first time, but like so many trips in my past, there would be no tourist activity. I remembered conducting business in Washington DC without seeing museums, driving through New York City without stopping to take in the city, and visiting Sydney just as a waypoint toward scholastic achievement. London, I thought, would be remembered through one pending interaction with a professor I had never met. Certainly not what I envisioned for my first visit to such a historical destination. A place Bren and I had promised to take one another someday as dorky American tourists.

As we approached, I felt my hands get antsy. We turned off of Temple Place toward Strand Lane. High above of us and directly next to the beautiful Somerset House, Shen and I entered into King's Building, the largest full-use building on the Strand Campus. As we passed, I marveled at the marble statues of Sophocles and Sappho located in the foyer. A large staircase to our right was my preferred option to move toward the sixth floor and Sunden's office, but Shen bypassed the stairs in route to the elevators located to the right side of the main hall. I followed her, not allowing the potential of vertigo from the elevator to weaken me any further in her eyes. The building was a beautiful eighteenth-century structure, well-kept despite its age. *What an amazing place to study.* It was difficult to keep my mind on point. This was probably a coping mechanism for not wanting to accept the reality of why I was there.

The elevator ride seemed long. Being around a relatively silent Yaravela Shen was wearing on my anxiety. She was stoic, held what seemed to be an ostentatiously straight posture, and demanded second glances from the few people we passed. Male and female equally marveled. The Shen from more than two years ago, the one that tried to look pedestrian in her official police garb, was no more. The Shen I had known, since waking up in a stupor twenty-four hours ago, wore makeup and outfitted herself well. She dressed conservatively with a snug fitting black pantsuit equipped with a white button-up blouse and form-fitting jacket. But she had the ability to turn the most boring of outfits into a sensual display meant to test the composure of conservative onlookers. I, on the other hand, blended in with ease. I looked every bit the part of research student in the humanities. I wore khakis over business casual black loafers, a powder-blue button-up dress shirt, and a black short coat. I kept the coat unbuttoned and placed a pair of black-framed, generic glasses around my inconsistent eyes. More than ten years ago, I had Lasiks on both eyes, but the astigmatism in my right created unnecessary

134

blurriness at times. It helped to wear glasses at night or in dark buildings. I've also been told I look smarter in glasses. Guess I'm easy prey to our profiling habits as humans. I guess we all are to an extent.

With a ding, the elevator halted at the sixth floor, uninterrupted the entire way up. We quickly found our bearings, using the closest office numbers we could find to direct us which way to depart the elevator. The way was right, the time was half passed two, and we were arriving within Sunden's designated office hours posted on the King's College webpage. We strolled down the long hallway toward Sunden's door. There was an eerie silence shrouding the hall, giving me the most sinking of feelings. Despite the day being Friday afternoon while school was in session, Shen and I encountered precious few people, and none since arriving on the sixth floor. The sinking feeling came to a head as we turned a corner. We both knew we were too late the moment we saw the tape. The tape was colored yellow, and it draped over the door that led inside Sunden's office.

We both checked the door in the off chance it was ajar. It was worth a shot to see if some junior officer was distracted from their duties in securing the room. Locked. A short and deathly air of shock weighed us down before Shen pulled out her phone. It was headline news yesterday. It read:

> *Developing story from Westminster as Professor Agda Sunden, an immigrant from Denmark, was found gruesomely murdered in her University office. Sunden, 47, was a professor of war studies at King's College London. All mourn in the community as a truly beloved professor and human has been lost. No details have been released about what police are calling a truly disturbing act of violence.*

I breathed in and out as I tried to compose myself. *She was a lead and now she was dead. Coincidence at this point was completely off the table. Sunden was murdered because she was onto something. The same something that I was apparently onto. The same something that I needed*

135

her help to delineate. The same something, I felt too stupid to comprehend on my own. How did we get all the way to her door without knowing this had happened? Sure, it was probably reported while we were flying. Okay, but still! How did something like this happen right as we were on the cusp? My mind raced in a search of possibilities.

"Does it say who found the body?" I asked as Shen continued to search for more details. Shen pointed to the door across the hall from Sunden's office.

"Dr. Richard Joyce it says. Guessing that's our man." She smirked. Knowing before I knocked that it was a futile cause given the rather ghostly nature of the entire sixth floor, I decided to give it a go. I knocked three times, and then four more times before accepting the inevitable defeat. Of course, neither Dr. Joyce nor anyone in the department was actually present today. Why would they be given that a colleague was just murdered?

"I'm guessing nothing about suspects? Guess that doesn't matter. Where do we go from here?" Shen shook her head before pointing at the caution wrapped door.

"We go there." I took a turn to shake my head slowly. I was trying to feel out whether or not Shen was serious. Of course she was serious. What choice did we have if we were truly dedicated to finding these answers? It's not as if the police would grant us access to Sunden's materials while they were investigating her murder. Time to make a decision.

"Screw it!" I said before lowering my shoulder and flinging myself toward the door. Nothing. Not a budge. Yaravela smiled at this. She smiled again at the expression I made. She smiled at my humiliation as I tried to hold back my grimace. My move as a blunt instrument was a touch misguided on the reinforced door. I wasn't a weak person, but that door made me feel so. I waited for Shen to pull some kind of lock picking tools from her pocket. That didn't happen. Instead, she pulled out a silenced Beretta 90-Two from her fashionable Coach purse. She directed it toward the door, and without warning, she fired two times. Nothing gave way at first, and so she fired two more rounds of .40 Caliber at the deadbolt. This time, it gave way. She tucked her Beretta back into the purse and pushed the door open into Sunden's office.

There was a reason for the caution tape. For some reason, I was simply expecting a ransacked office turned over. What we got was something that would make seasoned crime scene investigators shudder. Blood was splattered around the room as if a dog bathing in tomato juice had just shaken off. There was no body, but the scene was that of pure horror. I felt the cold chill overcome my body and sensed the same revulsion overtaking the battle-hardened Shen. I didn't know a human could bleed as much as we were seeing. Flashes began to pop in my head. Images of Bren lying in blood, of Hogue sinking in blood, kept appearing even as I tried to remain composed. Shen reached over to grab my hand.

"Are you okay?" Her speech broke the silence that the room of death had taken since we set eyes upon it. She tried to make eye contact, but I wouldn't let it happen.

I nodded and spoke quietly. "Where do we start with this?" Shen shook her head once again, not offering any insight. "I think we need to go." Shen began to agree. We obviously hadn't thought this move through and let ourselves yield to the moment.

"Is there anything you see?" She had crossed a threshold. I could see her mind at work. We were here, we had already shot four rounds into the door, and we had already seen the blood. What was the harm in searching just a few moments? I could tell that was her line of thinking, despite the moment of apprehension that preceded it. Again, I tentatively agreed. After what I had been through, did I really care about repercussions or decorum anymore?

We used our eyes to scour the office for anything unusual, but it appeared as though everything of value had already been bagged by the police. There wasn't a laptop, no visible traces of an external hard drive, and all loose notebooks were gone. There were books scattered around the office, but nothing pertinent. This was, in true pun fashion, a dead end.

After realizing the search was in vain, Shen and I respectfully moved toward the door. We hadn't touched anything, which was good since my fingerprints were on the Interpol list. Dejected, we both made our way out of Sunden's blood-soaked office.

My periphery caught a glimpse of his left fist, giving me the millisecond I needed to duck away from his punch. I felt the wind before I heard the crack of the doorframe. A dent and a roar followed from the Monster. The hardened wood that stymied my shoulder, had just broken pieces of the Monster's hand. You could hear the impact of bone to solid wood. Before I could register my own response, I saw Shen's Beretta seemingly float from her purse. She was about to pull the trigger when the Monster used the back of his injured left hand to slap the gun away from Shen. He roared again, feeling the gun sting his broken fingers. I swung at the Monster with my right fist closed and connected with his scarred left cheek. I felt the connection force his cheek and teeth together. Despite his enormous size, the strike did some damage. It left my right hand weak, bruised, and shy. Shen kicked at the Monster's right knee and hit her mark soundly. He then defended himself with a response equal to the task. He pushed at me with his right arm, obliging me to make an elaborate flailing motion toward the opposite side of the hall. I hit my head against Dr. Joyce's door and slid down in pain. Before I could return to my feet, I felt the boot of the Monster swing at my face. Without time to avoid the kick, I moved just enough that it broke my glasses and gave my eye-socket a thorough jarring. He reached for his gun situated in the small of his back. He could barely lift it out before Shen's foot connected with it and it flew from his grasp. She quickly swung another kick toward his knees, but was rejected by his right arm. He used his powerful right fist to jab at Shen's face. She blocked the jab, but still felt most of the impact. She went down hard. I searched the halls for something to throw while the Monster's attention was elsewhere. I couldn't find anything. I saw him gathering his Kimber and knew I needed to make a quick decision. I reached in my jacket pocket where my cell phone was stationed. I pulled it out and threw it as hard as I could toward the Monster's face. The phone shattered as it hit the bridge of his nose. He roared once again. Shen then kicked the back of his knees, knocking him off balance. He fell to his knees directly in front of me. I lined up his face and swung my leg like I was kicking a game winner from sixty yards. My loafer connected square to his cheek and nose, bringing the Monster to the ground just long enough for us to struggle away toward the stairs and safety. I didn't know how or why, but I had survived yet another encounter with a blunt tool meant for my destruction. Would I ever be rid of such a terrible nemesis?

Chapter 25

The world seemed so controlled from the Sniper's Mark 8 Leopold scope. She saw her targets talking, read the very lips they spoke from, but never heard their voices. She never saw any semblance of adrenaline or fear, at least not in respect to her. Some say there's a calm before a storm. What they don't say is how calming the aftermath can be. How a storm can destroy humanity, but leave the earth still, calm, and new. The Sniper took comfort in her simple storm leading to calm. One blast would ring in the air for several seconds, death would follow the path of her storm, and a sudden calm would overtake her subdued victims. This was the fate of most of her victims. All of her targets except one. The elusive Thomas Appling. The one that got away. Perhaps the one that was meant to get away.

Perched beneath the east side clock at the Somerset House, the Sniper peered through her scope. She viewed pieces of the struggle between Thomas Appling, Yaravela Shen, and the Monstrous Macedonian she had seen several times through her Leopold. A few years ago, he was insurance on the off chance her skills would require it. *That's business for you,* she thought. Now in London, she was the insurance policy. She was there to clean up the mess.

A calm breeze cooled her fingertips. Outside of her eyes, they were the only piece of her that could be seen if she were spotted. She just couldn't shoot in gloves. She needed to feel the trigger herself. She needed to feel connected when she struck someone down. As she positioned her weapon, her ever reliable Remington 700 sniper rifle, she pondered just how she could have truly become what she was. How she could be used as a weapon. How, under the direst of circumstances, people could become the animals they tried so desperately to separate themselves from.

She pulled down the legs of her bipod and placed them gently on the stone railing. There could be no mistakes this time, and her rifle needed to be stable. Daylight was dwindling, not necessarily because of the time, but the clouds that concealed all traces of the sun. She pulled the bolt back halfway to ensure that the .308 round was securely stationed in the chamber. She pushed and locked it back down into position. She pulled the butt of the gun into her right shoulder, feeling it press firmly in her glenoid cavity. Her right hand caressed the forestock before making its way down beyond the trigger guard and toward the stock. Her fingers felt good arranging themselves around the handle. Her cheek pressed gently against the left side of the stock. The tip of her index finger was all she placed on the trigger. Her right eye focused through the scope and onto her target.

There was no hesitation. She pulled back the trigger and released the round. From her military grade suppressor, most of the violence of the shot was subdued and no muzzle flash could be seen. The bullet screamed through the sixth-floor window of the War Studies department, breaking glass prior to penetrating the male skull on the other side. She kept her eye on the target to validate her kill. The calm after the storm. No movement could be seen. He was dead and her job was complete.

She quickly packed up her gear. She placed her rifle in a backpack guitar case she had custom-made to conceal her weapon. She grabbed one of two side handles and toted the case and herself into safety. When concealed within an abandoned office of the Somerset House, she pulled off everything mysterious about her outfit. Most notably were the black mask and cloak she had been wearing. She placed her garb in the guitar case, fixed her hair, and pulled the case over both shoulders. From there, she reached into her blue jean pockets and dialed his number. One ring was all it took:

"Is it done?" Deliverer wasn't much for pleasantries. The Sniper nodded in person to no effect, but also answered:

"Yes. He's dead." Deliverer sighed in obvious confliction over his choice.

141

"You see now why we obey every single instruction?" The Sniper nodded once again but did not answer. She didn't have to. He carried on anyway. "He was like a son to me. From nine years old, I raised him. I gave him purpose, and now he's gone." The Sniper stayed silent, but wondered how he could have such feelings for the man he had just ordered killed. "You see; I can have unforeseen mistakes. When dealing with life and death, it happens. But, if more than one or two are made then trust is gone. That said, I am a lenient man." The Sniper held back from scoffing at Deliverer as he continued his lesson. "What I can't have is disloyalty. Understand?"

"Yes sir." She didn't need to say much to the man who had taken everything from her. The man who used leverage on people to commit atrocities. The man who could look a child in the eye while he broke their neck. The man who supposedly just lost a son-like figure in his life. No. She didn't need to say anything. This wasn't her first lesson. She had missed before. If she were to have a chance to live, it would be her last mistake. She only knew that life was worse for her when she didn't obey. When she wasn't one-hundred percent submissive to his agenda.

"Now. Go kill Mr. Appling. If you succeed, it will be the last thing I ever ask of you. If you fail, I will kill everyone you hold dear, not just your husband." Deliverer ended the call. Bren lowered her head. This is what happens when evil breaks what used to be good.

142

Chapter 26

We bypassed the elevator this time, bolting down the stairs as quickly as we could. Déjà vu crowded my mind. I had thought about the day I rushed down the stairs at the McMullin Building at Newcastle at least ten times a day since the Monster first appeared in my world. Part of me wished so much that it was recorded. How funny my panic induced floundering down those stairs must have looked. Then again, I couldn't blame myself. Grace doesn't usually accompany panic.

The stairs in the King's Building were not as narrow as McMullin. This led to a slower but far more elegant descent for me and Yaravela. Luckily for us, it appeared as though my kick to the Monster's face was enough to buy us some breathing room. We didn't hear him following as we arrived at each platform from the fifth to the main floor, and we weren't about to lose precious time to glance back. I think we both felt intense relief when the elevator door stayed shut upon our arrival near the foyer. We didn't stick around to see how far ahead we were. In my experience, there are rarely times you take your foot off the pedal when your competition is even to you. When they are far superior, like I felt the Monster was, you never stop when you gain a lead. Bad things happen when you let your guard down, or simply lose concentration when moments become intense. Just like in football, there's something about a prevent defense that bolsters your competition. The swing in momentum very rarely helps those that soften up on their adversaries. We weren't prepared for the Monster to show up, but yet again, luck appeared to be on my side.

We sprinted out of the foyer, passed the nearly dilapidated faux Roman Baths on Strand Lane, and exited out toward Surrey Street. We looked both ways to see if we could find a cab. My whistle was pathetic outside of a modest attempt to harmonize. Shen's was not. She placed her index and middle finger in her mouth and let out a vicious and attention-getting whistle toward a prototypical London cab. The vehicle was nothing short of adorable puddling toward us, but we didn't stop to gawk as we immediately hurled ourselves into the back seat.

"Just drive!" I said with a bit too much pizzazz for our driver.

"Easy does it. Where we goin'?"

"Just out of here!" Yaravela snapped.

"Alright. Alright. No need to whine about!" He spoke loudly before muffling a "tossers" under his breath. "What, are you on the pull or somethin'?" the taxi driver said before accelerating toward Temple Place. He looked at me and raised his eyebrows several times in reference to Yaravela. We ignored the slang he spouted off. Neither of us really knew what he was talking about anyway.

All three in the cab were on edge as we made it to Temple.

"Left here!" I spoke up, realizing that we couldn't risk driving back toward King's College. The driver abided. He was mid-fifties, bald, and wore a worn down blue polo shirt. White chest hair flourished out of the collar. Bags under his eyes, as well as the subtle but strong hint of body odor abounding in the cab, suggested he had been working a thousand-hour shift. We didn't intend to make small talk, and he didn't attempt to ask us why we were in such a hurry. It seemed as though all three of us were keen on this nonverbal arrangement.

We hadn't planned this far ahead. We both intended on finding Agda Sunden, questioning her, and then traveling to the next stage of our journey. So naïve. There was no contingency for Sunden being killed and the Monster arriving to kill us. Shen looked at me as though I stole something from her. I could almost feel her resentment of me. She didn't ask me about a next step. I assumed she didn't because she knew my answer would only piss her off that much more. She was right. I would've shrugged my shoulders like an indecisive koala bear if she did. This gave us both some down time to think following the cataclysmic turn in our plan.

As our cab passed London Bridge on the north bank of the River Thames, I realized we were driving toward the airport where we arrived.

"Drive north." I said to the driver and to the perplexity of Shen. I shrugged off her gaze as we drove up a few roads I didn't pay attention to before turning onto the A11. From there, we drove in silence. We let the driver pick the road of his choice as he scoffed under his breath and maneuvered the cab softly along London's roads. The change from the stress of Sunden and the Monster was a very welcome adaptation for me. I breathed and ignored Yaravela's stare which, I could tell, was still fixated.

Victoria Park appeared outside our window. It was calm, which was something I needed.

"Stop here." I spoke and popped out of the cab without giving Yaravela a chance to retort. She paid the driver in cash, and he left us to our own devices.

"What are we doing, Tom?" She spoke, and I could again feel the agitation begin to boil in her. I walked into the park. I wasn't necessarily ignoring her, but I needed the safety of a tranquil environment to think. I felt her hurry to move closer to me. She grabbed my shoulder this time. "Tom?" She was scared. I never thought about it being possible in someone so stoic, but there she was. Her demeanor so human. I pulled her closer to me in a hug of comfort:

"I'm so sorry." I felt her tears wet my shirt. She needed this from me. She was alone in this world and so much of her future was riding on me. I never thought about it. I was blinded by my own fears of her. My own very understandable fears of her, of course. Nevertheless, here we were with only each other to lean on. Two people so vulnerable in the prospects of a decent future. Here we were, under the few trees amongst the greater buildings of one of the world's most iconic cities.

We detached from our short embrace.

"I'm fine. Sorry." She shook her head and wiped away any residual tears. She composed herself, and we both moved toward the center of the park. I think in that moment, Yaravela knew that I needed something quiet and something safe. There was a calm about us as we meandered around a small pond connected to a Japanese style garden. Ducks

145

congregated around the bank, waiting for tourists to toss them bread. Their sweet quacks made me feel as if nothing else was going on in the world. I took a seat on a bench underneath a large maple tree. Yaravela stood like a soldier in front of me before finally letting herself relax her guard. She took a seat on the opposite side of the bench. We both stared into the pond. The gloomy day couldn't cast a shadow on its beauty. The ducks continued to offer background chatter to improve the overall ambiance.

I breathed in deeply and let my mind float. This is how it happens. This is how it always happens for me. I finally, for the first time since solitary confinement, allowed my mind to wander. It didn't take long before an epiphany arose from the ashes of my brain. My thought process was simple. Roman Baths erected from the cisterns of Somerset House. It was a simple thought at first. Then it developed. The cisterns made me think about the cisterns on my historic property. The cisterns in which I spent hours digging through history. A time-lapse history that told the story of my farm prior to the use of landfills. A history told in glass bottles, empty medicine bottles, broken china, and outdated ink containers. It was archaeology, and I fashioned myself a much less adventuresome Indiana Jones. I transferred my thought process toward my current situation. Why was my research so important? Why was it so damaging to this organization that had tried so hard to eliminate me? Then it hit me. I spoke it aloud so Yaravela could share in the epiphany:

"It's not the what. It's the where."

"What?" She said perplexed at my words which broke our silence.

"This has nothing to do with what my research will prove. It has to do with where my research was taking me." She still didn't follow, but began slowly nodding in encouragement to keep elaborating. I still had more to divulge, but I could see her mind begin to churn with mine. "What makes me different, and what made Sunden different is GPR. I was going to use ground penetrating radar at Platæa. Whoever wants me dead, whoever killed Sunden, it has to do with GPR at Platæa. They needed us not to scan that area. There's something buried there." Shen interjected:

"But what?"

146

I shook my head. "I don't know. But whatever it is, people are willing to kill to keep it hidden."

Chapter 27

Turning into a killer is not as far off as many of us like to pretend. There are a handful of reasons we kill. Of course, over time, these reasons have evolved. Nowadays, most prominent of the reasons for those of us who aren't sociopaths, are love and hate. Two powerful and unstable emotions that have the propensity to collide. Two powerful emotions that have a paper-thin margin between them, despite being one another's opposite.

In Bren Appling's case, it was always about love. She would die for Tom. Still, to this day, she would easily take her own life so that he could live. So he could have a long and prosperous life of his own, but life doesn't work that way. Threats aren't made that way. To Deliverer, it was Tom or it was Tom and everyone. Tom was non-negotiable and was always going to die underneath the power and madness of Deliverer. It was up to Bren to make sure that Tom was the only one.

Bren remembered the first threat from Deliverer. He knew things that he shouldn't have known about her, about her family, and about her husband. She received it while out working. It was otherwise a simple day. Two spays, one neuter, three nail trims, an anal gland expression, and a truck load of flea preventative. She was about to leave the house of a feisty Calico named Bottoms Up. Bottoms needed meloxicam for a lingering arthritis issue. Bren had stopped by his house in the neighborhood of ten times over the last few months. Her client, Wendy McGregor, was needy but could pay for the extra attention. Wendy was divorced, but took a chunk of change in the settlement. She had four acres of prime, main-channel lake frontage, a brand-new Land Rover, and one companion, Bottoms Up. Bren smiled as she left the house, thinking that if more Wendys existed, she wouldn't even have to advertise her traveling veterinary service. There aren't many, but the Wendys of the world find the best possible options for their pets. Bren was the best option for Bottoms Up. She cared for and loved cats, which was hard to find in a veterinarian, and she also showed up at her doorstep to care for Bottoms Up no matter how trivial the concern. No car rides listening to him moan and pee on himself. Dr. Appling was the best option for Wendy's precious feline.

As she approached her truck, she noticed an envelope was tucked behind her windshield wiper. It made her nervous immediately, given the long driveway needed to approach Wendy's home. She thought about leaving it, and even hopped in her truck without grabbing it at first. She stared at the envelope for a moment before peering around 360 degrees from the safety of her locked Tundra. She then opened the door and stepped out cautiously. She pulled the envelope from the wiper and returned to her truck. It was a white envelope sealed with one strand of scotch tape. It was addressed to Dr. Appling. She removed the tape and opened the envelope to reveal a typed letter. From the beginning, it left her unsettled and terrified.

> *Dr. Bren Appling,*
>
> *You do not know me. You never will. You will call me Deliverer. The reason why I'm called this is unimportant at this time. I will first start with a simple warning. You may not reveal the contents of this letter, nor any correspondence I have with you, to your husband, Thomas Appling. You also may not reveal the contents of this letter to anyone you know, have known, or will know in this life. I hope that is clear that you will not reveal this letter, nor any correspondence I have with you, to anyone living in this world. My redundancy is here to stress the importance of my rules. I will reveal the consequences of such bold action as this letter continues. To the point. Your husband, Thomas Appling, along with several others, must die. It doesn't matter why. All that matters is*

149

that they must die and that you will help make it happen. I will provide you with instructions and you must follow them. I do not tolerate mistakes. If a mistake or any disobedience occurs, I will take from you. I will take your family. I will take your pets. I will even take the unborn baby residing within you.

Now that I have your clear and undivided attention, I will continue. There are no ways around what I'm asking you to do. It's simple. You kill my targets how I order you and in the order I tell you. If you don't, I will still kill all of your targets, but I will make you watch as I kill everyone you and your husband love, including your husband's unborn child. I will give you one example of my power. One single example will be clear in tonight's local news. You will hear my name and only my name. You have no other options, Dr. Appling. Do as I say.

Sincerely,
Deliverer
Instructions will follow

Bren trembled in fear through the entire letter. It was never a hoax. No one knew about the baby, not even Tom. She had the equipment, and conducted the first ultrasound herself. She wasn't much for surprises or false alarms. She had just missed her period. She would be less than five weeks into the pregnancy. She stared out of the truck 360 degrees once again. Nothing at all. She stared back at the letter and read it twice more. Tears rolled out of her eyes. Suddenly, a knock on her door jolted her and sent a shock greater than a bolt of lightning through her body. Her heart reached intimate levels with her uvula. The panic became frustration.

"Dr. Appling!" Wendy spoke from outside her window with Bottoms Up in tow. Bren composed herself to the best of her ability. She wiped away the tears and the look of panic that shrouded her face. The power to compose themselves under pressure was something a lot of veterinarians have. You simply deal with the issues as they arise, one by one. She then pulled the handle to release the door. She stepped out:

"Yes, Wendy. What's up?" Wendy shrugged off any emotions that weren't focused directly on her feline.

"Nail trim! I almost forgot!" Bren's outside remained calm. On the inside, she wanted to tie Wendy and her bad timing to the back of her truck and tow her into the lake.

"Sure. I'll meet you inside. Let me get my things." She forced a smile through her pain. She, like her husband, was a master compartmentalizer.

"You're a life saver!" Wendy screamed in excitement with too much vigor for the favor. She then gave Bren an awkward and uncomfortable hug before jogging Bottoms Up back to the house. Bren took a moment. She leaned against her truck and tried to imagine dreaming the letter. She hoped that when she returned from the nail trim it wouldn't be sitting on the driver's seat of the Tundra.

Her mind was elsewhere, but Bottoms Up received the best and most thorough nail trim he ever had. She tossed Wendy a bag of homegrown catnip prior to gathering up her bag and returning back to her truck. For a moment, all the normalcy of the nail trim gave her comfort. It all came shattering down when she opened the door to find the letter sitting exactly where she left it. It wasn't a dream. She hadn't fallen asleep at work or hallucinated. Her life would never be the same, and she had no idea what to do.

In the present, fresh off of killing the Monster from high above on the Somerset House balcony, Bren pondered the phone call she just had with Deliverer. He had already taken so much from her. A short time after the letter, about two weeks, Tom was off for Australia and his graduation. She'd accompanied him with clear instructions to kill Hogue and to never let Tom see his ceremony. Prior to killing Hogue, she replayed the threatening newsfeed over and over again from the day she got the letter. The headline had read:

Delivery driver kills eight. Disappears after crashing into maternity ward.

The headline still gave Bren chills. The most sickening and heinous act she had ever heard of. The biggest disaster in Tri Cities history, was all to prove her a lesson in his sincerity. To make a statement to her and her alone. There were no other options. Bren Appling had to abide by his rules.

Her first shot. The first time she turned into the Sniper and the first time she ever killed another human being, Bren was composed. She calmly pulled the trigger for the greater good of her life. The second target; her husband and at the time, father of her unborn baby, and the man she had been in love with for nearly eighteen years, was harder to square up in her scope. Tears flowed fast. She suspected he was panicking and knew she had already caused him pain. She pulled the trigger as the tears blurred the vision of her right eye. She knew she would miss. She wanted to miss. She released the shell and sent two more shots toward her husband. By the time she saw the Monstrous man in her scope, she knew her life would never be the same. There would be no turning back. Her only hope was that one day she'd be able to find a way to solve the puzzle and save her family.

Bren grabbed her stomach now, holding back guilt-induced nausea. The pain she went through was nearly incomprehensible. She made a mistake in what would've been her only assignment for Deliverer. From that point, Deliverer made her pay. With her husband in jail and ultimately doomed, she visited him one time with tears in her eyes. She was forced to lie to him about Atlas' illness, Deliverer's way to make him hurt while he was in jail and out of reach. She was forced to console her husband and feel empathy for his cause, all the while, reeling from a future that he would never know existed. Her punishment from missing with the second shot. Her punishment for not killing her own husband, would insure that any future task would be completed with, as Tom would put it, the obedience of an ancient Spartan hoplite. Deliverer would insure that Bren Appling give birth to a healthy baby. From there, he planned to use it as the ultimate leverage until Tom Appling was killed. Tom's very presence in prison allowed her to carry secretly to full term. By the time the trial came to close and Bren, Diane, and Lori arrived in the audience, Tom Appling was already a father.

152

Bren hated herself for what she had become. She hated Tom for placing their family in harm's way, even if he did it unknowingly. She hated Deliverer for making her play dead while the Monster was ordered to kill her husband right in front of her. She hated Deliverer for the text message she sent and then deleted from her phone. She hated the world and what it had done to her. She was a good person. She loved her husband and her family. Now, two years later and after putting Tom through so much pain, she would be forced to finish the deed she started. Tom would never know her struggle. He would never know why. He would never know that the ghost of his wife would come back to take him down with her.

Chapter 28

It was the first solid theory I had come up with. It was also more than just plausible. I had no other explanation for why someone would be interested in me, let alone want me dead. The link wasn't some group that needed to save Herodotus' name. That had long been tarnished by a myriad of historians. The only thing that connected me to Sunden was GPR. The item that would reveal all of my research, the key to my nightmare, was GPR. Something had to be underground at Platæa.

We still sat on the same bench pondering the implications of our recent discovery. As the park became darker, the clouds disappeared to produce the brightest of full moons. It was a deep orange harvest moon appearing just above the tree line. The moon lit up in the pond in an eerie way. The water was dark and still. The reflection of the moon was bright, almost flamboyant. The contrast to my eyes was blinding, but too beautiful to stray away from. I arose from the park bench, gathered a nearby stone, and tossed it underhanded toward the center of the full moon's reflection. A plunge of hysteria spread the once still water to the edges of the pond. Ripples dissipated as they extended their reach further from the center. They hit the bank only to backtrack from whence they came. They became smaller and smaller until the water was the same still as before. There had to be a metaphor in the reaction. Was I a series of stones throwing a cog into this organization's plans? Was my fate as inevitable as a stone trying to disturb a still pond? The stone would undoubtedly make waves, but in the end, the pond would always win, and the stone would always sink to a muddy grave. Was my fate so certain?

"The stone must hit with a force strong enough to remove the water." I said this out loud. Yes. I said this out loud. I almost wanted to punch myself for the vain whimsical depth of my approach. However, my logic, although demanding clarification, was sound. Yaravela was gawking into the moonlit pond with a glazed over expression. She stared at me as though she didn't hear a word I said. I continued without needing her to ask the question. "We can't skip across the surface of this, dropping in stones one at a time." I tossed another into the pond for effect. "If we do, we'll eventually run out of stones." I ignored her smirk as she watched the reaction of my stone disturbing the water before calming once again. "We have to figure out a plan to unveil whatever it is they are hiding. This means we need to have a plan to strike them with a deadly blow. In my metaphor, this is a stone that removes the water completely. In our situation, this means to find whatever it is they are hiding and unveil it to the world. We must expose them. If we don't, we will always need eyes in the back of our heads."

Yaravela began coming around to my thought process. Goofy as I was, she couldn't deny the logic around my words and the reality of our situation. We simply weren't going to harm this organization unless we had some sort of leverage against them. We weren't going to gain any leverage by running around in their circles, playing in their game and living ten steps behind. We finally had something. Now, we needed to attack it.

Shen picked up a flat stone. She squeezed it between her thumb and index finger. Underneath, she allowed the stone to rest on her middle finger.

"Or." She pulled back her arm and tossed the stone side armed into the pond. "We could simply gather what we need from them on the exterior." We watched as her stone skipped on the surface of the pond five times prior to jumping out toward the opposite bank. She winked at me prior to finishing her point. "We gather everything we can without rushing in guns blazing. Then, we simply cut a drain on the edge of the pond and watch all of the water drift away."

Her metaphor was also good, and I was very touched that she played along with me. We were starting to feel like a team. It gave me the

155

comfort of not being an absolute cheesy dork. Perhaps half of one, anyway. The two of us needed to build a chemistry if we were to trust one another in the unknowns that were still to come. I think we both felt that formulating a plan together would build that sort of trust.

We sat on the bank of that pond as the moon rose high and lost its clout amongst a sky full of hazy city stars. What used to be so impressive, appearing as if it were truly positioned next to the edge of the earth on the horizon, was now a run-of-the-mill full moon. Sure, it was bright and beautiful, it just didn't have the same impact as before. The water was darker now, and a scattering of clouds seemed to move too fast across the sky as the minutes floated by in our indecision. We were in agreement. We needed action, but we also needed to take care in our approach. Foremost in this, was that I was still being watched. The Monster at King's College, the one that had nearly taken me out once again, was proof of this. I was still so far behind this organization. It was time for me to drop the niceties and become blunter with Ms. Shen.

"It's time you tell me everything you know, Yaravela. Who is after me? How did you become involved? Why have you turned? I need to know everything. I can't move forward unless I can trust you." I spoke and immediately regretted the use of the word trust. It was insulting given that she had saved my life three times. Or, at the very least, once a few moments ago. It wasn't like I had verification on the other two, other than her word. *Hell, she told me she killed the Monster. Was that a lie? She did say no bodies were found. She didn't have to say that if it was some kind of trick. What was real?* I started to feel a bit uneasy about my new partner again. I could justify her being the worst of enemies and the best of friends. *What twists hadn't I seen in this? She obviously helped me get away from the Monster this time. It looked real to me. Could it have all been a ruse?* I was looking her in the eyes. Her dark gray eyes. I was almost expecting her to pull out a similar object in which she used to cut down Ricketts. I was panicking again. What was the endgame for her?

Yaravela Shen did something I wasn't expecting. She didn't get defensive at the mistrust. On the contrary, she acted as if I had every right to be skeptical. She stayed calm and collected, a true professional.

"Tom, I'm afraid you will be disappointed in how little I know." I kept my stare on her, unrelenting as she continued. "I don't know who is trying to kill you. I simply know a name. I never met him in person. He is simply called Deliverer. I received the first note." She cast a confounding stare into the water with her mouth agape in disbelief over the amount of time. "Shit, it's been more than seven years." She shook her head. "That's when he stole my family, Tom. That's when they took everything I lived for." Her head became still, and her eyes hollowed out in a glaze beneath the moon. "They, or I guess he. I don't know how many there are. All I know is he told me that he would keep her safe if I did exactly what he ordered. He was terrifyingly convincing. He knew everything about me. Things he shouldn't have known. He made threats. He made threats that were so evil. Then, he proved himself."

I could see her trembling now. I didn't ask how he proved himself. At this point, I had seen enough of his carnage to know what he was capable of.

She continued. "I began complying with all his demands. The hours became days. The days became months. When the months became years, I started losing hope that I'd ever see her again." I could see tears fall from her dark gray eyes. One fell straight from her eyelash. Another attached itself to her cheek, and rode the curvature of her face before falling off at the chin. I could finally see the pain she spoke of before. "In the first few years, he would play videos and recordings of her. He would send clips of her talking with threatening messages to keep me in line. These videos became fewer and farther between. By the time he ordered me to kill you, I hadn't seen or heard from her in so long. I was already in the police academy. Ms. Yaravela Shen." She laughed at her name. "I guess I am her now. I've been so many names that it's hard to keep track at this point. Identities change when you've done the things I've done, Tom, but I did them all for her." Her tears began to fall faster, thickening in their stream down her cheeks. I felt awkward next to her without comforting, but this was no time to get weak.

"Ricketts? You said he would kill me?" This brought her out of the deep cry. She composed herself, sniffed in the air, and wiped her eyes and nose on her shirt.

"Yes, Clive Ricketts. I didn't know at first. Apparently, Deliverer liked having leverage on multiple coppers. It's not like we knew one another. I was supposed to kill you that day like I said. I might have, too, but then I began to realize the value you were given. I began to realize how important you were to Deliverer. There were at least four people trying to kill you that day. I had never seen more than two sent at once. Anyway, when Ricketts broke protocol and pulled the feed, I knew I had to act. I don't know what he had on that man, but it would've killed you. That's how it worked. He uses leverage. He uses the worst imaginable leverage, and he gets what he wants." I broke her train of thought.

"Why did you risk it? Why then?"

She began to nod. "Because she's not alive anymore, Tom. Deliverer made a mistake after five years. As I said before, the videos and recordings became more sporadic over time. Well, she never got older, Tom. She never got older and he played the same exact messages. For the first few years, I didn't notice. Fear gripped me and guided me to act without question. Then, about a month before my order to kill you, I heard something in the background of the message. It was faint, but I had heard it before. The sound was a boarding call at an airport. I'm not sure how many times he played the same message to me. But I finally picked up on it. I finally realized that it was the same recording as before." I could see the look of defeat on her face. She was so disappointed in herself. How many had she killed falsely because of this mistake, and for how long?

"He had you killing people. He blackmailed you with something he no longer had? Was this a child that he took? Your daughter?" She nodded, again defeated.

"We have to stop him, Tom. He's evil. He's pure evil. He stole my daughter from me. He stole her, and he killed her. I don't know where he is. I don't know his name, or really anything about him. All I know is that he needed you dead, and I had to keep you alive. I have done everything I can do to keep you that way. He killed my little girl." I nodded now as she cried, feeling comfort in our mutual loss. Was I being naïve? I didn't really care. Her story was too convincing to care. The pain on her face was too real to be fabricated.

"We need to get ahead of him. We need to do something he wouldn't expect, right?" Shen agreed with a subtle nod. "Like you said, we can't show up at Platæa guns blazing."

"We can't fly into Greece either!" She spoke and I bobbed my head again in agreement. She was right. This Deliverer knew we would be in England and set a trap for us. What's to prevent him from doing the same thing if we showed up at an airport in Greece?

"Chunnel?" At first Shen said nothing. Then, after a moment, the wheels in her mind began to turn.

"That could work. Take that train into France and drive. It's the most inefficient thing outside of backpacking our way there." Shen smiled through the tears.

"Yep, and we show up from the north where there's nothing. It will, at the very least, help us get off the grid. Help us skip a stone on the surface." I winked at her, in full realization that we didn't have much to go on, but it was a semblance of a plan.

"We will still need a real plan, right?" Shen questioned rhetorically. "You know, a plan to actually find whatever he's protecting."

"All in good time." I replied and smiled. It's not like we were bursting with options. We couldn't show up and immediately start scanning. We'd have to have some help, of course. At this point, I guess I was more concerned with getting to Greece alive.

Chapter 29

A personal post man, code name Hermes. That's what it takes to operate everywhere around the world in true secrecy. Who knows how many post men Deliverer has throughout his network. Hermes wasn't too interested in meeting the others. Unlike the recipients of these letters, Hermes' reliability was completely contingent on the good old-fashioned bottom line. He would drop the notes with exact attention to detail. He read every single word of every single letter. This was important to understand the nature of the man he worked for. He received the emails, printed the messages, placed them into envelopes, and made the drops. He followed the instructions line by line and awaited his next destination. Today, that meant flying to Barcelona.

He arrived at Barcelona El-Prat at 9:36 a.m. local time. A white Koenigsegg Agera R awaited him in short-term parking. One thousand horses roared to life upon the start of the engine. This would be a fun day. He placed the car into gear and nearly flattened a pedestrian as the beastly auto struggled to be contained. He opened up the Swedish beauty upon reaching C-31. From there, he traveled west. By the time he could easily view the Mediterranean Sea, Hermes hit 190 MPH. Suburbs surrounded him as he blazed through, cursing the slower traffic in the fast lane. What normally took fifteen to twenty minutes, took eight in his Agera. He exited toward his final destination, a tropical restaurant named Chiringuito Iguana Sitges. The beachfront restaurant was quiet, only hosting a few tourists this early in the morning. He pulled into a sandy parking spot and cut off the engine, slowly rising from the driver's seat out into the sun. His white beach shirt and board shorts were the perfect complement to the seventy-three-degree sun. His giant Rolex

Yachtmaster, equipped with a platinum bezel, glistened freely. His aviator Ray Bans, spiked hair, and medium frame completed his ensemble. To the average onlooker, the man looked as though he bathed in cologne instead of water. He looked this way far before the ability for these people to actually smell him. Some would say sleazy. Some would say handsome. That's how different this world is in their perception of people.

The letter he printed prior to leaving for Barcelona was tucked into the back-left pocket of his board shorts. He didn't rush to deliver the note and leave this time. One of the perks of the job was the variance. It kept him on his toes in each individual situation. Hermes sat down under the large white dining tent. He chose a cheap lawn furniture chair facing the beach and propped his legs up on the chair to his right. The other two chairs under the four-chair table would have to go without him bestowing a presence upon them. A server showed up to his table and politely offered a menu. Hermes refused, but ordered a Coronita in a glass bottle. He sipped the beer while watching the waves float in from the Mediterranean. After two Coronitas and thirty minutes, Hermes found his mark.

Charlie Waters arrived on the Sitges Beaches with his wife, Jodi. The Waters were cruise-ship vacationers from East Lansing, MI. This was the couple's fifth time in Barcelona. They had seen the city, and the last three cruises found themselves taking in the sun of a nice semi-private beach walk. The Waters were prototypical tourists. Their wide eyes at the surroundings, copious upon ridiculous amounts of sunscreen, and ghostly white bodies were living proof that they traveled from a much cooler, and much more boring, climate. Hermes had waited for thirty rather pleasurable minutes for this type of couple. They fit the bill for what he needed, and the amount he would offer them in cash would more than cover their skepticism.

Hermes waved his hand and produced a rather comical Spanish accent. "My friends!" He stopped just before bouncing into the confused couple from Michigan. "I have been playing a game with my friend Miguel. We are each sending notes to the other from our restaurants. I own the Iguana behind me." He pointed back toward the restaurant he

161

had just patronized to the tune of two beers. The couple nodded and smiled widely, a defense mechanism to mirror Hermes' own smile. "You see; I send him a note from two strangers I see going his direction. I give them one hundred dollars for doing me this service. If the couple eats at his restaurant, he sends me back two hundred! I let the couple keep one hundred for doing me the favor. That's two hundred for delivering a note and eating some great food!"

Charlie was a bit unconvinced, but willing to go with the flow on vacation. "Let me get this straight. We get a couple hundred bucks just for walking in the direction we're walking? And then we eat something?"

Hermes smiled. "No gimmicks. That's the deal." He pulled out a crisp hundred-dollar bill along with the envelope addressed to Miguel Navas. He gave them both to Charlie. "Can you do this for me, my friend?" Charlie looked at Jodi and then back to Hermes.

"I don't see why not!" He snatched the money and envelope from Hermes with a vigor only known to those who vacation. You see, life on vacation is all about possibility. If the same guy walked up to the couple in East Lansing, Charlie Waters might call 911. But here, on vacation, the entire mindset changes. Charlie Waters was exactly who Hermes was looking for.

"It's called Latitud Norte. Just ask for Miguel Navas. Tell him the note is from Jose." Hermes smiled before jogging back toward the restaurant and out of the couple's sight.

Charlie and Jodi inspected the hundred-dollar bill. It seemed real enough. They walked with more than a pep to their step on the way toward Latitud Norte. Water splashed on their content feet on the roughly eight-minute walk. Sand clutched to their bare toes, washed away, and then resurfaced again. The never-ending cycle of the beach walker. It was the never-ending cycle that a couple like Charlie and Jodi Waters would love until the day they died.

Upon arrival at the raised deck canopy of Latitud Norte, Charlie Waters asked for Miguel. The server looked at him oddly before calling over to the bar. He spoke in Spanish with an obvious tone of question. A few quick moments and Miguel Navas appeared. He moved closer to the Waters and reached out his hand for a shake.

"I'm Miguel. What can I do for you?" He squinted his eyes and positioned a look of reluctant hesitancy across his face.

"Hey, I'm Charlie and this is my wife, Jodi. A gentleman at the Iguana gave me this envelope to give to you. He said when you saw it, you would give us two hundred for him when we eat something here." Miguel replaced his look of hesitancy with exasperated laughter.

"Oh he did, huh? Well, you can tell Rodrigo he's really funny!" Waters shook his head.

"No, not Rodrigo. This is from Jose." Charlie smiled, thinking this was all a prerequisite toward a few hundred bucks and a nice meal.

"What!" Anger overtook Miguel. Charlie and Jodi stepped back in fear over the turn.

"Easy. I'm just the messenger." He placed his hands in front of him in a defensive posture. Miguel looked as though he wanted to gut Waters alive. He composed himself for a short second.

"Jose is my son! He's been missing for a month!" Charlie and Jodi both appeared in shock over what was transpiring. "Do you know something about him?" Both the Waters shook their heads.

Jodi spoke when Charlie didn't. "We were just told this was some game you play between the restaurants. We were given money to drop this note to you. We are tourists." Her plea was convincing enough to ease Miguel. Jodi had the look of a plush and boring middleclass life written all over her. She didn't exactly ooze the ability to lie with a straight face. He shook his head and a tear began to surface.

"I'm sorry. I didn't mean to get so angry." He looked down the beach toward the Iguana before checking out his second envelope since Jose went missing. He ripped the seal on the envelope and another tear came rushing down his cheek when he read the contents. He breathed in and out, coming down off his high. He smiled through his obvious discomfort. "Have a drink on me for the miscommunication." He showed Charlie and Jodi toward his bar. They hesitantly moved toward the bar, thankful they weren't crucified by Miguel on the spot.

Charlie and Jodi sat at the bar. They were too nervous to make casual conversation. Charlie saw Miguel pull out three beers from a deep freeze filled with ice.

Miguel placed them atop the bar. "Here, have these on me." Miguel opened the top of all three and gave the couple from Michigan cheers. A bit of liquid eclipsed the top and splashed down toward the bar. He smiled to insinuate there were no worries and that he would take care of the mess. Then his disposition changed drastically. He sighed, before becoming scarily serious. "I just hope Jose can forgive me for what I have done. I hope you can as well. It's not my fault." He pulled a twelve-gauge pump shotgun from under the bar. He shot Charlie point blank in his face as Jodi screamed in terror. He pumped the shotgun, redirected it at Jodi, and fired once again. Compared to the blood, the mess from the beers would be nothing.

Hermes held the phone out of the window of the Agera. When the second shot sounded, he pulled his arm back in the car and ended the call without a goodbye. He ignited the engine once again, perched his arm out of the window, and peeled away from the Iguana. He had done his job. He would be paid handsomely for it by the man on the other side of the line. The man who needed to test Miguel Navas' resolve in protecting Jose. Charlie and Jodi Waters, two innocent tourists from Michigan, were now casualties under the wake of Deliverer. This was one of many scenarios Deliverer had Hermes conduct in his long career as the Post Man. The work was good and business always seemed to thrive. So many letters. So many threats, so many tests, so many deaths.

Hermes didn't remember them all, but he always remembered the first couple. Fran and Jim from Philadelphia. It must have been more than ten years ago at this point. He remembered reading the headlines, wondering if the two-hundred grand was worth the young couple's lives. They were honeymooners in Key West. He watched with binoculars as Virginia Patterson shot them both in the head with her 38-special and then turned the gun on herself. Such a negative result; Deliverer just couldn't stand the ones who weren't up to the task. The ones that were idealists or too religious for his blackmail. The ones who chose to kill themselves and take the easy way out. Or the ones that would kill the marks before, only to allow the guilt to consume them into murder-suicide. "What a waste" he would say to Hermes before disconnecting the phone. Luckily for Hermes' job security, this wasn't the typical result. He calculated that ninety percent of his marks were able to pass this type of test. Ninety percent of people were more than willing to kill in order to keep the hope of their loved ones alive. So many of them would kill for years without question or hesitancy. Love was turned into the greatest weapon. A weapon that made Hermes filthy rich. Conscience you might ask? To Hermes, the money always outweighed the people. Plain and simple.

His cell binged, barely heard over the one thousand horses he sat in front of. He read the message. This time, he was headed to Munich. He debated whether or not to drive his Koenigsegg all the way there.

"What do I have in Germany?" He couldn't think of it off the top of his head. With so many locations and so many jobs, he could hardly distinguish where he actually lived in the world. Where he actually left some of his choicest of cars. He popped the address in Munich into his GPS. Thirteen hours appeared as the estimated time. He pondered for a few moments. "I can make it in six."

Chapter 30

Yaravela pulled out her phone and began a quick search for transportation services to take us to the Eurotunnel Terminal. I almost slapped the phone from her hand but contained myself.

"We shouldn't use our devices? What if they're still watching you?" She smiled, almost mocking my naivety.

"It's encrypted and not the same one I used when I worked for him. I'm good at not being noticed. He hasn't found me yet, and I've been out of touch for more than a year."

I thought, *That's right, she stayed in Australia on the force a full year after I was imprisoned. How did she do that?*

"What did you tell him about what happened? What did you say about what happened in that room? Obviously not the truth I'd imagine if you were supposed to kill me!"

She nodded. "I told him that you killed Ricketts. The same story I told everyone. He never really believed me, though. I could tell he didn't have the same trust as before. Then, a month later, my life was in danger. He sent someone to kill me. Amateurs." She smiled in a sadistically beautiful way. It was the oddest thing. Something so scary being so beautiful. Feeling righteous in a way. She was not a good person. Her past was littered with the deaths of so many innocent people, but she had a way about her that felt like she was guiltless. A certain sexiness about her that trumped the cold-blooded killer.

"How many?" I blurted it out. I intended to ask how many times she had actually killed people. I wanted to know a number as if knowing would give me closure or comfort. I quickly rephrased, knowing that wasn't something I was actually ready to know. "I mean, how many times did he target you during the year?"

She smiled. "Nice save." She winked at me in full knowledge of what I meant the first time. She played along though. "Three. After a month, he sent some old lady. She tried to poison me. After two months, he sent another. This time, it was some little kid. He must've been seventeen, but he looked like a child. He attacked me with a Kabar knife like they use in the military. Needless to say, I was able to take care of that." I shook my head, not really needing the gory details of how she countered against his knife and slaughtered a kid.

"And the third?" I broke in when there seemed to be too long of a pause.

"Just before I vanished. This time, it was real. This time, he sent someone that knew what they were doing. Someone that was better than me. I arrived at a friend's apartment for a drink, living what used to be a cover. No one answered her front door. I decided to go ahead and let myself in like I had done before. It wasn't unusual, and she never actually locked up. She was a very free spirit. When I arrived in the kitchen, I could see her dead at the feet of a large man. He was in her living room. It looked like he had stabbed her, but I couldn't really tell in such a short glance. He was the picture of calm. I remember almost admiring how calm he was. Even though I knew for certain I was about to die. He lifted a silenced pistol and fired." She pulled up her shirt to reveal a scar on her stomach. I gasped in astonishment, clearly seeing a very serious wound. Something that looked more like a surgical wound than a gunshot.

"How did you make it away?" I broke in again as her pauses were becoming more regular.

"He left me for dead. Her neighbor, a blind woman that I had never actually spoken to, heard the shot. It's not like a silenced pistol is actually silent, especially to a blind person." She chuckled a bit before continuing. "Anyway, the walls of the apartment complex were thin. I got to the hospital about an hour after I was shot. Well, according to the chart in the room. They were able to rush me into surgery to remove the bullet. That's why the scar seems so ludicrous." I gave her the no you can barely notice it look. She rolled her eyes and continued. "I was

167

unconscious when I arrived. I didn't have identification. When I woke up, hooked up to an IV with a pain in my stomach, I knew I needed to get away. Not from the hospital itself but from that life. It simply became too dangerous. I pretended to sleep whenever nurses came around. After a few hours, I worked up the strength to simply stand up. There were no outfits or anything, but I'm decently resourceful. I poked around the closets and found a pair of scrubs. It took a bit of ducking around, but I made it work. From there, I just walked out of the hospital like I was supposed to. Australians tend to be so lax." We both smiled at that one, having very similar perceptions of that continent's inhabitants.

I had more questions, but none of them were really relevant. I wanted to know how she escaped from there. How she managed to stay hidden from this Deliverer for so long. Was there some type of training camp he used to turn these everyday people into killers? Or was this some kind of sick on the job training? I didn't bother. She was more suitable than me for handling the particulars of our escape from England.

She continued typing into her phone. About ten minutes passed before an Uber showed up at the park. It was a silver Mercedes E-Class of some sort. It was probably a few years old, but ever since my incarceration, most cars on the road looked relatively new. That is, most with the exception of the adorable London cabs and double-decker tourist buses. The driver was probably mid-thirties. He was clean cut, thin, and wore a relaxed smile. He seemed chipper even for the late hour, something close to 3:30 a.m. He wasn't the normal after hour cabbie. Certainly not someone you could associate with the second *Home Alone* movie, where a snarling beast with a glass eye peered through Macauley Culkin's soul. I quickly wondered whatever happened to that kid. Then just as quickly, I no longer cared.

The drive toward the Eurotunnel took roughly one and a half hours. Initially, we discussed taking turns at sleep, but at this point Shen and I were both on red alert, making sure our driver wasn't going to turn on us. I'm sure our overly sensitive, almost hyperactive personas, made us look like we were high on something. That, and the time at which we were picked up at the park must've added to that perception. Luckily, he didn't try anything weird. He was calm the entire journey. It was professional, clean, and we arrived at the Eurotunnel just after five a.m. local time. This left us a touch more than an hour to wait for the train Shen had booked for Brussels. It was direct and would put us on the path we needed toward Greece.

The Channel Tunnel, or Chunnel as it's often abbreviated, is a modern marvel. A high-speed railway system connecting the United Kingdom and France underneath the English Channel. Yes, a rail system built underneath a great body of water. The system was first proposed in the early nineteenth century. It took nearly two hundred years of diplomatic aggression, World Wars, and the *Treaty of Canterbury* to finally ignite England and France to commence digging in the Channel. In 1994, the first passengers were able to travel between Britain and France without setting foot on a boat or airplane. I couldn't help wonder how the tunnel would've worked if it were around during the World Wars. Which countries would've benefited the most? Would such a network be one of the first targets for the Hitler led Germany? Or would such a network create the necessary logistical framework for keeping the United States out of both wars? Hypotheticals and nothing more. I've always enjoyed passing time by pondering such irrelevant items. I find that it keeps me sharp, but I am a historian by trade. It's hard not to play in hypotheticals when you realize how fragile our very existence has been throughout time.

Time, the same time that felt like it was moving at warp speed not too long ago in the park, was correcting itself while waiting for the Eurostar train. The relative nature of circumstance to the perception of time is well documented, but come on! We waited in the large center, and I stared at an enormous clock with a ticking second hand. I guess you'd call it a travel center piped full of shops, restrooms, and a food court. It didn't really matter. I felt like we were there for the entire day. I remembered elementary school back in Sewanee, Tennessee. I hated school. I especially hated elementary school. I had way too many exciting things to get into when my real day actually began at three p.m. School was simply a tedious nightmare that was perpetuated by power hungry teachers, mean children, and its incorrigible necessity. What a burden it was to me. What a burden it was until I finally began researching with Hogue. I remember staring at the clock, waiting for the seconds to drift away. Anytime the classroom had a ticking second hand, it always felt so much longer. For whatever reason, the second hand that continuously moved, felt as though time was moving faster. It wasn't puttering along and mocking me with its pathetic attempt at moving. I swear some of the time it looked like it took a step forward, only to drop back nine tenths of that step before trying again. The Eurotunnel travel station clock had the same impact on me some thirty years later.

We didn't help each other with the time in the station. Perhaps we were coming off our highs from the uneventful Uber drive. Perhaps we were simply thinking about a plan. Perhaps, and this is the obvious explanation, we were simply exhausted. No matter the reason, we hadn't spoken more than a few casual words to each other since arriving at the station. This, despite my mind boiling over with the number of questions I wanted to ask her. Then, out of nowhere and just prior to our train arriving, I asked something very authentic. Something real that I never asked my friends that were in the military who had had similar experiences with death. I guess I was always too concerned to ask someone that was killing for their country.

"What's it like? You know, killing another human?" She was taken aback but not upset by the abruptness of the question. I watched her formulate a response. She seemed so calculated. She never spoke unless it was toward an end goal. I liken the approach to basketball and dribbling. It's called a "pea" dribble when you go somewhere that doesn't have a purpose in the movement. Dribbling just to dribble and not within the scheme of the offense. Talking just to talk is how so many people communicate. Not Shen. She never "pea" talked. At least, not with me in the few days I had known her. I could tell she was debating with herself. Would she be real? Would she truly open up to me about the feeling? Or would she be cliché? I think she chose a combination.

"It feels different each time. Every person is so different. You feel a connection with them. This intimacy that you can't get from anything other than love. There's a high moment. You can tell why there are battles for territory and supremacy in the wild. It's like we are built to desire this power over each other. Call it survival of the fittest or whatever. Anyway, like I said, each time is different. Sometimes you feel shame. Sometimes you feel just. Sometimes you feel nothing." She adjusted herself and stared me directly in the eyes. It made me uncomfortable considering the subject in question. I looked down before returning my eye contact. "I'm guessing you want to know about Ricketts? Is that why you're asking? It makes sense considering you were in the room." I nodded. It wasn't that I even cared about Ricketts prior to her talking. I simply wanted to know more about her in general. I needed to know her more than the surface elements.

"Yes, you winked at me prior to—" I didn't finish that thought before continuing. "What were you feeling in that moment?" It was a moment that I felt such horror. A moment that changed my life, for better or worse, forever. Again, I didn't really care. I wanted to know more about her and her response would give me that. She smiled at me now. The conversation didn't seem like it was about death at all. It didn't seem like it was about killing another human being.

"Freedom. I felt free from Deliverer. I felt free from a burden that had consumed me for years. When I winked at you and made the decision to disobey orders, my actions no longer mattered to me. Finally, and for the first time in so very long, I made a decision to save someone. I made a decision to save someone that I didn't even know. I had an inkling you might have answers to help me, but I saved you because it was the right thing to do. I saved you because I needed to stop being used by that evil Creature."

Her answer was long winded, and I liked that. I liked listening to her explanation. Whether or not this was real, it felt good to hear. It felt good to know that she needed to begin making decisions from a decent moral standing. It seemed like that started with me. Whether for the right reasons or not, Yaravela Shen had made a choice not to follow Deliverer's instructions starting with me.

"And when you stabbed his neck?" I got straight to the point. The moments preceding the action were great, but I really wanted to know about the moment of impact. The moment she took another person's life. The moment she thrust the screwdriver into his neck. Her smile drifted away, and she became more serious.

171

"Adrenaline. The point of no return. When you reach a point that could change your entire life if you made the slightest mistake in the planning. With Ricketts, I did very little planning. I seized an opportunity and went with it. Luckily it worked." I started to break in since she was dancing around. She knew she was prior to my talking. She raised her hands in defeat. "I know. I know." She closed her eyes, seemingly putting herself back in the moment: "It was so easy. The screwdriver went in his neck smoothly, and I knew right away he would be dead within a few seconds. Joy. It felt good killing that man. I felt good killing him. It's not like I knew him, but sometimes people just give you that. Ya know? They ooze something that makes you dislike them. With Ricketts, I could tell he was an asshole. I was ridding the world of someone who didn't have a positive impact. Someone who was exceedingly negative in every step he took in life. Someone who brought others down. Someone who could simply be present in a room and bring the energy level down. A drain on society." She didn't have to continue.

I knew what she was talking about. Ricketts seemed like an asshole the moment he stepped in the interrogation room, but what if he was simply like her? What if he was just another tortured soul trying to incriminate me to make his job easier when he was the one wielding the weapon? What if he was stripped of his humanity by Deliverer?

"What about someone you felt was good?" It was the question I truly wanted to hear an answer to. I could imagine killing someone who was a terrible person. What I always had a hard time understanding, were people that would kill someone good. I think all of us fancy Dexter's approach. A serial killer that put his murderous urges to good use in society. He killed bad people to make the world a better place. What about the true sociopaths that kill indiscriminately? The Ted Bundy's or John Wayne Gacy's of the world? The ones that killed children. Perhaps even the man called Deliverer? The orchestrator of our torment.

"Intense shame and self-hatred. Every step feels so wrong. The planning and the execution, even trying to convince yourself that you are doing it for good, feels terrible. Trying to save someone by killing someone else, especially someone you don't know. A mother or a father. It doesn't matter. It took me years to finally realize that. It was so

172

justifiable before. The intense longing I had for my baby. The depression I felt over her absence, and the anxiety over her safety overrode any emotion to stop me. I simply didn't care. All I cared about was protecting her. The shame I felt for not protecting her in the first place overwhelmed. Now I know everything I've done was for evil. My love for her doesn't trump the evil of the man I was killing for. I'm a monster, Tom. I will always be a monster because I fell victim to a monster's desires instead of my own."

***

The boarding call brought us back to reality. We hadn't even noticed the slick locomotive that entered the station. The somber pieces of our conversation had shed light on the realities of our situation. The realities of the man we needed to stop in our quest. I didn't blame Shen for killing for her child. I knew I would've killed if it meant protecting my family. Most of us would. Most of us would choose to kill a stranger to protect those we love. Whether this means a burglar trying to harm them or a psychopath using leverage is really a moot point. We protect those that we care about. It's only natural, I thought, that Yaravela would become a murderer if it meant saving her daughter. At the time, she obviously felt that what she was doing was justified. Now, only in the knowledge that her daughter was likely dead, had she realized the scope of the situation.

We both moved toward the train. We scanned our tickets and arrived in our seats three minutes prior to our 6:13 a.m. departure.

***

While we boarded, a hidden eaves-dropper listened to the conversation and watched every step. She felt intense pain seeing Tom and not reaching out to him. Not telling him all she knew. Not telling him she was alive and well. But like Shen, Bren Appling had a little girl born into the world of Deliverer. Like Shen, she was trying to do all in her power to protect her. All she wanted was the three of them to become

173

a family. Now, that dream seemed so far from her grasp. She had to protect everyone Tom held dear, but at what cost? If it came down to it, was she any more ready now to slaughter her husband than she was in Australia two ago? Could she really do the deed when the time came? The question to herself was rhetorical. She had had a scope on Tom's forehead a few moments earlier. She watched his mannerisms and realized how in love with him she still was. This was a man she had grown up with. Someone she shared her most intimate details with. Someone she trusted, loved, and ultimately tore apart without his even knowing it. She knew Tom. She knew now, that she was dead, that he'd stop at nothing to find vengeance against Deliverer. She knew Tom would stop at nothing to harm the people who killed his wife. She knew also that if he succeeded, the likelihood of his killing his own daughter in the process was almost definite. He simply had no idea that he still had something left to lose.

Chapter 31

His absolute favorite time of year. Like a symphony, the packages dropped from the sky. *Pat pat pat*, like the keys of a piano or the slow start to a powerful summer rain, they fell to the earth. Deliverer tried to watch each and every one. Tried to feel joy in each and every one. The feeling was pure bliss with a hint of anxious reverence at his accomplishments. It was beyond the excitement of a first kiss. It was better than his first time sleeping with a woman. It was everything. All his trials. All his tribulations. Everything wrapped up in the falling packages he witnessed each and every year. Displays of pure perfection.

It had been thirteen days since their meeting in Athens. The location was Alpha, more commonly known as Platæa. The number of aircraft flying by and dropping packages, ten. The total number of packages, one hundred and seventy-five. An entire years' worth of dedicated work, every painstaking detail accounted for, all wrapped up in one beautiful compendium. And then, just like that, the packages stopped falling. It was over. All one hundred and seventy-five had fallen. This time, he counted every single touchdown to earth. He smiled widely when the last one came crashing to the surface. He sighed in a feeling of immense self-satisfaction. Then, just like that, it was time to work once again:

"Move!" He spoke the word and ten men moved from the safe zone and toward the battlefield of Platæa. The battlefield was enormous. The aircraft were able to drop efficiently, but the spread of packages was significant. This was unavoidable with one hundred and seventy-five individual drops. Like shadows, the ten men moved onto the field. They dressed all black from head to toe. Their faces were concealed with dark scarves that intermingled with their gear. The moonless night sky accentuated their night vision goggles' effectiveness. The left lens was perfectly normal, using infrared for ease of sight in the dark. The right lens was special, offering each of them the ability to see a digital signature that corresponded with each package. In the darkest of nights, this offered them a solution to pick up each and every package without mistake. There could be no mistakes. Strict inventory had to be taken, and the packages had to be unloaded precisely. Five men would pick up seventeen packages. Five men would pick up eighteen. Deliverer wasn't a huge fan of the lack of symmetry, but it wasn't like he would choose to lose five packages to make one hundred and seventy. Adding five would've been immensely challenging, but there's always room to improve with next year's tally. One hundred and seventy-five represented his highest total to date. What an amazing year he had just orchestrated. He marveled at himself and his achievement. The sardonic smile returned in full force.

The packages varied drastically in size, but the value, at least for Deliverer, was the same for each. Each package represented endless possibilities. All opportunities unique in their substance. One by one, Deliverer watched as the packages came in. He inspected each one prior to checking them off his list. Like ants, the ten in black continuously brought in the packages. The process, as times before, took most hours of the night. When five a.m. local time struck Deliverer's watch, no traces of the night remained across the landscape of Platæa. Like ghosts, the packages, the ten, and the aircraft vanished from the scene. Deliverer, or Emory Chance in certain settings, stayed behind to inspect his work. The ten were paid in cash at drop-off locations. None connected. None lived locally. Most lived on the other side of the world. They never spoke a word to Deliverer or each other, but each one had shown up each year, and for every drop. Six hours of work, sixty-thousand dollars apiece. To some, it was the only thing they would do for the year. This made Deliverer laugh at the banality of their lives. How simple these creatures are.

The landscape began to come alive as farmers rose early to check crops around the battlefield. They were each old, tired, and showed the signs of wear across their faces. Seeing the historian around the site wasn't unusual. He was well known and he spoke their language fluently. Many of them had conducted personal conversations with Chance in years past. Many had been interviewed by him and his student, Thomas Appling, just a few years ago. Chance enjoyed his notoriety during the day. While only a few moments earlier, it would've spelled disaster for Deliverer.

Most of the field was covered in wheat, a testament to how precious crop-bearing land was to the Greek people. Only thirty percent of the land in Greece can support the growth of crops. That means, sacred land like that in front of Platæa. Land that staged a battle that altered the face of human history, would rarely be used to research the past. There wasn't a national landmark. Barely a trace of the battle fought survives in the present day. There are a few exceptions, of course. The ancient city of Platæa itself and a few churches scattered about the field of war, like the Byzantine church called St. Demetrios, are among such exceptions. And then there's Gargaphia, an ancient spring mired in controversy for its role in Herodotus' interpretation of the Battle of Platæa. An ancient spring, it's said, that Artemis once bathed in. Every time Emory Chance moved by the suspected location presented by Thomas Appling, he scoffed and spit on the earth. Not because Tom was wrong, but because Tom was one of the only modern scholars to present a worthwhile explanation of the Battle of Platæa.

The spring called Gargaphia represented all that Chance resented about Thomas Appling. Gargaphia was the cornerstone that gave Tom's theories such life. Theories that placed a direct threat on Chance's life's work if left unchecked. Prior to Appling, Chance's meticulous plan was seemingly faultless in its execution. There hadn't been a historian or archaeologist in more than two thousand years who had given a truly compelling theory of the Battle of Platæa. The battleground was perfect. Vast, unspoiled, and almost forgotten through time. The perfect blend for Chance's operation.

Then Appling, an American student in Australia, submitted his thesis proposal. He came up with a viable alternative that threatened the very existence of Deliverer's work. A ridiculous coincidence that gave Chance some of the strongest fatalistic inclinations he had ever come across in life. From there, he made sure to infiltrate Newcastle. After all, he was basically a celebrity offering to act as a reader on Tom's paper. *The most noted historian in the genre just stumbled in one day to help a nobody study Platæa? Please,* Chance thought. He had set up assets to monitor any new research proposal in ancient history, classics, archaeology, geology, or any other field of note. If someone had an interest in land north of Athens, Chance would know. For years, as expected, there was nothing. Then, along came Tom with the very proposal that could set flames to his business. At first, curiosity about the subject quelled any thoughts of aggression. He positioned himself to act as Tom's second committee member at Newcastle. He even traveled with Tom. He helped him. He needed to know everything about the man that could cause him harm if left to his own devices.

The more he learned, the more Emory Chance hated Thomas Appling. He hated him with a fervent passion likened to a cat given a bath in flea preventative. Tom Appling's very presence on this earth made Chance's skin crawl. The thought that the hatred sprang from jealousy enraged Chance even further. Unlike most of his marks, the ones that didn't mean anything to him, Tom represented a lust for punishment unlike any other. How could a business-man, from Tennessee no less, stumble upon something so keen? How could he possibly have insight or a workable theory? The simple thought produced redness in Chance's face. His vessels bulged and heat figuratively sprang from every pore. Deliverer wanted to punish Thomas Appling's life well after he would perish underneath his own blade. Deliverer would continue punishing him by punishing his friends, family, neighbors, and associates for as long as he held breath in his lungs.

Deliverer allowed himself to calm down. He was still in control of Tom's future. He delighted in the future pain of his pupil. The rage turned into a hysterical giddiness likened to school girls seeing their favorite boy band. Prior to leaving Bœotia, he visited the city of Platæa during the day. It was a city that would see little more than regulated investigation over the years. Archaeologists would come and go every now and again but never conduct anything worthwhile. Holes would be

178

dug and filled back in. Like many sites in the ancient Greek world, the interest was cyclical, and such cycles had made Deliverer one of the more powerful underground men in the entire world. He breathed in the fresh breeze sweeping in from Mount Cithaeron. The wind, always gusty it seemed, felt sublime. He stared down toward the field of war.

"I'll be back soon." He muttered and allowed a smile to creep in. He walked past the ruins of the ancient city where large stone walls once stood to protect the inhabitants. The remains were but a fragment of their reign in history. What a time it must have been. How many times were these walls sieged by angry Thebans or those from Attica or the Peloponnese? It's doubtful that history would tell us more than a few. For a few moments, it's almost as if Dr. Emory Chance wasn't Deliverer at all. He was born a Hyde that would eat away at the very mention of a Jekyll, but sometimes and rarely, he let the academic out. For a few moments, he was simply an ancient historian who appreciated the times past. The moment didn't last. Upon entry into his black Mercedes G-Class, Deliverer reached for his phone. It was almost like reaching for a portal of death at this point in his life. There, he scrolled through the potential. When he arrived at a South Korean named Nam Kim, he saw the opportunity he was looking for. Hermes was three spaces down as a text recipient. Prior to starting his engine, Deliverer wrote a message. It was plain and simple. He already had something that Nam Kim longed to find. Now, Deliverer would use it to cause a panic that would leave dozens in scattered hysteria. At this point, it was simple. Business as usual.

Chapter 32

There was always something about riding the rails I found relaxing. I wasn't sure what the allure was, but I was a sucker for it. Perhaps it felt like one of the safest forms of transportation to me. Don't get me wrong, things could go awry on a train or subway line, but perhaps the attachment to the rail itself gave me a feeling of comfort. Being on a rollercoaster always seemed to give me similar comforts. Despite the very intention to thrill the rider, the rail system seemed safe and secure to me. I could see the security winning over Shen as well. For the first time, I witnessed her letting her guard down in public. For a while, she would close her eyes only to jolt awake. It was that sensation of falling that creeps in when someone is sleeping where they aren't comfortable. What a shitty experience that is. So tired that you fall asleep anywhere, but your mind plays a cruel trick on you. I remember waking up in similar circumstances. Outrageously high heartbeat coupled with a feeling of humiliation when absolutely nothing was wrong. How peculiar the finer details of life can be.

It didn't take more than a few minutes on the two-hour and fourteen-minute train ride for me to feel calm enough to drift away as well. I knew we needed our sleep, and an almost empty early morning train would be as good a time as any. Who knew what the world had in store for us upon reaching Brussels? There would be no way to know if anyone was following us until it was too late. Point being, we would have to be on guard from the moment we left the Eurostar.

Our train had upgraded interior. It was brighter and sleeker on the inside than some of the older models. Four seats per row with plastic tables stationed in front of the passengers. For respect of the other guests, the seats folded back, but they might as well not bother. Despite the ability, even on planes, I couldn't let myself lean back. Something about being rude to the person behind me prevented the action. I tried to be hyper vigilant and be kind to strangers. There wasn't a length of time I wouldn't stand idly holding a door for someone. I tipped servers twenty percent even if they were bad. Perhaps even when they were the worst. When they were good, I made an attempt to cover all the bad tips they would receive for the evening. Even in business, I wanted others to make money in addition to myself. I cared so much that I designed agreements specifically so others would take at least fifty percent of the proceeds. I enjoyed giving to charity in both time and money. Selfishly, it felt good to give.

As the train approached the channel, we were both sleeping soundly. We would feel the residual effects of our positioning later that day. Something about public transportation lulls travelers into the deepest of sleeps and makes for the worst neck cricks. Still, it beat not sleeping at all.

***

The Sniper had watched as her targets boarded the train a few cars ahead of her. She gave them a wide birth before taking her seat far out of their line of sight. It wasn't easy lugging her Remington 700 around inconspicuously. Not with metal detectors and a modern world bent on stopping terrorist activity. Luckily, this wasn't a plane where an actual x-ray would be taken. These were simple detectors, and she wasn't a normal terrorist. No, her guitar case wasn't lined with some type of metal defying rubber. She simply used racial profiling in her favor. Her belt was metal, and her faux guitar had metal strings. Her rifle and pistol were taken apart and scattered throughout the guitar case like parts to a musical instrument. The detectors would pick up the metal, but the assumption was that it was simply her guitar. Racial profiling did the rest. Cute, white, American girl in her thirties. Hardly the greatest terrorist threat on the racial profiling watch list. She'd simply be a nice, calm, and ignorant tourist. Nothing to worry about.

Upon entering, she pulled the cell phone from the left back pocket of her jeans. She had to check in. If she didn't, she knew Deliverer would assume the worst and that was never welcome. It only took one ring and Bren could hear the anticipation in his voice.

"Is he dead?" Deliverer answered, baiting Bren into lying to him like the Monster before her.

"No. But I will do my job when the time is right." Bren answered calmly. She heard relief in his voice, something she felt was odd.

"Glad to hear that, Ms. Appling." Again, more baiting. Baiting the emotions to snap back. Not only was she still a Mrs. and would always be a Mrs. in her mind, she was also a Dr. "Change of plans." Bren shrugged at this. What could he possibly want now? "I've decided I want Tom to make it to Greece." Bren flashed a concerned face that no one could see. She didn't speak. What was this? Why the change? She already knew this was some personal vendetta against Tom, but what sadistic plan did he have now? She would have an answer to that suspicion soon enough. "Instead, I think Mr. Appling's role in my world isn't quite over. He hasn't quite seen all the things he needs to see. Death is a little too easy at this point."

Bren shivered. What was he getting at?

"There's just one hiccup, Ms. Appling. I've already alerted some people that Tom will try to reach Greece. Unfortunately, I decided I needed him to get here after I told them. Oh no. What to do, what to do." His game was starting to take shape in a very cruel way.

"What do you want from me?" Her tone, defeated and nothing more. The same defeat she had given in to so long ago. Deliverer soaked it in. He wanted nothing more than for her to feel pain, for all of Tom's loves to feel pain.

"Well. I guess I need you to keep him alive for me. I don't see any other way. I'm just too busy to make so many calls at this point." Bren's heart dropped before he put the cherry on the sundae. "If he doesn't get here. Well, I guess your baby girl is no longer needed." Click. He hung up. He didn't wait for a response.

His directions were very clear to her. The Sniper, Bren Appling, had a new mission prerogative. How twisted this was. Instead of placing a

182

bullet in Tom's skull, what she thought was terrible enough, she now had to keep him alive for whatever torturous ending Deliverer had in store. What would he do to him there? She shuddered at the thought and revisited her circumstance. If she didn't keep Tom alive, if she didn't insure Tom would suffer first hand by Deliverer, then their daughter would die. He would kill the daughter Tom never knew. The daughter Tom would never know. This man truly hated Tom. He truly hated all that Tom was. The hate seemed to grow with each and every day Tom lived. It seemed that he would stop at nothing to see him suffer. Was it because he escaped? Was it simply because he was who he was? Bren didn't know the answers. She simply knew that, for now, she had to keep him alive. She had to insure his journey continued. The hope of this being over for the man she loved faded into the distance of her mind. Tom would die. She knew there was no other way. Why did he need to suffer so much before? Why did he have to suffer the immense pain of loss? Hogue; his education; his research; his time in prison; toying with his mind using the we're watching notes; the Bloody American moniker; being chased by a monster; constant danger; a baby he would never know existed; the cancer; the images of death; and his very own wife slain. Hadn't he suffered enough? Bren shook her head. She wished that a bullet in her own skull would solve all of Tom's problems. How easy it would be to take her own life at this point. How quickly she would if it meant the safety of her family. But no. The suffering for all of Tom's world had to continue. For now at least, it gave her more precious time to try to save him from this nightmare.

Bren proceeded to get comfortable in her seat, all while uncomfortable in her own skin. The faux leather headrest was worn, but still comfortable on a mind tormented to the extreme. She sighed and let her mind drift to the only sanctuary it had left. What life would've been like…, what life would've been like if she had her baby and things were normal. If Tom came back from Australia with his PhD that week and not two years later. How she would surprise him with the news of her pregnancy. How, even though it was a girl, she had a plan to cover the nursery in sports paraphernalia from top to bottom. Chicago Cubs, Tennessee Titans, Tottenham Hotspur, and Kentucky Wildcats. If he knew about their daughter and was able to raise her, what an amazing father he would've made. If he was teaching classes at the college and she had the normal worries of a wife. Worries about the coeds hitting on the cute young professor. Thinking of how mad she would get before Tom would set her at ease with some hilarious anecdote. Of whether or not he would get tenure.

Worries about whether or not to kill him, understandably, never made it into these imaginations. Wow, how life's course had derailed the plan. How it intervened with the plan in the most disturbing of ways. What was Tom thinking at this point? Was he numb from the pain of loss? Was he dead set on avenging all of his losses? The loss of his own wife? Punishing the one who gave him the scar on his cheek? The one who saw few alternatives other than killing him just a few moments ago to save his little girl, his future Wildcat. Oh, how life had changed. Oh, how her life had turned from a fairytale into a living nightmare.

Now, she too, had to rest. They would be coming for him. They would be after him like their very lives depended on it. They would have no choice. These people were simply fathers, mothers, brothers, sisters, grandparents, husbands, or wives just like her. Each would be trying to kill Tom because they had no other alternative. Each almost assuredly innocent. They were simply in the wrong place. They simply loved too much for a world run by Deliverer. How many would there be? Where would they come from? Bren's mind raced. How would she defend Tom without him knowing? Sleep? No, she wouldn't be able to sleep. Not now. Not until her baby was back in her arms. Not until Tom was free. Not until Tom was free from all of this torment and pain. She eased her shattered thoughts of failure by repeating a mantra that Tom gave her while helping her through her first solo surgery in vet school.

"One step at a time. You've made the first cut and now you have to finish." No matter the mess in front of her, when she took a breath and could hear Tom's voice saying these words, time slowed and her apprehensive fears and insecurities faded away. She calmly pondered whether his voice would be the guiding force used to finally finish him. She had, after all, made the first cut.

She stared out of the window as the sun began rising over Dover Castle and the White Cliffs. It was sheer beauty. Such beauty in a world that seemed so dim. It made her feel so small as a piece of the universe. How, despite her struggles, the same sun would rise to illuminate the beautiful cliffs each and every day. It didn't matter if she killed her husband. It didn't matter if Deliverer killed her daughter. The sun would still rise to issue beauty and life upon humanity.

"So many don't deserve this." She spoke out loud but to no one in particular. And just like that. Within a moment. The beautiful sunrise was gone, consumed by the Eurostar entering the Chunnel. Concrete walls surrounded her. It was as if she was free for a moment with nature only to be locked back into her predicament. Darkness once again overcame the train. Darkness once again overtook Bren Appling. "One step at a time. You've made the first cut, and now you have to finish."

Chapter 33

In my mind, I was now Jason and the Golden Fleece was at Platæa.
I didn't know what my fleece was. I don't think Jason really knew either.
Just knew it meant power. Just knew it was important enough to die for.
I looked over at a sleeping Yaravela Shen. I wanted to say it out loud to
actually wake her. I settled with under my breath and without the risk of
breaking her momentary peace.

"I guess that makes you my Argonauts." I laughed at my own joke.
I was cracking myself up. Perhaps it was the excitement, the torment, or
simply the anxiety. Perhaps it was the unknown in itself. So much
unknown. So many frontiers yet to eclipse in this adventure. This was a
story of legend. A myth in the making.

"Appling, his Argonaut, and the plight of the evil known only as
Deliverer." I mumbled quietly in my finest 1930s movie announcer
impersonation. There were monsters, tragedies, and unknown treasures
at the end of the path. I could romanticize it in my head all I wanted. The
reality of myth is not as glamorous as the stories. The deaths were real.
The perils were just that, perilous. The characters were not heroes, and
my Argonaut was a self-admitted murderer. Her cause belonged only to
her. Perhaps that's how we all are. All heroes of our own story. Most,
villains of someone else's.

Living in my very own saga made me realize just how much I had
already lost. I felt that all I had left was the actual story itself. How it
played out and the characters intertwined in my struggle. No wife, dead.
No family, endangered. No career, stolen. Pushed to the edge. The true
fabrication of an ancient legend in the making.

As I marveled and feared my own legend, the train began to slow. My Argonaut, Yaravela Shen, began to awaken from her short slumber. We made eye-contact. It was intense and significant. We were both painstakingly aware, that once off the train, we would encounter the unknown. Would there be monsters? Almost assuredly I thought to myself. We didn't speak, but we kept our eye-contact. As the train stopped, I nodded with conviction. Now or never, I thought to myself. I could tell she agreed and I could see the humanity in her eyes once again. Despite being more prepared for an epic adventure, she was scared. She had experienced this man called Deliverer. She was aware of the atrocities he was capable of. She knew he wouldn't be defeated without a monumental undertaking.

The doors burst open, breaking our concentration. It was time. I sighed out loud to prepare myself for my first breath into the unknown. The breath was long and over exaggerated. I made eye-contact once again with Shen:

"Ready?" She didn't answer. She simply stared at the floor before standing. Her vulnerability had once again outstayed its welcome on her outer shell.

"Let's go." Her voice was confident, making me wonder how she murdered the sleeping beauty that was next to me just a few moments before. I nodded and failed trying to shed my own fears of our circumstance. My shell, despite the numbness associated with loss, despite trying to insert myself into an epic tale, was weak and susceptible. I had to get in a better frame of mind or risk falling into another panic. The Stretch Gillman. Yes, the Stretch Gillman. Creature flapping around like a wacky waving inflatable arm flailing tube man. I pictured Bren laughing at my impersonation of this creature. I smiled brightly and my fears began to wither. There was little I could do to change my fate. Might as well embrace the struggle in getting there. A new perspective. How quickly I could make that happen, especially when feeling behind someone else close to me. I used Yaravela's stoic personality to alter my own existence in Deliverer's world. Sometimes adapting to others, although disgraceful on certain occasions, has

187

immense advantages. I was ready. We were ready. Time to rise and embrace our fate.

The Eurostar station in Brussels felt anything but an epic journey of Jason or Odysseus. It was modern, clean, and reminded me of an airport back home. Perhaps reminded me of Hartsfield-Jackson International in Atlanta. The exception was the ground. Here, so much tile surrounded the Channel Terminal, but the tile was surrounded and overtaken by shops and mobs of people. That, in itself, reminded me of the major airports of the world. For someone not used to traveling by train, it was an interesting phenomenon. Perhaps it was me denying the use of cities for so long as I studied. I already missed the countryside. This feeling was compounded with a strong sense of uncertainty about my fellow humans. Which one of these would morph into a monster bent on taking me down? I began taking notice of each one, it seemed to their chagrin. It's not like people enjoy being noticed. At least, most of us don't, not in this setting anyway, not when there are so many unfamiliar and judgmental eyes surrounding them. That made my wandering eyes suspicious. In a world filled with people staring straight ahead or down to the earth, my gazes around to monitor my surroundings seemed to make people uneasy. I understood, but I didn't care. I needed to believe that I was the hero in my own story. I laughed once again without the use of externalities. Shen smirked and continued moving forward. I could see her shake her head at me. I could almost see a smile present itself on her face. That was quickly outmaneuvered by her defense mechanisms and replaced by her deathly glare straight ahead. It was amazing how the beautiful Shen could scowl away the weakness such beauty could plague upon most women.

I didn't have to micromanage Yaravela Shen. By the time we were outside of the station, she was on the phone. Who was she calling? I didn't really care if it was for our benefit. She was on the line for minutes. More people were walking by us. More potential threats. I was uncomfortable, and it was noticeable. We were too vulnerable out in the open. I began moving southwest down Place Victor Horta. Shen followed, but I could see a minor query in her body language. We turned west on *Ru de I'Instruction* and walked a few minutes until we reached

188

a small restaurant called *Van Wijnendaele*. We ducked in and were immediately surrounded by the strong smell of shellfish. It was potent and turned my empty stomach in the most uncomfortable of ways. We hadn't eaten anything in what felt like days. I was about to order when Shen sat down and ended her call.

"Don't eat." She scoffed, disappointed that I would have the audacity to eat at such a place. I was halfway toward the counter when she said those devastating words. I rotated back reluctantly toward her small, coffee house-like table.

"Why? Everything ok?" I sat down across from her.

She nodded. "Yes, fine. Just don't eat this stuff. Five minutes." She opened her hand when she said this to display all five fingers. She then lifted herself up and left the restaurant. I followed, not questioning anything.

We waited for less than five minutes before a car pulled up from the northeast on Rue Eloy. A middle-aged man quickly popped from the driver's seat and opened the back door of the white BMW 5-Series.

Shen turned toward me and smiled. "Come on. Get in." She moved into the car first as the driver held the door open. She scooted toward the opposite side of the car to allow my entrance through the same, rear passenger-side door. The driver with glasses, black hair, salt and pepper beard, and a suit that belonged on Jason Statham's *Transporter,* closed us into the vehicle. Beige leather consumed us in the sedan. I had a look of wonder on my face, but I still didn't question anything. Between the home in Mexico, the strange chartered flight to England, and this lavish treatment in Brussels, I still hadn't asked any questions of Ms. Shen. Was it out of fear? Did I really want to know? Or, was I simply single-minded toward a goal? It didn't really matter. The questions, much like my acid-reflux after eating buffalo dip, were imminent, but contained for the time being.

Fifteen minutes stood between us and our drive toward Dilbeek. More specifically, a small park behind a magnificent castle called *Gemeentehuis Dilbeek*. There, between a fountain pond and the castle, stood another man. This man was dressed in blue jeans, a white button up without a tie, and a pair of black sunglasses. He stood next to a beautifully restored graphite Land Rover Defender. In his hands, he held a manila envelope.

Shen and I waited as our chauffer stopped the car beside the Defender, quickly sprung from his seat, and let Shen out of her door. I let myself out and watched her nod to the gentleman in the white button up. He gave her the envelope and keys for the Defender. Then, he and the chauffer moved into the BMW and disappeared down the road we came. My mind filled with even more questions. Before I could ask another, Shen smiled once again and winked at me.

"Come on. Get in!" The same demand as before in the BMW. She moved toward the left side of the car and got into the driver's seat. Completely astonished, I moved into the passenger's seat. By the time I closed the door, Shen had ignited the SUV. She was about to place it into gear when I stopped her.

"Wait! How?" I was lost for words at this point. How did this happen so easily for us? I knew I was with an experienced assassin, but how did she pull this off on such a whim? "How did you do this?" I kept going.

"I have some connections, Mr. Appling." That was not the answer I wanted to hear, but the exact answer I expected.

"I'm Tom, Yaravela."

"Sorry, Tom. Is something wrong?" She almost mocked me with her confusion. Of course I would see something weird, but she was playing it off like it was no big deal.

"This!" I raised my hands to show Shen where we were. I looked into the back seat where suitcases were stationed with a cooler. "That! This isn't normal! How did you make these things happen so easily? The plane? The house in Mexico? This car and these supplies?" I looked around and saw a few pistols with boxes of ammunition, first aid kits, flash lights, and more. Shen began to nod, understanding she needed to be a bit more candid with me.

"Ok. I understand your concern." I nodded my head rapidly to insinuate a "ya think" kind of gesture. She continued: "I still have some connections leftover from my life as Deliverer's assassin. It's not like he paid me, but we had drop points all over the world. Well, at least in most major cities. There's a reason why Brussels was the first destination on this side of the Channel. Why not use his resources against him? He never communicates with these tools, it's beneath him. All orders come directly from his operations people like me. It's perfectly safe. You have to trust me, Tom!"

I didn't. I didn't trust what she was saying, but I didn't have many options. What she said wouldn't explain the plane or the house in Mexico. Although if she did use Deliverer's plane it certainly would explain why we were spotted so quickly by the Monster. I let that marinate for two seconds:

"Whoa! That's how he found us!" She passed a bewildered look toward me.

"Who?" I was getting a bit frustrated at her now.

"The Monster at King's College! It's not too suspicious or coincidental that we flew in with Deliverer's resources and then were immediately found by him." She smiled to my further frustration.

"Perhaps you're right. But the pilot didn't kill us. Neither did the chauffer. Neither did the guy that dropped off our new car. It doesn't matter at this point anyway. We need to go." She placed the car into gear and looked at me. "So, we know they are onto us. Get us out of here." She tossed her phone in my lap. She looked at the phone and back at me and raised her eyebrows to insinuate that I was in charge. She wanted me to navigate our journey to Platæa.

"So. This is where your resources end?" I was obviously being sarcastic, but she answered anyway.

"You just navigate us and let me worry about the resources." She was back to being calm and collected. "You're in control of the road. We both know they will be coming for us. We both know you don't trust me. So, here we are. One of us has to trust the other. I'm willing to be the first to take that chance. Find our way, Tom. Find a way to Platæa. Get us there. You fancy yourself Jason. Well, lead me there, Tom."

I was embarrassed now that she heard my quip about her being my Argonaut. I guess that didn't matter. She was obviously willing to let me lead us. Perhaps she thought they would be more likely to anticipate her path than mine. Perhaps this was something I needed in order to trust her fully. Perhaps she knew I needed some control of the process. I was, after all, the hero of my own story. I began to smile once again as I breathed and took delight in our resources, especially the cooler in hopes it was stocked with edible food and not explosives or something.

"Ok. I guess we are provisioned." I reached back toward one cooler. I opened it up and found nearly twenty bags and several pre-prepared salads. I opened a bag and found myself looking at a well-prepared sack lunch equipped with a ham sub, chips, an apple, and a cookie. More of the same from the other bags. I reached toward the other cooler that I assumed would have drinks. It did. We were stocked full of food, drinks, and a myriad of provisions that were yet to be explored. I looked over to Shen and tossed her a sack and a bottle of water. "Alright, Argonaut. Lift anchor and onward to Platæa."

Chapter 34

Germany, France, Switzerland, Austria, Hungary, Italy, Croatia, Albania, and Serbia. Nine countries and nine letters with the same end goal. Stop Thomas Appling before he reaches Greece. Hermes printed the pictures of Thomas Appling and Yaravela Shen. He printed letters demanding that they be killed or someone close to the recipient would die. Bren was under the impression that Deliverer wouldn't call off the ones he sent. In truth, he was much crueler, sending several more even after the phone call. Win-win for Deliverer. Bren Appling would suffer trying to keep her husband alive. If she succeeded, he would get to torture Tom in front of her. If she failed, she would see Tom die knowing it was up to her to stop it from happening. Either way, it meant more torture and the suffering of Tom Appling and his family. All good news for Deliverer.

Hermes tucked the letters neatly into envelopes. He delivered the letters. Each letter was delivered perfectly. Now in Spain once again, Hermes would deliver the final letter. Ten individuals from ten individual European countries. It all culminated with Miguel Navas near Sitges.

Ever since the letter that killed the Waters family, Miguel hadn't been back to the bar on the beach. He tried to keep a low profile as the investigation carried on. No one ratted him out. They were all like brothers to him. He grew up with those boys at the bar. Each owed him in some way or another. They all said it was some tourist that murdered Charlie and Jodi Waters. They said he disappeared after it happened, before they called the cops. Suspicion was high for Miguel, but evidence was lacking, and no arrest could be made.

Miguel lived in a two-bedroom bungalow in the hills of Canyelles, north of Sitges and his bar. He still had the shotgun that killed the Waters family. It was hidden under a loose floorboard in his bedroom along with a box of fifty shells. He sat on his couch for hours during the day, being a little too liberal with a bottle of tequila. He wore a stained white shirt that festered with so much body odor it seemed to condemn the use of a shower. It had been nearly a week since he committed his atrocity. He had only slept a few hours since then. Demons filled his nightmares. The blasts and the blood couldn't be washed away, no matter how much he consumed. After a long draw from the bottle, he clinched his silver cross in his tired hands and prayed to God. He prayed that the pain would end and that he would be forgiven for his actions. He prayed that Jose, his beautiful son, was still alive. He prayed again that Jose would forgive him for what he had done in his name. He lifted the bottle once again. What few drops were left in the bottle touched his numb tongue as tears again sprang from his eyes.

The ring of the doorbell sent a shock down Miguel's spine, causing him to drop the bottle. It broke, shattering to pieces on his unkempt wooden floor. He didn't rise to attention. More like he wobbled to attention, swaying back and forth to what felt like an upright position. He stumbled toward his entrance. He was vulnerable and didn't seem to care if danger lurked beyond the opening of the door. With a fling, Miguel swung the door open expecting to see the police. Perhaps he would've been happy to see the police. He certainly would've welcomed the police in contrast to what was now at his feet.

His third letter. The very envelope sent shivers throughout him. His intoxicated body no longer held up, and he fell harshly to his knees. His arms tingled with adrenaline and panic. He knew he needed to open it, but he hesitated. Outside air flooded his home, a welcome sensation after Miguel's putrid odor, his piled sink, and his overflowing garbage. A minute went by. Miguel didn't look around the neighborhood for the person who delivered the letter. Despite his drunkenness, after the first two times, he knew it would be a wasted search effort. He stared down, hoping the letter would simply dissolve in front of him. Hoping the entire ordeal was a tequila ridden nightmare. Minutes floated by, and the letter rested firmly in front of his knees. It wasn't going away.

There wasn't any resolve in his heart when he reached down. He was simply worn from trying to crush the letter with his false hope. He clutched the manila envelope between his thumb and index finger, as he used the door to hoist himself back to his feet. He slammed the door upon reentry into his home. He maneuvered his bare feet past the broken glass from the tequila bottle before collapsing onto the couch. He tossed the envelope onto the coffee table and heard a loud smack that piqued his curiosity. He reached toward the envelope once again and opened it. Inside, he found two eight by eleven pictures of people he didn't know, a letter, and a USB thumb drive. He placed the thumb drive and pictures on the coffee table and unfolded the letter.

> *Dear Miguel,*
>
> *This is your friend Deliverer. I have one task for you. One and one alone if you perform it to my satisfaction. Inside this envelope you found two pictures. It doesn't matter what their names are as they will certainly be traveling with aliases. You must kill these two people. Currently, they travel in Europe. They are on a path from England toward Bœotia, Greece. They must be neutralized prior to arriving in Bœotia. If you are successful, I will give you back your son unharmed. No tricks and no further obligations. Our business will be done. If you are not successful, he will die. Simple enough? Good.*
>
> *Sincerely,*
> *Deliverer*

Miguel dropped the letter on the table by the jump drive. He quivered as to what would be on it. For a few moments, he didn't move. Finally, he rose to his feet and walked toward the kitchen where he had left his laptop upon the retrieval of his last bottle. He picked his laptop up from the Formica countertop and opened his pantry. There, he found a new bottle of vodka, the last of his liquor stash. He opened it prior to booting up the computer. One swig, then two, and finally three. He moved again toward the couch and the coffee table. He placed his laptop on the table, opened it, placed the jump drive in the slot, and turned on the computer. After a few moments, the computer came to life. A few clicks stood between him and the contents of the drive. He proceeded clicking until the video popped up. It was Jose. Miguel reached out and touched the computer with tears filling his eyes as the young boy spoke.

"Daddy please help me. There is still time." His son. His three-year-old son spoke in Spanish on a loop. Miguel listened as his son pleaded with him for help, fifteen times, twenty times, fifty times. He heard it more than one hundred times before he slammed the computer screen down. He curled up on the couch and let loose. Tears left his eyes faster than he thought possible. In hysteria, he searched for the bottle once again. When he found it, he took one long swig before slamming it down on his computer. The bottle shattered and the computer crashed through the glass coffee table. Shards of glass attacked Miguel's legs and hands. He didn't feel the pain. He could only feel the pain of his son. He could only feel his duty as a father. He slowly rose to his feet and clutched the two pictures in his hands. He moved toward the bedroom where he retrieved his shotgun. He grabbed his keys and moved toward his garage. Once in his car, he looked at both pictures. He felt hatred for the two figures he didn't even know. He only knew one thing as he started his car. They had to die.

**

Hermes watched from a distance as Miguel backed out of his garage in his Seat Leon compact. Hermes was inconspicuous now. He wasn't driving his supercar this time. He was simply a fly on the neighborhood wall, blending into his surroundings and making sure his tenth robot was activated. He didn't know where Thomas Appling was on his journey. He didn't really care how the ten components would try to find him. Probably with some sort of aid contained in the package, he imagined.

He was simply the messenger, and he did his job well. Now, he was ready to sleep. After ten drops in twenty short hours, even the use of his own jet didn't curb the intensity of the travel. As Miguel sped away in the distance, Hermes moved closer toward the abandoned house left in his wake. He pried open the garage door and made his way inside. He balked at the smell as he entered, but he was too tired to turn away. He moved past what was obviously the master suite and toward the second bedroom. There, he found a baby room and a couch. He poked through Miguel's closet for a moment. He found a colorful blanket, placed it on the couch, and plopped down. From there, he pulled his cell from his pocket and dialed.

"Is it done?" Deliverer answered.

"Yes, all ten are in pursuit."

"Good." Deliverer ended the call, and Hermes tossed the phone to his side. He curled up on Miguel's couch and closed his eyes. He would sleep soundly as ten others struggled to save their very existences. The irony wasn't lost on him, but he didn't care. In the morning, he would check his bank account. There, like always, would be a deposit. This time, his twenty hours of flying, printing, and delivering would be worth one million dollars.

Chapter 35

After two years, what was another few days? That was my thought process as I tried to narrow down a route from Brussels to Platæa. Avoiding cities was of paramount concern. I figured the more people around the greater our chances of being spotted by one of Deliverer's "assassins." This, and I felt it wise to choose a route that almost no one would go if time was of consideration. My plan was simple: avoid major cities, travel incognito, avoid people whenever possible, and travel like we didn't know what a map or GPS was. All while sporadically changing our method of travel. I would use Shen's resources if at all possible. I was willing to change vehicles, or travel by boat. Hell, I would take a hot air balloon if it meant being spontaneous and unpredictable. Everything would be kept to myself, and I would make up things as I went. At least, it all sounded good in theory.

"South on E19." I spoke and Shen obliged. From the minute sample size, she was an excellent driver. She handled the manual well, and I could barely feel the gears shift due to her skillful use of the clutch. I kept Shen's cell on Google Maps, viewing potential routes to Platæa as we began our journey south from Brussels. The traffic was eerily light on E420 as we bypassed Charleroi toward N5. Tension overcame the car merely one hour into the drive. It was as if Shen and I were expecting something to happen at any given moment. When I thought rationally, I settled my mind. Why would someone know where we were? Unless our car was bugged somehow, but it's not like we were confronted in the Chunnel or in Brussels. Assuming, and it might be a large assumption on my part, that Shen was on my side, then it didn't seem likely we were in any real danger until we reached Greece.

Upon reaching the French line south of Couvin, the drive through the countryside couldn't have been more idyllic. It was quiet and uneventful despite our anxiety. There was scarcely a soul on the road upon entering Parc Naturel regional des Ardennes. That's when the road began to narrow. Almost one lane. Trees engulfed our Land Rover. The sunny sky above disappeared as the automatic lights flicked on to give us both a short scare. We both smiled at our gasps. It was similar to driving at dusk, but we hadn't reached noon. I could almost feel my pupils enlarge from the sudden change. I gripped the handle in front of me. A defenseless passenger at the whims of the French road. We kept moving forward, the Land Rover cautioning around each blind turn in the park. The few miles lasted an eternity. Finally, we saw the light shining through at the edge of the trees, north of Harcy, France on D22. We reached the edge of the forest, and my pupils immediately constricted to the point they were no longer present in my brown eyes. The sun hit the Land Rover like an alien death ray from high noon. I could see Shen squint slightly, long enough for the periphery of my eyes to catch glimpse of the Volkswagen van thundering towards us. With a cat-like reaction, Shen twisted the steering wheel and veered the Land Rover. I could feel the passenger tires lift from the road as our vehicle swerved left toward a house on the edge of the forest. The van shot into the forest, creating a deafening clap against a multitude of large trees. Shen angled the wheel back to the right. We could hear and feel the wooden fence posts graze the Land Rover, scratching the driver's side of the car from front to back. Jostling about, with a clip and screech, we blew through a barbed wire fence into a pasture. Our all-terrain tires skidded to a stop just before reaching a massive set of evergreen trees on the opposite side of the pasture.

Stunned beyond words, we both broke free from the constraints of the SUV. Adrenaline pumping on hyper-drive, we both came close to hurling but thought better of it. Instead, instinct took over as we began a short, panic-induced jog toward the park and, eventually, the van. We were simply two people who had narrowly escaped a car accident, worried solely about the other driver's safety. We waded through brush and trees to find the van on the wrong end of an unforgiving hardwood.

199

Steam sprang from the radiator and fastened itself to the tree. The door was jammed as the momentum of the crash had turned the van into a compact. I pulled with all my might, and the door reluctantly unlatched. The airbag was full of the blood from a mid-thirties woman. There were no passengers, but there was a set of car seats mangled in the back from the impact. Despite the horrific scene in the driver's seat, something even more disturbing rested calmly on the floorboard beneath the passenger seat. What had obviously been stationed in the seat itself prior to the crash, now looked to be a discarded pile of mail. The confusion in the mail couldn't hide what could be seen clearly above the rest, a picture of me.

I ran around the van as Shen tested the driver for a pulse. The passenger door unlatched easily in comparison. Probably due to a jolt in my resolve. I flung the door open and reached down for the discarded papers and photos. I made haste to flip through as Shen released her finger and shook her head.

"She's dead." I looked back at her, unfazed by the death but rattled by the driver's material.

"So are we." I replied to Shen. I pulled out a second picture with Shen's likeness and showed it to her. She couldn't speak. I could see fear building in her. We were both in trouble. I peered through the rest of the package, but couldn't read it. "German?" I asked Shen. She shook her head, still in shock of the photo.

"We need to go, Tom." I agreed. I grabbed the letter and photos and we ran toward the Defender. How had they found us?

***

The Sniper slowly crept along D22, never more than a few minutes behind Thomas Appling and Yaravela Shen.

"They're sitting ducks." She thought to herself as she opened her door and approached the van. She knew how this German woman found Tom. It was her. Prior to Deliverer's orders to keep him alive, he ordered her to place a miniscule tracking device in Tom's bag. The satchel was a gift from her. It must've been ten years old by now. He took it everywhere with him. Shen must have grabbed it when she saved Tom. She would have smiled if the bag didn't mean such danger to him now. "Stay lucky, babe." She said out loud upon reaching the Volkswagen. She stared at the dead German woman in the front and choked up when she saw the two child seats in the back. She shook her head at the evil shrouding Deliverer's world. "I'm so sorry." She spoke genuinely. She knew it wasn't her fault. She imagined that the seats were empty by Deliverer's design and could only be occupied again by their mother's compliance. She felt nothing but sorrow as she pulled the pistol from her pocket and placed a bullet between the woman's eyes. There would be no loose ends. No risks taken. Dead had to stay dead. She pulled out her cell and snapped a quick picture of the woman. She didn't know if her death might have a chance to save the children represented by the empty car seats. She didn't know if she'd need some sort of proof that she killed the woman. It didn't matter. She knew it was better to be safe.

Bren moved back to her car and calmly closed herself in. She unlocked her phone and unveiled the map that pinpointed Thomas Appling's bag within a few feet anywhere on the planet. He was on the move again. It was only a matter of time before another caught up to him. She didn't know when or where it would be, and she couldn't count on the next being so sloppy. She needed to stay closer to him. Perhaps next time, it wouldn't be a soccer mom. Perhaps next time, it would be a trained killer like Shen or, she winced at the reality, herself. She turned over the ignition of her rental, a blue Opel Mokka. She placed the car into gear and began driving toward Renwez, France, D988, and the husband who didn't know she existed.

Chapter 36

"What just happened?" I screamed from my passenger seat but wasn't looking for a response. We were both in shock. I saw Yaravela's face when she saw her picture. She was scared. This wasn't a plot by her. Both of us were in the dark. "How do they know where we are, Yaravela?" My question wasn't accusatory and I think she took some delight in the change despite our circumstance.

"I don't know. What just happened!?" She echoed my sentiment, and the confusion cast a haze in our loosened, but still fully operational, Defender.

"What do we do?" I asked. Shen shook her head,

"What can we do? We have to keep going." I nodded, realizing that this wouldn't end without our dying or gaining some sort of resolution to our quest. I decided to blurt out a line that someone might hear in a movie.

"We solve this or we die trying." It was simply the grim reality of our situation. I snatched the letter written in what I thought was German. "We need to know what this says."

Shen agreed in part, but she was familiar with the handy work, almost intimate with it. She spoke with resolve. "I've seen more letters like that than I can count. All in the same font. All with cruel demands. I don't know German, but I know what it says. Well, I know the gist of it anyway."

I looked toward her as we merged onto D988 from D22 and continued south past Renwez. She looked over and grimaced at the sight of the letter, reliving the times when she was the recipient. Reliving a time, she fought for her daughter's life. Reliving a time before the realization that she would never get her back.

"This is a note demanding our death," Shen said.

"Well, that seems pretty clear," I nervously spouted. I always tended to lean toward heavy sarcasm when I was scared.

"Yes, I supposed it is clear. Basically, the letter says that you must die." She paused for a moment. "And I guess I must die." She looked again at her photo now resting on my lap, stationed offset so she could see both of us. "Or, whoever Deliverer has taken from the recipient of the letter will die. In my case, it's always my daughter." Shen shed a tear remembering in the past tense. "Or I guess I should say, was always my daughter."

"This needs to end. This monster has to be stopped, Yaravela." The statement was a duplication of the mindset we had before, but, for whatever reason, things clicked for me now. It clicked for me that we were up against someone who was pure evil. Someone who stole children, killed whomever he pleased, and used people like pawns on a chess board. It clicked for me why someone like Shen, with seemingly nothing left to lose or fight for, would be so passionate about taking him down. She nodded, seeing that I was finally becoming aware at the totality of what we were up against. This was no longer the romantic adaptation of a myth in my mind. This was about stopping injustice. Putting an end to the horrors of someone who didn't play by the rules of morality. Someone who wasn't ruled by a conscience. We had been the prey for far too long. It would be unwise to think we weren't still prey, but we needed to hunt with all that we had left. We had to get to Platæa, and we had to stop him.

For hours, roads turned into other roads as we made our way south. We hugged the borders of Luxembourg and then Germany. The beauty of our surroundings in the French countryside went largely unnoticed. I remember passing vineyards and mountain ranges. I remember smelling the sweet yeast of fresh bread in small towns, but we were simply too focused on Deliverer. Too focused on Platæa to care about living life to the fullest and embracing the little things.

I switched over to begin my shift at driving around dusk upon our entry into Switzerland near Basel. The Defender felt good to drive, and I took delight in getting a shift with more undulations in the earth. Everything was rather smooth until we reached Altdorf and the meat of the Swiss Alps. We decided it made for a nice stopping point for the evening in lieu of risking a nighttime drive through the unfamiliar mountain roads. After a quick search online, we stopped at Hotel Reiser and took seats at the hotel restaurant called *The Raven*. The atmosphere was rather difficult to describe. Stucco tavern came to mind. It was kind of like it didn't really know which way to go. Antique or modern? Well, it chose both and, in a way, it kind of pulled it off. Warm food felt good going down. I think both Shen and I could've eaten anything warm at that point. Our last hot meal had been in Mexico, quite a few miles behind us now. Like the ambiance, the menu varied drastically between cultures. Items from Japan, Switzerland, and Thailand made appearances. The special was recommended, and we both indulged. Shen had a glass of red wine to cool her nerves from the German van that tried to end our lives. She then had another and then one more.

A French couple sat in front of us toward the end of our meal. We could hear them arguing, but couldn't delineate anything they said. Shen didn't seem to notice, but for some reason, I felt as if their arguments were centered on us. I thought I was being paranoid. An easy thing to do given the circumstances. Then, in similar fashion to the Volkswagen van, the couple charged us swinging their steak knives hysterically. I guess I wasn't being paranoid after all.

The man charged me. I thought about that being a bit misogynistic, but then became a bit overwhelmed with his charge. I thought how much more prepared Shen would be at handling the larger man than I was. Guess that was a stupid thing to think about with him coming down on me. Even inebriated, Shen repelled the woman rather easily. She perched back in her chair and kicked out with both legs. The French woman felt the impact in her midsection. She collapsed back toward her food and crashed into the table. The wait staff was in a frenzy over the development. I could see one trying to reach help on the phone out of the corner of my eye. Then, I deflected the knife of the man, and he occupied the entirety of my attention. I received a stroke of luck as his attempt took out a piece of my right bicep, but nothing more than a flesh wound. I swung my left fist and connected with his jaw. He staggered back from the blow. My ring finger throbbed taking in most of the punch and offering the man something extra to remember it by. His eyes seemed to fill with an uncontrolled rage. He was about to send himself on another charge when something familiar happened once again.

Flashbacks ensued almost as soon as the French man's face split open. Unlike Hogue, I didn't receive the pleasure of having him splatter all over me. We simply witnessed his blood cascade over what we presumed was his wife. She screamed and turned toward the window. As soon as she did, with scarcely a long enough time to register the sound from the first shot, another round pierced through the glass and penetrated her chest. She fell dead instantly next to the husband she had argued with a few moments prior to attacking us.

Shock and horror enveloped the restaurant. Quickly sobered, Shen grabbed my arm:

"Run!" We both fumbled over our table and held our heads low as we scurried away from the chaos toward the back exit. We bolted out the door toward the Defender we had yet to unpack for the evening. No more shots were heard in the background which I found very odd. I jumped into the driver's seat, started the engine, and peeled the tires. I accidently clipped a car in the parking lot, but I couldn't tell the type and didn't much care at that moment anyway. We took some backroads out of Altdorf into the Alps. My heart was beating so fast I thought I would pass out. I felt completely helpless, completely and utterly vulnerable. Shen was in shock but alert in the passenger seat. The stillness of the road couldn't contain the panic we both felt on the inside. I was driving too fast, making the multitude of turns difficult to navigate with the Defender. I kept telling myself to slow down, but my mind did not send the signal to my body for action. I continued to speed up. I was on the verge of losing control.

Shen placed her left hand on my right, where it was firmly attached to the shifter.

"We're safe. You can slow down." I cautiously began to come down off the adrenaline high as her hand quickly left mine. My right foot released its death stomp on the accelerator. Just then, from behind, high beams with the additional help of off-road lights blinded me from the rearview mirrors. The passenger truck or SUV, I couldn't tell which between the two, was barreling down on us as we descended from one of many peaks which plagued A2. The brush guard of the other vehicle connected with our Defender. I pressed firmly on the brakes, fearing that they would give out from the force of gravity if not the other vehicle. I could see the guard rail in front of us as well as our imminent death if we were to stay on the present course and career off the mountain.

I twisted the wheel to the right, immediately forcing the Defender to have an intimate relationship with protruding stone from the mountain side of the drive. The sound inside was deafening. Shen's window shattered, and she ducked toward the left to avoid being crushed by the mountain. The right front light of the Defender went out upon impact. The enemy vehicle's right front light and off-road lights were taken out as it, too crashed into the side of the mountain. Both cars skidded less than fifty feet to the cliff side death that awaited us. Perhaps it was adrenaline and perhaps it was muscle memory from my adolescence, but upon entry into the turn with too much momentum, I pulled the hand brake and banked hard right. The Defender almost flipped from right to left off the cliff, but held steady with its off-road tires. The vehicle to our rear disconnected slightly to lose grip on the road. The disconnection made their attempt at the same move futile. We skidded and grazed the guard rail before momentum carried us to the right and the safety of the road. Our assailant wasn't so lucky. We heard the squeal from his tires locking. I assumed he tried to apply the emergency brake. The vehicle crashed into and over the guard rail. We watched from our mirrors as the lights tumbled off the cliff and were enveloped in flames below.

I pressed the gas firmly once again. The Defender responded. There was smoke from the tires, but no crippling damage yet again. How lucky could we be? I looked toward Yaravela:

"Are you ok?" She nodded her head softly and tentatively.

"I think so. Shit. You?" I nodded in agreement and crushed the fear with a victory cry:

"Ahhhhh!" I ecstatically smiled in relief and jubilation. Near death yet again but still alive. Was I a fucking cat? I flipped on the single bright light on the left side to help illuminate our path. We needed to fix some issues, but neither of us was keen on stopping anytime soon. I simply hoped the Land Rover could make it through the mountains. I dropped it into second as we drove up from another ravine. We were alive. I didn't bother looking over to Yaravela. The last ten or so minutes were a complete blur.

"I wonder what the story was on that one?" Still I looked forward as a sudden calm hit both of us. Three attacks in the span of a long workday. Four in the last twenty-four hours. With the exception of my three-week slumber leading to Mexico, I felt like the adrenaline high was commonplace. What were we doing still alive? Deliverer's choice of assassins sucked something fierce. Where did those shots come from, and why didn't they target us? Once again, too many questions. Too long a road ahead to get caught up in the details. For now, I would simply tip an imaginary hat to our guardian angel.

Chapter 37

Midnight in the middle of the Swiss Alps. Scatterings of headlights marked the rare activity we encountered since our run in with the maniacal vehicle bent on pushing us over the edge. Stopping and sleeping was no longer an option, but it was becoming chilly in the Defender without the passenger window. We did our best clearing the glass on a remote shoulder a few kilometers back. Despite the efforts, Shen now sat in the back behind the driver's seat. We stretched a blanket to act as a temporary window, but we needed to shed the Defender in favor of something less conspicuous. An SUV that looked like a recent participant in a demolition derby was hardly incognito. While our last encounter certainly felt like it, we weren't in some video game. Although *Grand Theft Auto* came to mind when thinking about switching vehicles, it would certainly make things easier just to yank some Alps dweller out of their car and speed off into the sunset. Back to the point. Perhaps at this juncture it would be wise to shed everything for something less noticeable. The movie *Faceoff* came to mind. I wonder how long that surgical procedure would set us back? The mind works in a funny way throughout high adrenaline scenarios. I must've thought about twenty movies and games in the few moments following the encounter.

While I drove and pondered nonsense, Shen scoured the back of the Rover for anything unusual. She went through the coolers and took apart each meal. She searched the headrests for punctures, the ammo boxes, the plastic coverings, the seats, and everything in between. Nothing. No bugs. She spent more than two hours searching. Then, she got to my bag. The bag I had carried my research and laptop in. The bag Bren gave me as a present so many years ago. It didn't take long. Tucked in the primary pocket was a tiny little dot the size of a pencil eraser. I wasn't paying attention. She asked me permission to look in the bag and I granted it without concern. We were being chased, and I didn't care why it was happening. I simply wanted it to stop. Whether it was the Defender or something slipped into my bag was inconsequential. Turns out it was something in my bag.

"I wonder when this happened?" Shen spoke aloud and presented me with the tiny tracking dot before tossing it out the window. I shrugged:

"You think that's the only one?" Shen smiled, not enlightened or psychic enough to answer my question.

"Well, I guess we'll find out soon enough." She continued searching everything she could get her hands on. I was happy it was her. The task was beyond tedious, and I always sucked at the details.

We were beyond the Alps in Italy. Shen was still searching. Still probing through the Land Rover like a hawk scouring the ground for a field mouse. I had already decided not to drive the original route into Slovenia. I wanted to alter course completely. Also, I really like birds of prey. Not really on point toward altering course, but another random thought presenting itself. A magnificent osprey diving after a surface dwelling fish. Fish. Water. Yes, the water.

"Can you get us a boat?" I broke her concentration. She paused for a second to ponder what I was saying before slowly nodding:

"I don't see why not." I shared some of my thoughts on a new itinerary. I didn't reveal the raptors that led me to the epiphany.

"It'll be six hours before most people are out going to work. If we travel the Italian coastline south of Ravenna we will be around Vasto at eight a.m." I showed her the phone as I quickly pulled over toward a twenty-four-hour gas station near Verona, Italy. "There we have a few options. We can find a boat and someone to take us to Greece, or we can go south a bit more and take the ferry from Brindisi. Or, something in between." I pointed toward the options, but knew we probably needed to choose option three. We would miss the morning departure by the time we made it the extra few hours to Brindisi, and while this would give us time to get the Land Rover's light and window repaired if we were to drive it into Greece, it was too easy to be spotted even though we had shed what appeared to be our tracking dot. For the same reason, we weren't flying into Greece, we couldn't just take a ferry to a major port, at least not one in Greece. Shen agreed, and I could see her contemplating.

"Let me see the phone." She reached from behind me and grabbed the phone as we began traveling east from Verona toward the Italian coast. She sent off a series of text messages. I could hear the replies buzzing and her fingers popping on the text box from behind me for hours. Finally, as the sun began to rise and illuminate the Adriatic Sea, Shen let me in on her plan. "Ok. Get us to Bari. Someone will meet us there with a car. From there, we will take the ferry to Albania. It docks at Durres. We should be able to drive to Platæa from there."

We hadn't been attacked since relieving ourselves of the tracking dot. And despite its injuries, the Defender was still running smoothly down A14 toward Bari. We were getting too many looks as traffic started to pick up. I was becoming uncomfortable, almost expecting we would be destroyed at any given moment. Too many people. Too many opportunities to strike us down. I began rubber necking the cars that passed by. Too many to watch. Too many potential dangers. Still, despite the gawking at our beat-up Rover, nobody chose to strike at us.

Bari was a beautiful and historically significant place. It was just too crowded as we entered the city around ten a.m. local time. Shen felt the same but remained calm in her resolve for her plan. We exited east on SS96 toward *Zona Industriale*. We drove toward the industrial park until we reached an abandoned warehouse next to Roglieri Ittica, a large fish and seafood distributor. We stepped outside the Defender and stretched away the exhaustion and stiffness of more than twenty-four hours of driving. Fifteen minutes passed with nothing. The smell of dispatched fish nearly made the air unbreathable. We felt the air coat our clothing, a penetrating aroma of stench. Our clothing that was already decently ripe after so many hours without showering. Wow, had it really been since Mexico that we last had showers? That thought gave me a chill, and my obsessive mind immediately made me feel as though my skin were covered in some kind of raunchy ectoplasmic shell. I was a ritualistic shower taker and had been since I was ten-years-old. A shower every morning and most of the time a second after sporting events in the evening. It had been forty-eight long hours. We brushed our teeth with the supplies in the Defender, but our plans to shower and sleep in Altdorf took a rather unpleasant turn.

After another five minutes, a matte black BMW X6 M turned the corner. Low and behold, salt and pepper Jason Statham from Brussels stepped out of the car. His suit was pressed to perfection, and we could see him break his professional etiquette when he saw the state of us and the Defender. A smirk filled his face. He handed Shen an envelope and the keys to the X6. She returned the keys to the Land Rover. I watched almost dumbfounded again. How the hell does she do this? The pristine chauffer approached the Defender. I could see him stick his nose up as he grabbed the handle and let himself into the SUV. He drove out of the industrial park, leaving us without a word, but with a very sexy replacement to the Land Rover.

"Come on." Shen looked at me, and I followed once again without words. We left everything but our clothes, my bag, and Shen's cell behind in the Defender. She took the driver's seat in the X6. Upon entering, the smell of the X6 completely drowned the fishy exterior. New car. Brand new car smell. And the supple leather felt nice after the performance seats of the Defender. It almost felt disrespectful sitting in the beauty given our current state. I looked in the back. Stocked again. Coolers, suitcases, guns, etc. I shook my head and smiled. *Twilight Zone*, I thought to myself.

Shen opened the manila envelope and presented me with the directions. We drove on SS16 toward a quaint village north of the city. The directions were not to the ferry, but a residence. A two-story villa off Lungomare Ugo Lorusso. The place was a far cry from our accommodations in Mexico, but there, we found hot water to clean ourselves up. We both took long indulgent showers. It was as if we needed to wash away any thought of the dangers we were in and any thought of the danger we were about to be in upon entry into Greece.

I opened my suitcase to reveal a fresh pair of athletic shorts. *"Thank god,"* I thought to myself. Traveling in the same khakis and loafers from

211

our intended meeting with Agda Sunden might've been a more uncomfortable experience than the people trying to kill us. No Crocs, but a nice pair of Merrell hiking shoes would do the trick to go with a comfortable dark cotton blend tee. I didn't know what we were about to face, but I would do it dressed comfortably. I picked my teeth clean with floss, swished mouthwash, and brushed once again. I felt good. I was worn out, but I felt better mentally and physically. I found that a touch disturbing given the circumstances. Perhaps humans have one ceiling of shock, grief, and panic. The next stage perhaps was physical, or maybe some kind of unassociated mental torture, but prior to getting to that point I didn't see what could induce more stress than what I had already been through. The revelation set my mind at ease. I was seasoned and ready for the culmination of our journey.

We bumped into one another on our way out of our separate rooms. We both smiled. Peas in a pod. Both wanted to travel in comfort and were willing to shed any formalities associated with fancying ourselves up. She wore a comfortable pair of khaki shorts. They were like cargo shorts without the pockets. She completed the outfit with tennis shoes and a light-colored tee shirt, and shed her wire bra for something a bit more comfortable. Perhaps a figure flattering sports bra if something like that exists. She had her hair tied back in a single ponytail, and she only bothered with the subtlest of makeup.

A fresh pizza sat on the kitchen counter. We ate like we hadn't seen food in years. Perhaps our last meal disruption sparked an animalistic hunger. We felt safe. Safe enough to let our guard down for a few moments. I didn't even question where the car, the food, the clothing, or the house came from. They were all gifts, and I wasn't about to deny this gift horse. Not now. Not after the death that had become our shadow. The deaths that had followed wherever we went. Wherever I went. We talked about nonsense for around an hour. Mostly sports. Mostly English Premier League soccer and American football. Shen knew sports. She even knew college football from America. I found that a bit odd given her tame, but present, Australian accent.

The pizza was down to a final slice when reality crept back in. This wasn't a vacation and we both knew the dire circumstances. No pizza or shower could hide it. At least not for long.

"When do we leave?" I reluctantly got us back on point. Shen wasn't surprised. Our small talk could only go on for so long. There were still so many unanswered real questions between the two of us. Tension would eventually creep back into any conversation. There wasn't such a thing as a normal or pleasant casual conversation. I assumed this would be the case as long as we knew one another. This wasn't some Hallmark daytime movie special. The two of us were not meant to find adventure and then live happily ever after. The two of us were not meant to find love in one another. We might've been from the same puzzle, but we were both broken pieces.

"Ten p.m." She replied. I nodded and smiled:

"We should try to sleep." The sentiment was shared between the two of us.

I was restless for a while. On edge, fully dressed on top of the covers, just in case we were tossed into the midst of adventure once again. Eventually biology took over. I was exhausted. Therefore, despite circumstance, sleep arrived in full force. About an hour before our departure, Shen knocked on my door. I stirred awake and felt a numb sort of drowsiness. I'd slept hard and found my REM cycle. Perhaps that's when I was awakened. I rotated my head and felt the bones pop in my neck. I stretched and flexed my back to pop more out of place vertebrae. I sat on the edge of the bed for a few seconds to find my bearings. When I did, focus once again overtook my body and mind. Upon entry into the X6, the friendliness of our sports conversation departed in favor of professionalism. It was time to go to work once again. The ferry, and our next step toward Platæa, was fifteen minutes down the road.

Chapter 38

The signal, and any chance of intercepting the target prior to Greece, faded away. Anticipation flooded Deliverer's mind. Would he make it? Would one of the remaining assets ruin the reunification of teacher and student? The fear of the confrontation. The exhilaration of meeting his nemesis in battle. It was the making of Deliverer's own epic tale. Thomas Appling had proven himself the worthiest of adversaries. If it weren't for the resentment, Deliverer would've had the utmost respect for his enemy.

He picked up his iPad and pondered the implications of the map. Ever since the signal was lost, the coordinates of the assets' cells were scattered. Most of the dots began migrating toward Greece. A few had obviously boarded flights to do so. Then there was Tulio Esposito, the man from Milan. He didn't go toward Greece. Instead, he drove south and stopped in Bari. Deliverer pondered the implications.

"What are you up to?" He zoomed out of the map to check things out. Frustratingly, his phone rang. It was his personal line. The line he used for Emory Chance. He answered the call with one word. It wasn't his style to waste too many words on other humans. This caller, an unknown number to him, received the honor of a one-word answer.

"Yes?" He awaited a reply and what he received disturbed him.

"Good day." A man with a thick Australian accent replied. "My name is Rick Matthews with the *Newcastle Herald* in New South Wales."

He waited for a few moments and thought to himself. *Why would a journalist from Australia be calling?*

"Am I speaking with Dr. Emory Chance?" The caller waited for an answer. He almost didn't reply, but curiosity piqued higher than his instinct of self-preservation.

"Yes, this is. What can I do for you, Mr. Matthews?" Deliverer readjusted. The thought of the Italian near Bari started to fade away. Matthews' voice was crisp in the phone. It was as if he were talking directly into Deliverer's ear.

"I'd like to ask a few questions concerning Thomas Appling, your student from a number of years back."

Deliverer thought, *Speak of the devil. Or, think of the devil more like it.*

"Yes, Mr. Appling was a student of mine at Newcastle. What is this about?" Confusion showed on Deliverer's face. He felt a cringe of anxiety, but was too pompous to feel in harm's way from the likes of a reporter in Newcastle. The anxiety was driven by the sole mention of Thomas Appling's name. His nemesis. The Hector to his Achilles. He waited for Matthews to get on with it.

"Well, Dr. Chance, for starters…, why do you want Mr. Appling dead?"

Anxiety turned into shock. Shock into fear. *How? Why?* This was not Deliverer being accused. This was Emory Chance. Chance, the noted historian. The beloved professor. In a panic, he ended the call. He dropped his personal cell, an iPhone, to the ground and stomped on it. The antic didn't produce a result. He picked the phone up and hurled it at a nearby olive tree. It shattered to pieces. He breathed in and out. How? Why was this happening? How could he possibly know? If Matthews knew, who else did? He snatched the business cell from his pocket and dialed a familiar number.

"Yes, Deliverer?" A man answered. A man familiar with a particular routine commonplace between the two. Deliverer tried to contain his rage, but failed.

"I need a package from a new target." Deliverer ended the call. He used his phone to open his secure email, where he began creating a draft email.

Man called Rick Matthews. New South Wales, Australia. Newcastle Herald.

He saved the message in the draft folder to be opened and deleted by Customer. Customer wasn't on the other line, but he would get the message through the usual channels. This had happened well over a thousand times in the last ten years. Same protocol. Never a single hitch in the operation. Variables, yes, but never a single hitch. The operation was like a flowchart. Optimal results and contingencies. Never any mistakes.

He closed out of his phone and contemplated his next move. It was unusual for a call to throw him for a loop. This call was particularly unique. What was he missing? Where was there a hitch? Sure, Appling still lived, but not for long.

"I guess we'll find out soon enough." He pulled his tablet in front of his eyes once more to reveal the dots representing the assets in pursuit of Appling. "Where are you?" He stared down at Tulio Esposito's dot once again. "What do you know, Mr. Esposito?" He zoomed out of the map once again to reveal the crossings into Greece and smiled. "Soon enough."

Chapter 39

The *Grandi Navi Veloci* was more like a cruise ship than a typical ferry. Luxurious staterooms, multiple lounge areas, food, entertainment, and a beautiful view of the surrounding Adriatic Sea. Shen booked a two-bed cabin for us to hang low for a while until the ferry was safely out to sea. The accommodations were stately with exterior views of the moon hitting the dark sea. There was a private lounge area near the window, accompanied by a nice-sized bathroom and two double beds.

The sea was calm and the slight sway to the boat would only harm those worst plagued with motion sickness. My stomach was always strong at sea. I loved to scuba dive. I had even conducted some research in the Caribbean on days the sea was not so tame. I felt like it would take a hurricane for my stomach to churn at sea, but I had seen plenty of the other side of things. Certain people just didn't have sea legs. Unfortunately, Yaravela Shen was one such person. She wasn't vomiting yet, but I could see the discomfort written across her face as she moved immediately toward the bed and a tablet of Dramamine. I could almost feel her embarrassment. It was palpable in the room. She could maintain her resolve through gun battles and car chases, but the calm ocean had beaten her. What an ironic world. A world that could bring the best of us to our knees in the most peculiar of ways.

We were well out to sea when I decided to leave the cabin and let Yaravela battle her demons. I moved out of the cabin toward the lounge on the deck of the ship. It was a large room toward the back of the boat. The edges of the room were curved to accentuate the boat's features. Red seats, golden columns, and ornate lighting highlighted the features on the interior of the lounge. A large bar with medium wood and gold accents took up most of the left side of the room upon entry. A white baby grand piano sat in the corner opposite the bar to the right side of the room. It was all very retro. It was also rather calm. I assumed this was due to the lateness of the hour, around midnight local time.

I took a seat at a two-person table near the periphery of the lounge. A server came over and immediately spoke English. I smiled. I guess I was that obvious. I ordered a Cherry Coke. The server returned the smile upon my order. She was dressed like a cocktail waitress in all white and black. I considered ordering some food but decided against it. The waitress returned with my drink and it was fancied up. The addition of a small straw and plastic sword skewering three Maraschino cherries was a nice touch, making me feel welcome in a social world run by stronger drinks.

I sipped my Cherry Coke in peace for a few moments and watched as patrons came and went. A few young adults were attempting some kind of courting process at the bar. I wasn't very familiar with the mating rituals of young humans and alcohol, but I found the anxiety of both sexes rather amusing. It was as if everything was riding on that moment. Nothing else mattered at that point in time. The process from drinks to eventual copulation was everything that defined them in that moment. I had never been like that. Even if Bren and I had met later in life, it certainly wouldn't have been over drinks at a bar. I was calculated and reserved. I thought many steps ahead and rarely lived in the moment no matter the circumstance. I hated that about myself and longed for the day I didn't think about my next step. That day wouldn't be in the near future. Certainly not in a world where Deliverer still lived.

There was another single man in the opposite corner, nursing a glass of red wine. I felt his eyes on me. I was one step away from inviting him over if he made eye contact. One glance and he lifted from his chair to approach my table. He was polite and spoke English in a thick Italian accent:

"May I sit?" He motioned toward the chair opposite me. I obliged. He smiled and placed his half empty glass on the table. Before sitting, he made eye contact with the server and asked for another glass of wine and whatever I was having.

"That's not necessary." I said, but he refused to hear it. "Thank you. Very kind of you. I'm Tom." I reached out to shake his hand. He returned the gesture. His palm was sweaty and his hand was soft. He was a skinny man. Some six feet tall and perhaps 160 pounds. He had a slender frame even if he were to gain weight. We were polar opposites in that regard. I was boxy with broad shoulders and tough hands. I could tell my handshake was a bit too stern for his liking. My grandfather taught me as a young man to have a solid handshake and to make eye contact when meeting people. This man hadn't learned either of those lessons, but compensated with a social gesture of buying my next round. He pulled his hand away and sat down with fine posture.

"Tulio." A fine Italian name. One that I was familiar with.

"The one that leads." I said to his confusion. I immediately explained myself as he appeared ignorant to my words. "Your name. Tullius in Latin. The one that leads or name of a king. Cicero shared the name. The famous Roman. Writer and orator." Tulio looked me over.

"Yes, I understand." He finally caught a grasp of what I was trying to say. "And what does Tom mean?" I smiled. I knew the answer and felt silly at this point.

"Twin." I answered. "Thomas means twin." Tulio nodded and finished the remainder of his wine in a single gulp.

"And what do you do for a living, Mr. Twin?" To most people this was an easy question. To me, it had never been easy. I wore many hats. I guess the one that fit most easily was historian, but who should I be tonight? Was I Tom the historian or Tom the businessman? Was I simply Tom the traveler? Or Tom the Bloody American? I went safe and easy.

"I'm a historian. Ancient military history." He nodded several times as the server returned with our fresh drinks. He picked up the new wine glass and took another deep sip.

"Well, then Tom. I guess the knowledge of Latin make sense." He continued taking deeper sips of his wine. By the time I began more pleasantries, he was more than halfway finished with his new glass.

"And what is your profession, Tulio?" He had business of some sort written all over him. Pressed striped shirt with solid cuffs held together by white gold cufflinks. Designer belt and shoes that must've cost

219

thousands. All topped with a large white gold Breitling watch with a leather strap, designer specs, and slicked back dark hair. He was probably in his early forties.

"I'm an architect." He spoke under his breath as he took another sip of wine. I could tell now that the sip was out of nerves. Perhaps Tulio had some type of social anxiety he was trying to overcome with casual conversations with strangers. I didn't think much of it. He placed the glass back on the dark wood table. "Tom. Do you ever think about death?" The nerves made more sense to me now. He stared up from his glass deep into my eyes. I returned the favor, trying to get some kind of reaction from him that would reveal him as an enemy. The reaction didn't surface.

"Lately." I said softly as I took another sip of fresh Cherry Coke. He smiled and shed the intense eye-contact for something more casual. Tulio stopped beating around the bush this time.

"I'm conflicted, Tom. To be perfectly frank, I'm here to kill you." Almost choking on the swig of Coke in my mouth, I sat up in my seat in preparation to do battle with this man. He was so lax though. He said he was there to kill me but made no threatening gesture. He didn't act on the statement. He didn't move toward something to kill me with. I didn't say anything. "I don't want to kill you, Tom. You seem like a pleasant person. You seem like someone who has been through enough." I nodded and kept my eyes firmly positioned on him. I contemplated a number of exit strategies, but rested on the fact that I would be in a better position to counter him than to try an escape.

"I would rather our conversation lead to something more pleasant as well." Tulio wasn't shocked that I was calm. I found this odd. What were his intentions upon revealing his plot? What did he gain?

"France, Tom. I've been watching you since France. There were many times to strike. Plenty of times where you and your partner let your guards down. But that would be the case. You were…, how do you say? Ducks sitting." I didn't correct his language slip up. What would it prove at this point?

"But you didn't kill us. Why?" Tulio nodded.

"That is a question. Call it sport. Call it mercy. I couldn't in good conscious kill someone who was so susceptible, so vulnerable. I watched as others tried. The woman in the van. The couple in the restaurant. I didn't see the truck, but I saw the aftermath of the wreck. All failed. All tried to kill a vulnerable man but were unable. Suppose, eh luck or something." He finished off his glass once more and placed it on the table. He didn't order another.

"What does he have on you?" My question seemed to give him some incentive to smile in nostalgia over a lost love. We were both tortured souls in Deliverer's game.

"Yes. He has something I love very much. My partner. His name, Sebastian." I lifted my glass:

"To Sebastian then." I took a long sip and felt the cherry syrup surface underneath my tongue. It felt good. The flavors mixed so well. It was easy to digest, unlike my new acquaintance. Tulio was not a man who could be read with ease. I didn't know whether he would join me or try to kill me on the spot. I was under the impression that he didn't know the answer to that either.

"This man says he will kill Sebastian. He says he will torture him unless I do what he says. I'm no killer, Tom. I haven't killed you yet because I don't want to have to kill you, but you removed the tracking device." I nodded again:

"There's no one else to do it now, huh?" I spoke softly, knowing the predicament Tulio found himself in. I understood him. I felt sorry for him.

"There's no one else. I'm the only one who has kept contact. The only other who followed after Altdorf was not after you." *The guardian angel,* I thought to myself. I still tried to ignore the fact that someone was trying to protect us. I assumed someone Shen must've hired. Perhaps that was still the case. "When you stopped in Verona, I knew I had to do something about that. I couldn't risk being killed as I followed you. I slashed her tires and followed from a very far distance. I almost lost you several times. It was ex—exceden…"

"Exceedingly?" I helped.

221

"Yes. It was exceedingly difficult to track you without the device to help. I knew I was the only one left, so I followed, and I watched."

I could still see such conflict in his face. He was in a nightmare of Deliverer's making just like the rest of us.

"And here we are." He nodded, affirming the reality of a very shitty circumstance.

"Here we are."

We felt a small change in the sea. We rocked slightly due to it. Mortal enemies. Enemies that could've easily been friends or associates in another life. Returning stares. Almost tempting the other to make the first move.

"Another drink?" I offered this time. It was a show of respect for my enemy's dire circumstance. One of us would not leave that boat alive. He accepted, and I raised my hand for the server. Some more small talk and a final drink stood between us and our fate. One of us would be a killer and the other a dead man before we reached land in Albania.

The drinks came. This time we sipped them slowly. We didn't talk, but we did stare. We stared into each other's soul. We had known each other for nearly two hours in that lounge. Two hours of intensity. Two hours of the most intimate conversation. Two hours to meet and understand a man who would try to kill me. The man I would be forced to try to kill in return. I reached up my hand to settle the bill. The server brought us both folders with checks enclosed. We both paid cash and left the folders on the table. We stood in near synchronicity.

"It was a pleasure meeting you, Tulio." I spoke first and looked him dead in the eye. I presented my hand once more for a shake. He obliged me. I softened my hand this time. He noticed and smiled.

"The pleasure was all mine, Tom." He released my hand, nodded to me, and we both turned away. It was a duel. Not the typical ten-step duel, but a duel nonetheless. A duel between two men, their own conscious minds, and a world turned upside down.

I wasn't going to die that night. I didn't want to kill Tulio, and he didn't want to kill me, but one of us would die, and I wasn't going to chance it. I made an assumption that Tulio knew my cabin number. Being keen on strategy and not taking chances any longer, I had already studied the boat's layout. From the top lounge where we had drinks, Tulio had one logical path down to the cabins. What Tulio couldn't have known was that I already had a small silenced pistol in my shorts pocket. Call it an insurance policy gifted from Shen's friends. I was also competent with guns. Call it living in the south and being an avid collector. The pistol was a .38-Caliber Kel-Tec with a very short compressed barrel. I had my choice of hiding spots in the chilled open air of the Adriatic. I was keen on the spot where the gusts of sea wind could deafen any reverberation of a shot. Luckily, the small alcove was a location most would want to avoid if they were attempting a pleasant voyage. I wouldn't be able to hear him coming, but as he passed, I would be able to see the back of Tulio's head and the stripes of that shirt. I knelt down in the alcove just in case he used precaution in his pursuit of me. I figured the wine would eliminate the risk, but again, I wasn't taking chances. I finally, for the first time, felt in control. I felt like the predator and not the unsuspecting prey.

No surprises. Tulio was half-stumbling as he walked by less than two minutes later. I didn't say anything theatrical. I didn't alert him of my presence. My entire body was shaking. I was as scared as I could be, despite knowing I was going to live through the night as my enemy would perish. It didn't matter. It felt wrong stalking a decent man. It felt wrong killing because of Deliverer, but the decision was easy when it came down to it. Him or me. I balanced myself up and took a few deep breaths as I slowly crept behind Tulio. There would be no mistakes. I positioned the Kel-Tec less than a foot away from the back of Tulio's skull. I used both hands to position the small gun and pulled the trigger soundly. Tulio was dead before he hit the ground. The bullet passed clean through his head and now called the sea home. Blood congealed to his face from the wind and sprayed toward my face and clothes. Cold silence. I used the excess adrenaline to prop his limp body. I wanted to save him for his family to bury, but I couldn't risk him being found. Near the back of the boat, I pulled him up, and without a hint of grace, heaved him over the rail. His body cascaded toward the Adriatic, but I would smell his cologne for days. He would feed sharks and various other fish.

I would be alive. I would be an alive killer trapped in Deliverer's game like so many before me.

I placed the gun back in my shorts pocket. I took my shirt off to wipe the blood off the deck of the ferry. The fiberglass and spray of the ocean made it easy to clean. It was still warm as it stained my dark shirt. There were signs for a forensic team, but not the passengers or crew. I would be long gone, perhaps even dead, by the time the ferry would be analyzed. Perhaps it would never be analyzed. I breathed in deeply once more. All I could think about was getting back to the cabin. Getting back to a shower and a fresh change of clothes that were not soaked in blood. I could barely contain the shaking as I reached my cabin door. Somehow, I had managed to stay alive yet again.

Chapter 40

Shen was still asleep when I entered the room. I did all in my power not to wake her. The last thing I wanted was to talk about what just happened. Better that it be ignored completely. Wow, how quickly I was educated into Deliverer's world of evil. It was too easy. Too easy to kill someone. Too easy to have a casual conversation and then shoot someone in the back of the head moments later. Too easy to forget about Tulio's strife in concern of my own self-preservation. Survive and advance. Something so lost in modern society. The very nature of survival. Sometimes it's as easy as you versus them. That's how it was with Tulio. He was on his way to kill me. Probably on his way to kill Yaravela as well as she slept.

I kept pleading with myself that there truly was no other option. That didn't change the reality of killing someone so methodically. Gaining an advantage through deceit. How would Tulio know I was armed? I guess it didn't matter. The deed was done. He was dead, and I was alive. His time had come. Life was not through with me quite yet.

I snuck into the small bathroom and closed the door gently behind me. I looked at myself in the mirror. My bare chest was clean from blood. My face looked like I had been spritzed with a spray bottle of crimson dye. This again. So many deaths that were caused because of me and my research. I had someone else's blood on my hands once more. This time, both literally and figuratively. I closed my eyes and tried to compose myself the best I could. I opened them once again, and I cried for a few moments. No tears came out. It was a reflex never to cry. It wasn't acceptable for a male to do in my family. I'm sure they would've reconsidered if they knew the pains I was going through. The culmination of torture now stared himself in the mirror. Nevertheless, I took control of my situation. This time, I was the orchestrator of the blood that I was about to clean off. I turned and twisted the knob in the standing shower. I placed my hand in the flow immediately to feel the cold water turn warm gradually. When it hurt my hand, I twisted the knob back slightly to create my ideal temperature. I pulled my shoes, socks, shorts, and underwear off and tossed them into the corner atop my bloody tee that I had placed on a white towel. I intended on taking the towel with us and making a burrito out of the guilty clothing before discarding the package somewhere in Albania.

I entered the shower and pulled the glass door closed to seal myself in. I stood still under the water. The pressure was heavy. The water felt amazing pummeling my head and body. Blood eased off and circled the drain slowly and sadistically. The last remnants of Tulio. I placed my fingers, left middle and thumb into my eyes and massaged them as the water poured down my back. There I was, and there I stood for nearly ten minutes prior to actually cleaning myself. Then, I washed my face with scented soap and scrubbed myself from head to toe. No external piece was left unwashed. I couldn't bear the thought of Tulio existing somewhere I forgot to clean. I continued to allow the water to pummel me long after the soap followed Tulio down the drain. My fingers were prunes by the time I turned off the water and stepped into a clean white towel on the outside of the shower. There still, every movement was exaggerated. My face stayed long in the towel's care and I dried off each extremity with attention to detail like never before. I draped the towel around my neck and took care wrapping the second towel around my bloody garments. When finished, I pulled the first towel from the rack and wrapped it around my waist. I carried the burrito with me as I exited the bathroom.

I hadn't planned to tell Shen the news. I wanted to act as if Tulio never existed, but when I got out of the bathroom, she was sitting up on the bed looking straight at me. It was an eerie and uncomfortable sight. It felt like I was caught red-handed. She didn't use words to express her emotions toward me. She didn't need to. She pried me open without saying a single word. I stood in front of her and caught her glancing at my body, in particular my scars. When she noticed that I caught her staring, she didn't blush or show any emotion of remorse for her wandering eyes. Instead, she took a longer and more exaggerated stare up and down. Her candidness would've been sexy in a different circumstance. One where I wasn't mourning a dead wife or coming off the high of killing another human being.

"I have some. Not sure how to put this. I have news?" The confusion took a deeper hold over her face. "I just killed someone." This didn't break the confusion, so I floundered on how to move forward. She still didn't speak. "His name was Tulio."

"You asked him his name?" Her first words. A legitimate question. In her position, how would I know this man's name?

"We met at the lounge. He was sent to kill us. He was actually a good person." I began recapping the entire story from inception, ending with my shower and bloody toweled burrito. Shen's eyes were wide at this point. There was concern written across her face for my well-being. I think both of us needed the other at this point.

"Are you okay, Tom?" Genuine approach. Feelings and what not.

"I will be when this is all over." She nodded. Her sentiments, too.

We didn't sleep much the next couple of hours. We were due to land around seven a.m. local time in Durres. We reached the port about fifteen minutes early. I chalked that up to calm seas, but perhaps there was wiggle room in the travel times to begin with. Shen and I cautiously walked down toward the carport and our X6. There wasn't a crazy amount of movement going on like you would associate with a search for a missing passenger. That gave us tremendous comfort. By the time we arrived at the BMW, we were relatively calm all things considered.

The *Autoriteti Portual Durres*, or Port Authority, was to the south of the city. Durres reminded me a lot of Bari. An ancient port city with a touristic metropolitan destination built on top. Modern high-rises along the beaches marred any real reminders of the cities that rested on the land thousands of years ago. We didn't hang around Durres long enough to search for any old relics of the city that was. We quickly bolted off the ferry, passed rather quickly through customs, and began driving south on SH4 through the Albanian countryside. About three hours stood between us and the Greek border. It would be three hours filled with otherworldly tension and anxiety. We were getting too close to our destiny, too close to whatever madness Deliverer had in store for us.

Despite the suspense, the drive toward Greece didn't present any new obstacles. Our X6 floated down the roads as Shen pressed the throttle down. As we crept closer toward our goal, it became blatantly noticeable that we needed to create a plan with a high number of contingencies. We knew driving to Platæa, scanning the area, and unveiling Deliverer's buried treasure wouldn't be a practical strategy. At least four people had already attempted to kill us en route. The rest would surely be waiting at our destination once they didn't have a marker to follow. We didn't know how many would be there, but it was a safe assumption that there would be an ample presence of Deliverer's "assassins."

Luckily, I had a plan that had begun to take shape in my mind somewhere underneath the English Channel. That said, we still needed to figure out a way to get close to Platæa without dying in the process. That meant taking the mountainous roads to the west and not the open plain to the east.

We arrived at the Greek border at Ktismata. We were tight once again as we stood in a line that consisted of three other cars. The Greek officials made a mess out of the two in front of us, searching both. Our X6 was quite a bit more attention grabbing than those vehicles.

"Shit." I said out loud, thinking that the various weapons and supplies we had in the car would surely send us on a one-way ticket to some dingy Greek prison. There, the term fish in a barrel or sitting ducks would hardly explain the ease in which we'd be slaughtered. We began driving toward the line, slowing as we reached the customs station. Waved through with little more than a glance, hey didn't even look at our fake passports. We were in shock. We were in Greece. The excitement of arriving in the country was marred by the ease with which it happened. Shen looked over at me in the passenger side of the BMW.

"What the hell just happened?" I shook my head. It wasn't supposed to be that easy.

Chapter 41

It was my turn to drive. A beautiful and uneventful three hours placed us at the point where the Ionian Sea meets the Gulf of Corinth. At the point, we could either enter the Peloponnese or hug the coastline and go through Phocis to reach Bœotia. We chose the latter, in an attempt to keep us away from Athens and additional eyes.

Our good fortunes began wearing thin. The first oddity since the border patrol letting us enter was a small drone hovering overhead. It seemed to follow us mile after mile. I wasn't sure when it began, but by the time we reached Delphi, it was low enough that we could probably attempt to shoot it from the sky. We refrained and continued our journey as planned. We looked all around our positions in an attempt to catch whatever treachery was about to happen as soon as we could. Danger was in the air. The fear was like a blanket of clouds consuming our X6. We were on Deliverer's home field now. His game was being played all around us, but we kept moving.

Another hour passed, and we were ten minutes to the west of Thiva. The drone was nowhere to be found, but two black SUVs began following too closely. We sped up. So did they. Like the drone, they didn't try to engage us. They simply held their ground. On Route 3 just prior to Thiva, two additional black SUVs appeared in the road ahead of us. They were stopped and the writing was clear. We were being funneled into a trap.

We had to think fast. I made an executive decision to drive faster toward the stopped SUVs. Quarter mile to impact, one-thousand feet, seven-hundred feet, three-hundred feet. We saw the outline of their eyes. One-hundred feet, twenty feet. We could see the whites of their eyes. I turned the wheel hard to the left. I veered into the other lane and on-coming traffic before darting into an open pasture of freshly plowed farm land. Our X6 popped up on the churned-up earth. The SUVs from behind took chase. Dust flooded the sky and blanketed our assailants along with several farm buildings that showed their age. We bypassed a barn along with another dirt road that bisected the large farm. We felt every imperfection in the land as our shocks tried their best to hug the earth but failed beneath the speed. A dog appeared, and I panicked. I twisted the wheel too hard and at too high a speed. We veered around the dog, but hit an unforgiving patch of earth that tore into the undercarriage. A large stone caught our exhaust pipe and spun us up in a vicious spin. The noise in the cabin was drowned out by my adrenaline. I knew it was loud, I just couldn't hear it in the moment. The supplies from the back of the X6 sailed through the air. One stainless cooler nearly decapitated me as it ricocheted from the back toward the front windshield. We rolled three times before landing wheels up next to a large tractor and various other pieces of rusted farm equipment.

Our seatbelts and a copious number of airbags softened the blow. We were alive yet again, but upside down and sitting ducks. Shen was unconscious. I released my seatbelt and crashed toward the sun roof of the car. I felt the glass crack as it took the weight of my upper back and shoulders. I patted Yaravela's head. No reaction. I slapped her face gently and then moderately to see if I could awaken her. Nothing. I wouldn't leave her behind. I reached up to release her seatbelt and took the weight of her fall just as the sunroof took mine. I cupped her head and started screaming at her to wake up. After a few seconds that felt like minutes in this situation, her eyes opened wide. She let out a painful grimace before coming out of her delirium. I kicked toward my window, breaking what was left of the glass. I scurried out onto the plowed dirt. Dirt mixed with blood on my hands, and the sun shielded me from the cars approaching. I crawled free from the wreckage and turned to help Shen. A gunshot rang in the air. The shot was close. The echo lasted several moments. I continued my endeavor to save Shen. Another shot blasted aloud. It was even closer. My body wanted to freeze, but the adrenaline wouldn't give in. I tried to reach into the car toward my own gun. Another shot, this time I could hear the pull of the trigger prior to the blast from the shot.

"Just fucking stop, Tom." A familiar voice. One I hadn't heard in years. I loosened the grip on my gun and fell back toward the plowed dirt. I looked up at a figure blocking the sun.

"Dr. Chance?" My old professor smiled at me. He extended his left hand down to help me up. I accepted the invitation. Just prior to our hands touching, he pulled his away. I saw him lift his right hand. He had a pistol in it. The image of Wilson Combat from the magazine appeared. Then, with a thud, the butt of the pistol struck my forehead. It only took one blow to render me unconscious

Chapter 42

Water careened off my face, awakening me back to my nightmare. Shackles attached my wrists together. My arms were raised high above me. I was attached to some kind of hook. My feet barely reached the ground. It was just enough to tease the relief in my rotator cuffs, but not enough to relieve the pain. I wasn't conscious for more than a few seconds before realizing exactly where I was. I was in the center of St. Demetrios church, a marker for one of my controversial theories on the Battle of Platæa. I had spent so much time in the little church during my research that I knew the unique interior from anywhere in the world. It was small, but beautiful. Entirely made of limestone with a Spanish tile roof. Stained glass depictions of biblical events covered windows, and the arched door frames were cut into the stone by hand. We were smack dab in the center of my research, something Chance would've been well aware of.

Emory Chance stood in front of me. If anything, the time away from Newcastle had improved his overall look. He seemed thinner now. The sadistic smile across his face would brighten a room in Hell. On earth, however, the very sight of it might wilt the spring flowers.

"Why?" I foolishly asked. He shook his head. He was bright and lively when he spoke to me.

"Mr. Appling. Thomas Appling." He was enjoying the moment too much. What was going on? "You have taken from me Mr. Appling. Every time you refuse to die, you take from me a little more." I didn't respond. This frustrated him. I could see he was begging me to send him on a rant. I wouldn't give him that pleasure. Despite my efforts, he would oblige himself. With an over-the-top theatrical gesture, hands raised in the air like he was summoning power from the heavens, he continued. "Alas, I have kept you alive. Why do you ask?" I didn't but he was obviously going to have a conversation no matter what my participation level would be. "Because now, someone knows who I am. I need to know why." He grabbed my cheeks with his hand and positioned my eyes toward his for effect. His pudgy fingers felt soft in my short beard. His eyes were a creepy ice-blue. Blue to the point they were almost white. "And you are going to tell me everything." I shook out of his grip. This pleased him, and I immediately regretted giving him the satisfaction of participating in his game.

"I don't know what you're talking about." It was the truth, not that he would accept that. He shook his head slowly and clicked his tongue to the roof of his mouth to mock a perceived lie.

"No. I think you do know some things. Rick Matthews knows some things." He awaited a response and received nothing in return. *Rick Matthews? The reporter? What?* This was getting weirder by the second. Perhaps I died when Hogue was shot a few years back? I didn't obviously, but it seemed to make more sense than this conversation. He continued: "Alright, I'm going to tell you a story. It's a story of cheeks and nails. A story that gets me what I want. You have, no doubt, been privy to a man so large he filled door frames when he walked into a room?" *The Monster*, I thought. "Well, he responded as a young child to a particular set of treatments. In short, I strung him up by his cheeks in a similar position as you find yourself now. The pain is gradual and diversified. Sometime it's the teeth that hurt. Sometimes it's the jaw. Sometimes it's the gums. Sometimes the tongue gets so dry from the cool air that you want to cut it out. Sometimes the teeth feel frozen and the anticipation of them being tapped with a metal object, something like a hammer, is almost too miserable to fathom." He pulled out a hammer for effect and tapped a glass bottle. The bottle burst, making me feel phantom pain in my teeth.

"What do you want from me?"

"Well that has evolved. At first, I just needed you dead. Then, I wanted you to die slowly. Now, I want you to suffer before dying slowly." I looked down to him.

"Haven't you taken enough from us?" The use of plural had him flummoxed a bit.

"Nothing more than you have taken from me. I spent years working on theories of Platæa. You undermined everything I worked for. Then, you lived and forced me to kill my boy." He made a dramatic gesture more theatrical than grief-stricken. I looked at him in confusion. "Well, I couldn't let him keep failing me, could I?" I guess the Monster was dead. This was getting even weirder, but kind of relieving that he was dead. Since being strung up, I almost expected him to enter the church and squeeze my head until it popped. Yes, I had already envisioned this for myself. No, it wasn't a pretty image. I blurted out a sarcastic retort:

"Well, yea you could've." He didn't like my insolence but ignored me.

"And then there's you." He directed his attention behind me. "Little Missy Powers." Who was he even talking to at this point? I tried to turn my head. It rotated just enough to see Yaravela Shen hanging from a hook set up exactly like mine. *Missy Powers? Who's Missy Powers?*

Chance saw the confusion on my face and delighted in it. "Oh.... She didn't tell you?" He laughed like a cracked-out hyena. "Oh.... Aren't you in for a treat?" Shen said nothing. "Your disappointing partner in crime is none other than a newly fatherless billionaire, Tom. Here she is, the long-lost Missy Powers. Teen pregnancy. That didn't really end well, did it, Missy?" He threw his arms in the air to display her like a game show host would reveal a prize. His attempt at riling her failed. I was proud of that, and I didn't care what her real name was.

"You take delight in killing someone's daughter, Chance? You're beyond evil." I interrupted. I could see fury in his eyes. The man was truly psychotic. How did he hold this in as a professional? How did he contain all of this while I walked next to him in the field? While I sat next to him in the office?

"And how many have you killed, Tom?" I didn't understand his question. He elaborated: "How many legacies have you killed with your research?" I couldn't help but scoff.

"You equate the evolution of research with the taking and killing of innocent children?" The very thought that the two weren't equal baffled him:

"Oh, but they are equal, Tom." His ice-blue eyes seemed to glow in front of me. "You of all people should know the value of the human word in history. If you weren't stopped, you would've changed how Herodotus, the father of history, was remembered in time. You would've spit upon his grave. You would've spit upon Pritchett's grave, Grote's, Grundy's, and Kromayer's. You spit upon my legacy. You can't just stumble upon an idea that ruins the lives of those who preceded you!"

"That's what history is, Chance!" I interceded again. "That's what evolution is. That's the fabric in which knowledge is built. The old must die to foster the new. New techniques are born that build upon or simply dismantle the old. It happens in all research. It will happen to mine, too." Chance shook his head:

"But it won't happen to me. I've made sure it won't happen to me. No one will study these sights. No one will conduct research below the surface." I shook my head. There was no bargaining with this man. This wasn't the professor I loved working with four years ago. Perhaps it was, but it certainly didn't appear that way back then. "Enough of this!" He screamed. "Tell me what Matthews knows! Give me the names that know!" I still didn't know what he was talking about. I held silent.

"He doesn't know anything," Shen exclaimed in the background, finally breaking her silence. *Missy Powers? Why was her name so familiar to me?* I searched the corners of my mind until it hit me. It hit me like a freight train. *Was this Jules' Missy? Did I find her? Does that mean Jules' daughter was dead? Is dead?* I had too many questions and it seemed the short time I would be alive wouldn't be long enough to get them answered.

"Then I guess there's no reason he should be able to talk then?" Another scare tactic, but I assumed his scare tactics were backed up in reality. He reached into his pocket and pulled out an old oil rag. He stuck it deep into my mouth with enough force that I couldn't bite his hand. The taste was disgusting. It seemed to have lived in an automotive shop prior to my mouth. It gave me memories of the first time I changed the oil in my old farm truck, when I used a pan too small for the job, and the excess oil splashed into my open mouth. The memory was too bland for the occasion. Reality snuck in. Pain in my shoulders shot toward my neck and down my spine. My wrists pinched into the base of my hands from the shackles.

Chance left my sight toward the back of the room. I couldn't see where he went, but his immense presence faded to the distance, like he actually exited to a different part of the church. I used the relief as time to think. Some kind of timeout from the torture to compose myself once more.

I looked around the church where we hung. So many things began making sense to me. Chance knew my research would take me to Platæa to ruin whatever plans he had in the area. He left my committee and assumed that would be enough to destroy my chances at succeeding. His insanity must have an overwhelming amount of arrogance attached to it. When he was wrong, he tried to kill me. Perhaps he always wanted me to die. How deep did this go? The border patrol that let us drive right by? The Greek government itself? What were we dealing with? This went far beyond a self-righteous historian with a grudge. Shen interrupted my thought process:

"I'm sorry I didn't tell you." I made a muffled sound to let her know I was gagged. She took the hint. She began telling me a story I was already familiar with from my time as Jules Englewood's cellmate. She spoke of a kid from Atlanta getting her pregnant. Leaving her father and mother in Alabama. Grady Hedges. Being sold and trafficked out of the country. Tortured, abused, and abandoned by countless men. Nothing as bad as Deliverer himself. The man who found out who she really was. The man who used that, as well as her own daughter, against her. How she coped with her daughter's death. How she finally returned to claim her inheritance. All the resources made sense now. Shen, or Missy, could buy any help she wanted. But she was too prideful to let someone take care of Deliverer for her. She needed personal revenge on this man. I admired her for that. I was proud to be a positive part of her journey to make that happen.

Just like that, Deliverer returned. This time, he carried a long, sharp nail and rope. He let the rope drag behind him for effect. I heard each and every floor board bounce the end of the rope where the nail was tied on. Pop. Pop. Pop. The rope slithered like a well-trained snake underneath Deliverer's command. He reeled the rope in as he stood in front of me once again. He stared me directly in the eyes. I felt his cold blue eyes bring winter into my very soul. This time, he didn't crack a sadistic smile. He didn't make a calculated joke at my expense. His seriousness would've beckoned the attention span of a seven-year-old with ADHD. He spoke four words with such somberness that hurt me physically when they left his mouth.

"You deserve his pain."

Chapter 43

Chance ungagged me. He obviously thrived on the give and take of the exchange. It was working in his favor after all. I thought to myself about "his" pain. Then I remembered the scars on the Monster's cheeks. Those symmetrical scars. Between the dragging of the rope, the nail, and his threats, it didn't take long to understand who he was referring to.

His mood actually seemed to lighten up. Like he was re-energized by something else.

"You know what's worse than his pain?" Chance spoke directly to me once again, still holding on to the nail and rope. The similar rope and nail he used to torture someone he actually claimed to care for. "What's worse than pain is knowledge." He moved directly toward me. He pressed his index finger into the scar on my cheek from that fateful day in Newcastle. He smiled viciously through his gray beard: "Yes, much worse than physical pain." He moved away and took a seat in the pew in front of me. "I have a better story for you. The story of how I destroyed your life."

Chance was the master of mind games. He would bait and switch torture. Then, add in a mental game even more detrimental. Still looming always was, of course, the reality that the physical torture would come. He created an imaginary gun and exaggerated an aim at my face.

"That scar on your face is so beautiful, Tom. It was put there by my sniper." I didn't react as his smile seemed to grow with each word. He leaned back in his pew in the most self-righteous display of ego I have ever witnessed. "Your wife, Mr. Appling." He cackled loudly as I processed what he was saying.

What? Bren? My mind raced. I could sense that he could almost see the wheels of my mind turning, trying to work its way through his taunt. "It's true, Tom. She's been under my thumb for years now."

I took the bait. I couldn't help bursting out. "Bren is dead!" I saw her. I saw her lying in blood. Chance shook his head.

"Nope, she's quite alive Mr. Appling." I continued shaking my head. I tried my best to justify all the reasons it couldn't be Bren. I saw her dead in front of me in our own home. Then, Shen's voice began echoing in my mind. "No bodies were found." I never allowed myself to think about the possibilities. Not truly. She was dead. She had to be dead. My vision began to blur. Was it Bren all along? Did she send me the text in Tennessee?

"She would never do this to me." The statement was exactly what Chance wanted to hear. It played directly into his plan. He cackled once again and let out a sigh of pure ecstasy.

"Love, Tom. You humans all have it. It's pathetic and it makes you betray those closest to you. It turns you into animals. When you love things, you will do anything to protect them. This includes hurting other loved ones if the circumstance is right." He whistled loudly as I smirked at him comparing himself to something nonhuman. "Come out!" He shouted toward the lady chapel behind me and in front of Shen. It was basically a dressing room in a church this small.

There was a long pause. I heard soft, timid footsteps against the wood floor of the old Byzantine church. My peripheral vision caught the first glimpse, and I felt like life was both given and taken from me simultaneously. When she appeared in front of me, I was lost for words. I shook my head, trying to make the image disappear. Betrayed? I had been betrayed by my wife. The woman I had loved more than anything in the world. There she was, alive. Her hands were cuffed behind her back and her mouth was gagged by a similar rag like what had been in my mouth only moments before. Tears filled with emotion dribbled down her cheeks. The same tears flowed from my eyes when I saw hers. It was similar to what people refer to as a contagious yawn based on the sympathetic reflex non-sociopaths get when someone yawns around them. Only, these tears were meant solely for my sympathy and not those around us. I still couldn't speak. Deliverer didn't mind seizing that opportunity for more of his own rhetoric.

"You see, Mr. Appling? Alive and well." He snickered with delight, snarling like a tiger tearing into its prey. "She shot you. She played games with you. She would kill you right this second if I commanded as much." Bren looked down to the floor in shame. She began bawling, which only fueled Chance's derision that much more. Her tears hit the church floor, echoing throughout like a hollow room plagued with a leaky roof. I was stunned beyond words. What made her do something so evil? What did he have on her that was so hurtful? My mind was blank and my body was numb. This wasn't the Bren I knew. There wasn't a thing in the world that Bren wouldn't sacrifice for me. At least, that's what I thought. I tried everything to rationalize her actions. What had he done to her?

"Why?" I finally mustered a pained response and made eye contact with Bren. Her gag prevented speaking and Chance wasn't about to give us the opportunity. She just shook her head and let the tears fly.

"That's the thing, isn't it? Why? Why do these people accommodate me so much? Help me against anyone in this world? Become my assets?" He opened his arms with hands up to elicit another question from me to suit his cause. I didn't give in. He pulled out a large butcher knife and moved toward Bren. He positioned the knife over her head and down. He grazed her nose as he lowered it toward her neck. He allowed the blade to touch her neck, sliding it below her chin and shaving skin cells before stopping abruptly. The halt of the knife could be felt in the room. It was as if the knife stomped on the floor to alert us that it was positioned soundly for death and death alone. Silence in the room beckoned my plea for help. I shook my head.

"Stop! Please stop this!" He smiled and pulled the knife slightly to the right. Bren grimaced as the knife dug into her neck. Blood trickled down from the superficial wound. Like a bell curve, Chance's smile steadily grew and then subsided before he lowered the knife completely. I could tell that he felt each and every moment. He lived vicariously through our pain. Through the very suspense that made our hearts wince in fear.

"Leverage, Mr. Appling. Just like your friend behind you. It's simple leverage. You take something away that they want. You threaten someone they care for. You show them there is no other way. You keep using them until they dry up." More ego-stroking chuckles at his own brilliance. "You'd be amazed at how long you can keep someone's hope going." He positioned a sick stare toward Shen as he mocked, "Honestly, you don't even need the leverage for more than a few days most times."

Shen interrupted. "You're a fucking monster!" I could hear chains begin to resonate through the church as she struggled in anger. Chance's smile became outrageously big with jubilation.

"Yes! So many call me this! I was told that your daughter screamed for her mommy as they cut her from ear to ear." I heard Missy's shackles shaking ferociously. She screamed something inaudible and continued to fight her constraints to no avail.

"So you force people to do your bidding all while fabricating their hope? How do you live with this? It's disgusting. You're a putrid excuse of a human." My insults did nothing but make Chance happier. He loved his enemies calling him names. He delighted in their attempt to humanize him, in their attempts to make him subject to the morality and consciousness that plague mankind.

"I'm a genius, Tom. No one can claim to be as good as I am."

"Bodies? You're hiding bodies here?" I came to the disgusting realization. Hidden at Platæa were the bodies of all of Deliverer's victims. Missy's daughter was buried beneath us.

Chance nodded. "Yes, so many bodies! Now you see! I couldn't just let you ruin this for me. This is my life's work. No half-bit business-man, wannabee historian will dig here. No one will ever dig here." I wanted to ask how he was getting away with such an elaborate operation. How he had the government agencies working with him, but I didn't want to give him any more satisfaction. Bren had collapsed to her knees at this point. I saw that she could barely breathe. Chance kicked her in the back, and she collapsed to the floor face first. I shrank in fear over our personal fates, hanging on every word he spoke.

"Don't worry, Ms. Appling. I haven't killed all of them. One is always in need of loyal servants. Now, with my token son gone from your shot in England, I need to groom another who feels no pain and answers to me without fail. You others are too unpredictable. Too unskilled for all my work. And work is booming, let me tell ya!" I had no clue what he was talking about. I looked down at Bren as she slowly moved back to her feet. A look of madness was written all over her face at this point.

"Who are you talking about?" Chance just smiled again at Bren and then at me. I finally chose the words to shut him up. I guess he figured making my mind wander from Bren's betrayal was more damaging. I think he was actually right in this. I needed to change the script. I had, after all, a plan. "Well, I guess there's nothing else to do but die then." He was caught off guard by this. "Us, probably right here where we stand. You in a prison cell somewhere waiting for lethal injection or the chair."

He scoffed. "You're funny Mr. Appling." I nodded at this. Hell, I agreed with him that the next bit of information was funny.

"You see, Shen, or Missy, and I knew we had no chance of conducting uninterrupted research at Platæa. We knew we would eventually be caught. We were even ready to die as long as we made you pay." The tables were slowly turning. Now, I was the one who delighted in his confusion, and I had finally rendered him a bit speechless. I was ready for him to threaten and jump around like a child who'd had a toy taken away.

Chance floundered but used the pretense of an exhausted sigh to question me. "So then, what was your master plan?" Chance tried to remain calm. I had no clue what he was talking about with Rick Matthews, but I did know of something else that was going on directly beneath his nose as he delivered his self-serving monologue and basked in his own genius. I knew of a plan I had initiated to finally move one step ahead. One step ahead of someone rarely beaten. One step ahead of someone too arrogant to realize he could be outwitted.

"Simple really. Diversion." He looked around the room.

"Do you know the definition of that word? No wonder you couldn't get your PhD." He smiled, thinking I was bluffing for more time.

"Well, you might be right about that. Perhaps I was too stupid to get my PhD, but while you've been in here, someone else has been out there. Maybe I do know the definition of that big word." I used my head to point to the outside of the church. Chance's eyes got bigger, this time in shock. The change was a welcome relief from the evil default setting. I continued. "I hope Ditch Witch Model 2450GR was big enough for the project. I know it's fast enough. Amazing how fast these tools can scan an entire area. I guess in this case, it's not mapping out ancient history. I'm guessing it's finding all sorts of fun details to stop your operation, though."

Chance screamed, "You're bluffing! And if you're not, well, I guess I'll have to kill your precious Bren." He pulled Bren close and placed the knife to her throat again. "I will cut her to pieces in front of you. Tell me everything!" The tables had finally turned. He was in a panic. There was a variable I hadn't foreseen. It was standing quietly in the corner of the room.

"Normally that would get me, but right now I'm more worried about him." I motioned over to a young Spanish man holding a twelve-gauge shotgun who had been waiting silently in the corner for the last few minutes. He had snuck into the church without Chance noticing a few moments ago. "What are you going to tell him now that I'm guessing he just found out his leverage is already dead?" Chance maneuvered Bren in front of himself like a shield. Miguel Navas began slowing walking toward him with the shotgun pointed at his face.

"Where is my son?" Miguel had the look of alcohol and pain written all over his face. His clothes were torn and his eyes glazed. When he didn't receive a response, the rage boiled his blood over: "I said..., *Where* is my fucking son?" He racked the shotgun theatrically and came even closer.

"Wait!" Chance stepped back with the knife still fixed on Bren's neck. I saw an opportunity to ignite the Spanish man:

"Where's his son, Deliverer?"

"Yea, where's his son!?" Missy chimed in.

Chapter 44

There was no way Chance would get out of the church alive. Miguel Navas had the shotgun poised for delivery, and he wasn't about to let the chance go by. What puns were floating around in my mind quickly vanished. Chance looked at me in the eye. It was a cold stare that would be imprinted in my mind for the rest of my days. He didn't seem to fear the gun as long as he knew I'd receive pain. Moments ago, I thought I was in some sort of control. That feeling vanished. He still held one card in his twisted game. He spoke out-loud, but didn't acknowledge the man with the gun. His words were almost too calm. He had a painful sense of righteousness to his actions as if he were a pious martyr for something greater than himself. His words pierced every fragment of soul I had left.

"Your son is dead." He dug the knife into Bren's neck and pulled hard to the right, cutting her throat directly in front of me and sacrificing himself in the process. I screamed in shocked agony:

"Noooooooo!" Bren fell to the floor as the déjà vu of her blood began covering the wood. My nightmare had returned, and I was faced with watching my wife die a second time. Emory Chance opened his arms and smiled at Miguel Navas. He dropped the knife and looked toward the ceiling. Miguel pulled the trigger, blasting a close-range hole in Chance's chest. Chance flew back and collapsed over a small set of church pews and onto the floor in dramatic fashion. Miguel screamed incoherently, moved next to him, and shot once more. This time, half of Chance's head split off from the impact.

Bren was still fidgeting on the floor, trying to get my attention. My eyes hadn't left hers as I flailed in my constraints. She rolled herself over, spit out blood and her gag, and tried to mouth something to me.

"Dot." I didn't understand. Blood spewed from her mouth and neck. "Dot r." Her eyes rolled back and her muscles softened. My heart fell through the floor. My beautiful Bren had escaped death only to come back and immediately be taken yet again. What kind of world is cruel enough to play such a trick on me? I was speechless and defeated. Hanging in the same position, the Spanish man caught my attention:

"I'm sorry." He spoke loudly. He too, was defeated, despite killing our common enemy. He positioned the shotgun. I said nothing to stop him. With his exposed toe, he pushed the trigger down. The barrel in his mouth detonated, and blood exploded from the back of his skull. I didn't react. My mind was fixed on Bren. I continued looking at her. She was dead again. This time at my feet. This time, I witnessed it firsthand. I wanted to jump down and scoop up her lifeless body in my arms. I wanted to mantle over her and protect her, even though she was gone. I wanted to gather the blood and try to put it back into her body. Somehow, I wanted to, I needed to, reanimate her. Instead, I hung in the air without hope. Deliverer had ultimately won. He had reduced me to nothing yet again. I lowered my head and felt the tears cascade toward the floor. The uncontrollable tears that had been held hostage by my family rules for most of my life. There were no more barriers. No more strength to keep them in. Through the blur, I saw them mix with the blood still easing out of Bren's neck. The blood and tears gathered at a low point and pooled together. My misery. Bren's death.

Missy didn't say a word. One of her enemies had perished. Her new partner's heart had broken into pieces. A few seconds later, the door burst open. A very familiar figure stood in the frame with a pistol pointing toward the room. He must have heard the shots fired. I made eye contact with him. The tears continued to escape my eyes as he assessed the scene and ran toward me. He lifted me up. I didn't mean to be rude, but I bypassed him and collapsed to the ground to put my arms around Bren. How had this happened again? What did she try to tell me with her last breath? I pulled her into my lap and rocked with her in my arms. Her body was soft, limp, and cold. Her blood was still warm as it dripped onto my bare arms and legs. I pressed my lips on hers and pulled her head into my chest. I felt her head bounce up and down from the beat of my broken heart.

The familiar face moved toward Missy, and my sadness overcame the ironic moment that was to unfold behind me.

"Jules?" Missy questioned as my old cellmate lifted her off the hook.

"Missy?" Jules returned the question. The odd reunion was happening in the background. One that had taken more than ten years to fulfill. Missy Powers and Jules Englewood. Two kids who ran away. Two kids who got pregnant at the wrong time. The awkwardness of the moment was shrouded by my pain in the forefront of the room. The two people closest to my pain quickly moved next to me. Bren's blood soaked into my clothing. I was nearly immovable. Finally, after nearly a month, I was able to mourn my love. I was able to mourn my life. All those who were lost. All the pain. Everything that Emory Chance had plagued the world with. It was over. He was dead no more than inches from me. Blood was everywhere.

Jules Englewood touched my back after a few minutes of silence.

"We should get out of here, Doc." I slowly brought myself back to life. I was in shock. Few could've brought me out of my stupor, but Fluffy was one of them. He was a calm rock and I needed that in one of the worst moments of my life. I tried to gather myself by overcompensating:

"Did you scan the ground?" Jules nodded:

"Every bit of it, just like you asked. I ended with that dried-up spring." *The Gargaphia Spring*, I thought to myself. I had called the prison from England just prior to leaving for Platæa. I was granted an audience with a prisoner who would be released a day later. I booked him a flight to Greece while Shen took care of having the equipment ready for him. I didn't mention his name. *Why*, I thought, *would it have mattered?* Turns out, these two knew each other very well.

"What should I do with the drive?" He spoke of the hard drive from the ground penetrating radar unit. I knew people would need to have the information to put Deliverer away. I didn't know that he'd already be dead. That said, the macro nature of the case was far from complete. We had taken down our nemesis and rid the world of a terrible monster. So many more questions existed. None of which I wanted to answer, but I knew someone who would.

"Rick Matthews. We'll send it to Rick Matthews." He nodded and handed me a rag to wipe away her blood. I folded it neatly and gently rested it on her before he helped me to my feet. I didn't know where to go or what to do. Life has a funny way of showing you the pieces. With tears continuing to flow, a young child's cry appeared as a faint sound toward the lady chapel of the church. At first, I thought my mind was officially tapping itself out from the pain. Perhaps, the sound was residual ringing from the blasts? But I heard it again, and then, again. Soon, it became clear and audible to the entire room.

I quickly ran toward the sound. The girl was small and fragile. Probably less than two years old. She started walking toward me as I approached. Perhaps the comfort of any adult, even a stranger, throughout such a traumatic experience was favorable over the horrors of being alone. Instinctively, I ran over to shield her eyes from the carnage of the room. I picked her up and whisked her toward the side door away from the unpleasantness of death. That's when I saw something familiar around her neck. It was unmistakable. It was Bren's wedding band. Completely unique to her. Something I had custom made. White gold, a scroll work design, diamonds down the center. This was Bren's wedding band. *Dot r*, I thought to myself, remembering Bren's final words. *This girl was my daughter*.

Epilogue

The airport was hot, sticky, and slow. The custom agents at passport control were rude. Probably a testament to the miserable working conditions as the plug-in fans whistled in the background, the only circulating air keeping them sane. The pseudo baggage check upon exiting the airport was unorganized. Life in the Caribbean. Slow, miserable, and beautiful.

Missy Powers and Jules Englewood hailed a cab upon leaving the airport. A Kittitian named Trumpet blared a mixture of reggae and rap music and floored the gas when they said they needed to get to Christophe Harbour on the peninsula. Missy and Jules hadn't started dating or anything cliché like that. They'd united behind a cause that would be the second stage in grieving their lost daughter. They had become friends. They even both contemplated hooking up, but nothing had come of it. They both knew that there was too much pain associated with each other for a lasting relationship.

The drive to the peninsula was bumpy. Potholes, herds of goats, broken down cars, and mongoose crossings marred the journey. Solicitors with green vervet monkeys lined the beaches, doing all they could to trick tourists out of another few dollars. Trumpet's taxi van, *De Lime Lite*, struggled up the large hill that stood between the main island and the Peninsula. There, the roads became tougher and pot holes even deeper. Trumpet wove in and out of the danger zones like a veteran.

The schedule was tight, but nothing unmanageable. It wasn't as if Missy's chartered plane would leave if they weren't back in two hours. Christophe Harbour was full of bungalows, expensive beach houses, and a deep-water marina meant to attract the most illustrious of world travelers. The ability to buy citizenship in the dual tax-haven islands of St. Kitts and Nevis, however, attracted quite a few of the world's most dangerous villains. There were your run of the mill drug lords, your scam artists, and your escapees, but worst of all, there was Grady Hedges. The man who had sent Missy down a path of destruction and pain. The man who had ruined Missy's life and the one who acted as the chief catalyst in her daughter's eventual death.

It took approximately three months to find Grady's exact location. His schedule was easy enough to squeeze out of his new local workers. Missy and Jules used a fake meeting he would have with a local businessman to assure his attendance. After-all, Grady couldn't resist a good business deal. All the wealth in the world couldn't compare to the rush of a scam.

Grady's house was secluded in the Harbour. The privacy, meant for nude beach walks and raucous parties, would be the perfect venue. Trumpet pulled into the driveway as scheduled. He acted as a driver for a lot of the local businessmen. He was full of life with a kind nature about him. Not many things could rock him. He was cool, calm, and always stoned out of his skull. Between that and his ritual to begin drinking at eight in the morning, Trumpet wouldn't hear the gunshot, much less remember it.

Missy Powers reached under Trumpet's seat. The .38 Special was "hiding" exactly where it was supposed to. She checked each cylinder for its round before locking it back in place. She smiled widely at Jules.

"Let's go." The two moved toward Grady's house and knocked on the front door. Not an ounce of security at the house itself. Since Grady told the guards at the beginning of his drive that he would be expecting Trumpet, it was easy enough to drive right by. Besides, the local islanders were not known for being experts on security in the first place. Grady opened the door with a wide smile that faded just as quickly as it was fabricated.

Missy smiled. "Hi Grady!" Boom. The last words Grady Hedges would ever hear.

***

It had been six months since Bren and Emory Chance died in front of me. I would think about those moments each and every day of my life. The knife, the blood, and Miguel Navas. I heard good things coming from investigations, but I tried my best to forget and move forward with my life. More than one thousand bodies had been found around the grounds of the battlefield. The bodies each sustained post-mortem trauma from being dropped in sealed packages, or bags, from thousands of feet in the sky. The packages represented more than one-hundred different countries and people of all ages, but more than fifty percent were children under the age of four. I still shuddered thinking about the numbers. Mass graves covered up by archaeological investigations. Sites would be dug and officially closed by the government thereafter. Deliverer would drop the bodies in the sites and then close them for good. They were untouchable until my research presented a kink in his plan. My research would uncover the sites without needing the government's permission to dig. Even the government would have a difficult time controlling a quick scan by GPR. It took Jules but a few hours to get what we needed for evidence. It took but a few thousand dollars of bribes for the GPR machine to find its way to the site. The rest was as easy as pushing a very expensive lawnmower.

There were obviously many players, but much of the investigation died with Deliverer. I always wondered about how deep the conspiracy went. Officials in a corrupt Greek government plagued by debt, rioting, and unemployment? A terrorist organization killing people from all over the world? The speculation created quite a lot of work for my friend, Rick Matthews. I wondered where he was, or if he was getting close to the answers.

As for me, I was next in line. My robe touched the ground and my blue hood stretched low on my back. The doctoral hat was just as elegantly goofy as I could've ever dreamed. I wore various medals and chords I had been given. Six months and thousands of offers of honorary degrees. It seemed that everywhere in the world someone wanted an interview with me. They all wanted my story. When they had it, they needed a different take to keep the momentum. The public ate it all up. Hell, they were still feasting on it six months later. Hundreds wanted me to write a book about my experiences. I had to farm out my social media accounts. For a while, it was an absolute circus, and being a celebrity under these circumstances was torture in itself.

Of course, it took Newcastle ages to get back to me. The one place in the world that was running just as slow as I remembered. It was kind of relieving that one place stayed normal through everything. Finally, and officially, I would walk at my graduation, shake the hand of the head of school, and fulfill my three-year journey of pain. Newcastle rescinded my suspension and would graduate the Bloody American.

I had no idea what stood in front of me, but I would find some kind of contentedness picking up the pieces. Forgiving Bren was easy when I saw what she was fighting for. I read the letters. Disgusting letters that still make my stomach turn. She truly didn't have a choice. I still love her so much.

I looked to the audience with a genuine smile for what felt like the first time since that fateful day. Ethan was there with a leash holding Atlas and Nutty, who were both given special permission to enter and leave Australia without quarantine. If Deliverer taught me anything, it's use the leverage you have. Missy and Jules were there. Diane, my mother and Lori, my sister were all anxiously waiting in the crowd. And then there was Bren. Bren Victoria Appling bouncing in Lori's arms. I didn't call her Bren as I always found that creepy. Who wants a daughter with the same name as their dead wife? She would forever be my Vicky. It didn't take her long to forget the whole ordeal.

Becoming a father was my newfound priority. It is needed to keep me focused on a future without such pain. My little girl is adorable, thirty pounds of energy, wonder, and sassiness. The one positive piece that came from the church next to Gargaphia. The little piece of joy my wife died to protect. The sole survivor of the world run by Deliverer.

About the Author

Robert T. Jones is an author, ancient military historian, wildlife philanthropist, green business creator, and hobby farmer living in East Tennessee. With an intense focus on making the world around him better, Robert designs ventures that have the ability to leave a positive lasting impression. As an author, Robert pursues writing in multiple genres so he will have a truly diverse readership. Robert loves the challenge of moving from one genre to another and interacting with assorted groups of people.

In the same Caribbean evening, Robert caught three touchdown passes, watched a volcano erupt live, nursed a dive-induced fire coral wound, and had his car robbed. He has renovated an 1820s tavern where bottles once quenched the thirst of US Presidents, and pistols were hidden in the fireplaces. He can talk with an auctioneer's cadence, string a tennis racquet or do physical therapy on an owl. He has felt the joy of a bald eagle kissing him on the lips and lectured on business sustainability in Nova Scotia. Robert has defeated lymphoma, no longer has a gallbladder, and has been called color confused. He has lived and has many scars to prove it.